Mermen of Ea
Stealing the Wind

SHIRA ANTHONY

Dreamspinner Press

Published by
Dreamspinner Press
5032 Capital Circle SW
Ste 2, PMB# 279
Tallahassee, FL 32305-7886
USA
http://www.dreamspinnerpress.com/

Stealing the Wind
Copyright © 2013 by Shira Anthony

Cover Art by Anne Cain
annecain.art@gmail.com

Cover content is being used for illustrative purposes only
and any person depicted on the cover is a model.

ISBN: 978-1-62798-053-1
Digital ISBN: 978-1-62798-054-8

Printed in the United States of America
First Edition
August 2013

FOR Bob, the captain of my heart, who helped me find my Land's Zen. Special and heartfelt thanks to Tali and Aisling for sailing with me to Ea'nu and helping me to imagine the possibilities. Thanks also to Manda, Kim, Madison, Thea, Venona, Helen, and Rebecca for sharing some of their precious time to read for me.

WHEN two sailing ships engaged in battle in ancient times, the attacking vessel would do its best to sail upwind of the enemy and billow its sails fully, thereby stealing the wind and leaving the enemy "dead in the water." The assailing ship would then come about and ram the stalled enemy, cutting her in half and sinking her.

WHILE the world of the Mermen of Ea Series is not Earth, it is based upon our myths and traditions. "Ea," also known as "Enki" in Sumerian mythology, was the Babylonian god of mischief, water, intelligence, and creation. Ea was sometimes depicted clothed in the skin of a fish. Ea had the power to control water and was considered to be lord of the deep and the counterpart to Anu, the lord of the heavens.

ONE

THE sound of thundering hooves outside the door of their one-room hut caused the wooden table to shake and the lamplight to flicker. Surprised, Taren met Borstan's wide, fearful eyes over the top of the book he'd been reading.

Borstan jumped up from the bench. "Hide, boy! Quickly, now!" he hissed as he shooed Taren up and away from the table.

"Who—?"

"Go! Now! And not a word from you!" Borstan shoved Taren hard, and he scrambled behind the stores of rope and flour.

The heavy thud of a battle-axe nearly shook their wooden door from its ancient hinges. "Rigger Borstan Laxley! By order of Lord Grell, we seek recompense for your gambling debts!"

Taren peered around a flour sack. Borstan stood next to the door, his back flat to the wall, his eyes squeezed shut.

"Who are they?" Taren whispered loudly.

Borstan put a finger to his lips to silence Taren just as the men broke through the door. Only Borstan's body kept it from banging against the wall. Borstan yelped as four ironclad giants stormed the room.

"Borstan Laxley!" the leader shouted as he dragged a terrified Borstan from behind the door. Another man pulled the bench, their only bench, from the table and aligned it in front of the fireplace. "Tie him!" the leader commanded.

"No, please. No! I told his lordship I'd have the money to pay in a fortnight," Borstan shouted as they lashed him, face up, to the bench with his own finely crafted cordage.

Taren started when the first blow landed. He huddled in the corner, trembling like a newborn leaf, and buried his head beneath his arms. He couldn't bear to hear Borstan's mewling cries with each successive blow. On his cheeks quavered hot tears for the only master he'd ever known.

"Use the tar!" the leader shouted.

Taren snapped his head up. *No.* The cauldron over the fire held the boiling tar they used to coat the rigging they made. Borstan began to scream in earnest, and Taren, no longer able to contain himself, shot to his feet with a shriek, his voice cracking with emotion and youth. "No!"

The four soldiers turned to Taren in unison, one holding the dripping tar swab in his hand.

"Y-y-you… you cannot do that to him!" Taren forced out in terrified effort, fists balled at his sides.

The leader advanced on Taren, a wicked grin of rotted teeth filling his rat's nest of a beard. "What have we here?"

Taren backed up quickly. His heels met a flour sack and he fell on his ass, the sack bursting and caking him in fine white powder.

The brutes roared in laughter as the leader claimed the front of Taren's cotton shirt in one beefy hand and hauled him into the air with a single powerful arm. The man's odor was an acrid stench in Taren's nostrils as his feet left the floor. "Who are ye?" Taren's shirt pinched his throat as the man shook him violently.

Taren desperately batted at the man's mighty forearm in an effort to loosen the grip on his shirt. "Taren." The single word was a strangled breath on the air.

The leader leered at him. "Yer a right pretty one, boy."

"Leave 'im be! He's mine!" Borstan mewled.

"Yer what?" he demanded with another suffocating shake to Taren. Spots of gray filled Taren's vision. His tongue felt thick from the lack of oxygen. The soldier who had held him put Taren back on his feet. Taren struggled to stay standing.

"He's my apprentice! Leave 'im be. Leave 'im be." Borstan struggled against his bonds. Taren saw the red marks where the soldiers had beaten the old man begin to blossom into purple.

The soldier who'd held him now looked Taren over head to toe. "He's yer pretty little slave, ye mean to say!" All four soldiers roared in laughter.

"He's mine." Borstan's voice was less forceful this time. His gaze darted between Taren and the men, as if he were considering something.

"He's a bit spare, but he'd be an extra pair of hands for Lord Grell," said one of the other men. "No doubt he'll grow." In two big strides, Taren found himself thrown over one of the men's shoulders like the sack of flour he resembled. Blood rushed to his face as he gulped air into his lungs.

"Aye," Borstan agreed. Taren looked at his master with a dawning sense of horror. Surely Borstan wouldn't let them take him away?

The leader strode back over to Borstan. "Yer debt is ten silver coins, Laxley. Ye willing to trade 'im?"

"He's worth more than ten," Borstan replied.

"Master?" Taren looked to Borstan, but the old man would not meet his eyes.

"Fair recompense, I'd say. Will ye sell the lad or not?" The leader made a fist and covered it with his other hand. "Or perhaps we should talk some more."

Borstan's eyes widened and he nodded quickly. He did not look at Taren. "Aye. Fair recompense."

Cold terror clawed at Taren's gut, and he fought the powerful arms that held him fast. "No! No! You can't sell me! I've worked hard for you. I've done all you've asked of me. Please, Borstan, no!"

The leader nodded to one of the other men, who untied the bloodied and beaten Borstan. A moment later, the soldiers walked out the doorway with Taren, who continued to fight to free himself. "Borstan, no! No! No! Borstan, please! I beg you! Don't do this! Please, I beg you!"

Two years later

TAREN huddled beneath a tattered blanket as an icy wind blew through the cracks of the ramshackle dormitory. The mortar between the bricks had crumbled and the fire was a good twenty feet away, providing him little warmth. He didn't dare move closer—he had been beaten more times than he cared to remember by the other, bigger men with whom he shared the drafty sleeping quarters of Lord Grell's Inn.

He'd lost track of time since he had come to this place. The living quarters at the inn were far less comfortable than Borstan's hut on the edge of the docks, but the work wasn't nearly as strenuous. Still, Taren longed for the freedom of climbing the ropes of incoming vessels and standing atop their masts with the wind in his face. More than a warm place to sleep, he wished to work at the harbor once more, where he could pretend he was a sailor or, better, that he captained one of the great ships.

More than anything, Taren dreamed of the ocean. He closed his eyes and imagined the spray against his face, the rocking of the vessel beneath his bare feet. He imagined crouching on the masthead, looking out through the telescope, trying to spot approaching boats. He imagined hoisting the sails, watching them billow and fill, and feeling the vibrations of the deck beneath his feet as the ship caught the wind.

Sometimes he dreamed his parents' home had been one of the far-flung islands, or that he'd been born at sea aboard a great vessel. Sometimes he dreamed he was a creature who lived under the waves, chasing schools of fish and watching the waves overhead as he lay in the sand at the bottom. Sometimes he dreamed he was an admiral in the king's navy, ordering his men to fire their guns at an enemy vessel as he defended the Kingdom of Derryth. But whatever Taren dreamed, he always dreamed of the ocean.

Dreams were all they were, for Taren had never been to sea.

"You, boy," a sturdy woman called from the doorway. "What's your name?"

"Taren, ma'am." He got to his feet and repressed a shiver. It would do him no good to irritate Madame Marcus at such an ungodly hour—she would see his weakness as a complaint, and he didn't want another whipping.

"Cook's needing you in the dining room. A new ship's put into port. He wants an extra pair of hands."

"Of course, ma'am," Taren said, dropping the threadbare blanket by the wall.

Dining room duty was better than some chores. Cook might even let him scrape the dregs from the pots as they cleaned up. Taren's empty belly growled at the prospect and he followed the woman across the open courtyard, past an angry rooster who pecked at him when he strayed too close, and into the warmth of the kitchens.

"Cook, sir," he said to the large man standing at the ovens, his face dirtied with soot from the fires. "What do you need?"

"Grab the soup from off the counter, boy, and ask the gentlemen if they would like more."

Taren nodded and pulled a potholder from a hook beside the smallest of the ovens. The fabric of the potholder was, as with everything else, worn thin, and he felt the heat from the iron handle as he reached for the pot. A few months before, he'd have struggled to lift it, but his arms had grown stronger and he lifted it with ease. He ignored the pain as the metal burned his palm and scurried out into the dining room, retrieving a large ladle hanging near the doorway along the way.

THE light in the dining hall was far more subdued than in the kitchen. The candles burned a warm yellow and made the faded red fabric wall coverings appear less tawdry than in the daylight. Men crowded around the long wooden tables that ran the length of the room laughed and shouted, some singing off-key, most with large tankards of ale in their hands. The warm smell of sawdust and the sour tang of sweat mingled with the scent of the stew. At first, Taren had found the odors overwhelming. Now they comforted him.

Taren met Verita's gaze. She was one of the other servants and old enough to be his mother, but her inclinations were hardly maternal. Still, she had always been kind to him—as kind as could be expected in a place such as this. She nodded and got back to filling tankards, leaning over as she poured the men's drinks so they could easily see her full breasts and cackling when the men fondled her ample bottom. Later, he guessed, she would offer her services in their rooms, as many of his fellow servants did for the paltry coins they might receive in return. The master never complained about such activities, but Taren knew he expected half of what Verita and the others earned with their bodies. Taren had never been tempted to follow a guest to his or her bedroom, although he had been presented with the opportunity on many an occasion.

He felt a rough hand on his forearm and nearly lost his grip on the pot. "You're a pretty one," the owner of the hand said in a low voice. "Ain't he, Captain?"

Pirates, thought Taren, *judging by their looks and their rough manner.*

"Please," Taren said in a trembling voice. "I must serve the soup." Another hand grabbed his buttocks and squeezed. He couldn't pull away or he'd spill the hot soup on himself and possibly the man seated to the left of his antagonist.

The man seated at the head of the table—the "captain"—pursed his lips in appreciation. He raked his gaze over the open collar of Taren's shirt and the tight fit of his too-small britches; Taren felt hotter than he had under the blanket only minutes before.

In the past year, Taren had begun to grow from a boy to a man. He now stood taller than Verita and the other women at the inn, and although most of the male servants were larger than he, Taren guessed it was only a matter of time before he reached and perhaps surpassed their stature. This transformation had come as an enormous relief. He had no idea how old he was—eighteen or nineteen, perhaps?—and he didn't know his parents. For as long as he could remember, he had been the smallest of all the boys at the inn, and he had been given no reason to expect that it would ever be otherwise.

One of the men at the other end of the table laughed as he squeezed Verita's bottom. "Nice 'n' meaty," one of the men said as Verita cackled and wiggled her hips. "Nice tail on ye', woman."

"I want me a mermaid," another man interjected. "Now *that* would be a nice tail. Hear you have a few 'round these parts."

"Only a fool believes those stories," the first man said. "Don't you think we'd've seen 'em if there were any?"

The captain, whose eyes hadn't strayed from Taren, shook his head. "Something so beautiful wouldn't go near the likes of you, Charlie."

"They'd've swum away from you!" shouted another man.

Taren had long heard the stories of mermaids here in Raice Harbor. One of the other boys at the inn swore there had been a woman with a tail like a fish found near the water's edge. Taren spent enough time down at the docks to know that if the merfolk existed, they would hardly be whiling away their days in the filthy water of the harbor. Still, he often imagined what it might be like to swim beneath the water without having to surface.

"I heard tell of a mermaid who led a pirate ship full o' gold to wreck upon a reef," Charlie said as he emptied his tankard of ale. "They say the pirate Odhrán keeps merfolk as pets. Like dogs. Uses 'em to lure ships."

"Come here, boy!" the captain shouted, interrupting the men.

Taren did as he was told, trying to ignore the lecherous gaze of several of the men seated nearby. "What can I get for you, sir?" he asked as he'd been taught.

The captain, middle-aged with a coarse beard peppered with gray, was a broad-chested bear of a man whose relaxed manner and intense gaze spoke of confidence and power. Taren had to admit he was attractive. His skin was weathered from the sun and the wind; his eyes were a piercing blue. The weight of that gaze and the raw desire in his eyes frightened Taren and made him dizzy. *The master won't abide a servant taken without consent.*

Taren began to ladle the fragrant soup into the captain's bowl. He would endure the wanton looks and the fondling in silence, as he had done in the past. Then he would retreat to his duties in the kitchen, safe once more behind the wall that separated servant and guest.

"What's your name, boy?" The captain's voice was a deep rumble that seemed to work its way through Taren's ears and into his body.

"Taren, sir," he answered as he did his best to control the trembling of his hand. "Taren Laxley."

"Charlie's right. You are a pretty one."

"Thank you, sir."

The captain rubbed Taren's ass before Taren realized what was happening. He couldn't move away or he'd spill the soup, and he couldn't put the pot down on the table and risk Cook's wrath either. The captain pulled Taren's shirt from the waistband of his trousers before he could protest, and moved his hand from Taren's ass to Taren's hardening cock.

"Now *there's* a tempting treat," the captain rumbled appreciatively.

Taren's legs shook at the contact. The touch of the captain's hand was practiced, sensual. Taren tried to repress the moan that escaped from his lips. Taren was surprised that the captain's musky scent aroused him even more.

"You like that, don't you, Taren Laxley?" The pirate let him go and Taren sighed in disappointment. "Don't worry," the captain added, "I just wanted to make this a bit easier for you." He took the pot from Taren's hands and set it on the table, then pulled Taren closer to him by his shirt.

Taren looked around the room. No one seemed to notice that he now stood in front of the pirate with his back against the table, or that his cheeks were surely now as bright red as the feathers of the rooster in the courtyard.

Whereas before he'd have tried to escape the touch if given the chance, his own growing desire to experience the captain's touch once more had him frozen in place. He swallowed hard and trembled not out of fear but with desire.

What is wrong with me?

"I won't hurt you," the captain said, his voice low, his expression unfathomable.

"I know," Taren whispered. He shuddered in anticipation as the captain reached around him and slid his large hand under Taren's trousers and over his buttocks. This time, however, his hand was slippery. Taren caught the faint whiff of butter from the table and saw the smile on the pirate's face.

"Better like that, isn't it?"

Taren nodded, too overcome to speak.

The captain found the soft flesh of Taren's sac with his free hand and rolled it around. Taren gasped as he pushed back the foreskin with his large finger and swept over the crown. Taren nearly fell forward, but the captain held him upright with his muscular thighs.

He had never known such pleasure. The captain's scent was powerful, adding to the intensity of the sensations that ran through Taren's body like fire. The man's eyes held him captive as much as his hand. Taren fought the urge to reach out and touch the captain's rough jaw, to feel it beneath his fingertips.

The captain continued to play with Taren's balls, caressing the sensitive skin behind them and straying close to the hidden opening between his ass cheeks. Taren moaned and shuddered with each slippery tug on his cock. The captain pulled and stroked until Taren bit his tongue to keep from crying out. Taren no longer saw the room or the other men as the captain rubbed his hand up over Taren's tip and probed the slit.

"Ahhh," Taren groaned. He didn't care if anyone else heard. He couldn't hold back anymore. The captain found the tight ring of muscle with a buttery finger, not breaching it but stroking it tenderly.

"Lovely," the pirate captain said. "You please me well, boy."

Taren relaxed at the man's appreciative smile and reassuring words. He closed his eyes and gave in to the heady sensations, spellbound by the touch. He wouldn't have moved if he could have stayed there; he didn't want this pleasure to end. And when the pirate pressed his finger so that it barely breached Taren's opening, Taren came hard, his body shuddering with his release, his head reeling from the intensity of it.

"Thank you, sir," he managed to croak as he came back to his senses.

The captain chuckled and licked his hand as if it were covered in honey. "No need to thank me, boy," he said. "The pleasure was all mine."

Taren tucked himself back into his trousers, escaped from between the captain and the table, and picked up the soup. Thank goodness his long shirt hid the evidence of his release! He walked back toward the kitchen with a heated flush still on his cheeks, and he stood at the entrance, trying to calm his racing heart as his breath came in stuttered gasps.

Oh gods! Had Verita witnessed the entire sordid act? And what of himself? Had he *enjoyed* it?

No. Anyone would respond to such a touch. The thought didn't comfort him. And yet the warmth he had felt, having been satisfied by a hand other than his own—a *man's* hand, no less—still lingered.

He set the soup down on the fire to keep it warm and glanced over at Cook, who was happily tasting an aromatic stew in large spoonfuls, oblivious to Taren's return.

"I've finished, sir." Taren set about washing the dishes while he awaited further instruction. Perhaps he might be able to explain away the embarrassing stain as water from the sink.

He needn't have been concerned. Verita returned a short while later with a stack of bowls for washing, then left with the stew on her arm. She didn't say a word; she didn't even attempt to catch his eye.

MORE than an hour later, the dishes dried and replaced on the shelves, Cook gave Taren leave to return to the sleeping area. Taren had avoided any further contact with the pirates, and Verita had vanished after the tables were cleared, most likely to spend what remained of the night with a guest.

The faint color of dawn lit the horizon as Taren stepped into the courtyard. The rooster who had scolded him before crowed from atop a stone wall. Taren yawned deeply and strode with purpose across the dirt, taking care to steer clear of the other birds that were already pecking the ground in anticipation of breakfast.

He was nearly to the doorway of the building when he heard footsteps from behind him. He turned in surprise, confused as to why any other servants were up before the morning call. But it was not a servant he saw—it was one of the men from before.

"What can I get for—" he began to say, but a hand clamped tightly over his mouth from behind, cutting short his words. His heart pounded with fear as the hand pressed a piece of cloth against his mouth and nose and he inhaled a pungent odor. The world seemed to dim, and he remembered nothing more.

TWO

TAREN awoke in a large four-poster bed hung with heavy drapes. His body felt strange, as though he were a babe being rocked in his mother's arms. In his sleep-clouded mind, the slow rolling movement reminded Taren of the way fields of grain bent and swayed in a strong wind. He heard the sound of gulls and smelled salt on the air. Through the curtains, he saw a set of tall rectangular windows set with thick glass panes, much like those he'd seen on sailing vessels in port. Several of the windows were open, and the cool breeze caressed his face and chest. There was nothing outside but the blue sky, nothing below but waves.

We're at sea! Taren wondered how many miles they'd put between them and Raice Harbor. Had they sailed down the mainland coast before they'd set off, past the small villages that hugged the rocky coastline of the Derryth Kingdom and on toward the Eastern Lands? Or had they gone directly to sea, setting a course for the more tropical climes of the Luathan Islands? Taren had heard that pirates preferred the safety of the Luathans, with their calmer seas and sparsely habited shores.

Taren's excitement to discover he was no longer on land was tempered only by the next revelation: he was completely naked beneath the linen sheets. He tried to sit up, but his head spun and his vision clouded once more.

He struggled to remember how he had come to be aboard the ship. The vague memory of serving dinner resurfaced, along with a jolt of heat to his groin. He remembered the pirate captain—the deep blue of his eyes, his rugged features, his large hands....

"Good!" came a bright voice from the end of the bed. "You're awake. Captain's been asking about you. Said you'd been sleepin' like the dead. Wanted me to make sure you wasn't. Dead, I mean. Said old Shin gave you a bit more of Doc's sleeping draught than he should've. He was mighty angry with 'im too."

Taren started at the voice, pulling the sheets up over his chest. He felt as though he'd been sleeping for days. Perhaps he had. He needed to learn more about why he was here, why he had been taken from the inn. About the captain.

"What ship is this?" he asked as his eyes focused on the waif of a boy with shaggy black hair and freckles who was peering in between the drapes.

"The *Witch*," the boy said, his face lighting up with obvious pleasure. "The *Sea Witch*. Captain Rider's pride 'n' joy."

"Who are you?"

"Fiall. Practically raised aboard the *Witch* from a baby. And you're Taren."

Taren blinked in surprise that the boy knew his name.

Fiall giggled. "Didn't think I'd know that, did ye?" he asked. "'Course I would. You being the captain's new woman 'n' all."

"Woman? I'm not a wo—"

"Aw, I don't mean nothin' by that. It's just what we call the captain's favorites, is all. You know"—Fiall lowered his voice conspiratorially—"the special ones. The ones he keeps for himself. There's only one other. Bastian is his name. You'll be meeting him soon, I expect."

"Special ones?" Taren tried to force his fuzzy head to cooperate.

"The ones that sleeps in his bed," the boy answered with a knowing grin.

"Oh. No. I don't... I mean I'm not...." Taren's cheeks burned with embarrassment. It was one thing to imagine what it might be like to find himself in the captain's arms, but it was quite another to learn that everyone aboard the ship knew about it.

"It's nothin' to be 'shamed of," Fiall persisted. "I'd be right happy to be in your shoes."

"You... you're not a...?"

"Nah. I'm just the cabin boy. Besides, Captain don't like 'em young. Not that I'm young, mind you, I'm eleven years old now," Fiall said with pride. "Maybe in a few years...." Taren guessed Fiall realized he'd probably said too much.

When Taren remained silent, Fiall added, "I brought you some food. Captain says you'd be growin' more if you ate better. It's not much. Some bread and cheese. We'll get more supplies when we put into port in a week or so, seein' as we had to leave pretty fast on account of you."

"On account of *me*?"

Fiall smiled. "Seems like the captain took a likin' to you. Tried to buy you from your master, but he weren't havin' none of it. Somethin' about you not being for sale. Captain got a few of the men to bring you aboard."

That explained what had happened on his way back across the courtyard. Taren wondered if his former master had other plans for him. Maybe he'd planned to sell Taren to a merchant ship because of his rigging skills? Or perhaps what the other men had said was true—a pretty slave might fetch a pretty penny at auction. He'd heard the whorehouses paid well for boys with untouched bodies. The thought made Taren shiver.

"I'll leave the food on the table for you," Fiall continued, undaunted by Taren's silence.

"Thank you, Fiall."

Fiall offered Taren a crooked smile as he turned to leave.

"And Fiall?"

The boy turned and looked at Taren. "Yes?"

"Before you leave, can you tell me where I can find my clothes?"

Fiall blinked in surprise, then laughed outright. "You really are a one, aren't you?" When Taren continued to look confused, Fiall said, "You don't need no clothes down here. Later, maybe the captain will let you out on deck. If he decides you'll be needin' them for that, well, that's up to him. Nobody will touch you without his permission. The crew all know who you are."

And with this pronouncement, Fiall closed the drapes around the bed. A moment later, Taren heard the sound of a door closing. He was alone.

No clothes? He wasn't uncomfortable being naked—he'd worn rags that barely covered him before. Still, he felt vulnerable, especially when he thought of the captain.

Captain Rider. Taren wasn't so naïve as not to understand what it meant to be Rider's "woman." And after the other night, well, he was pretty sure that whatever that job entailed would be more pleasant than anything he'd been asked to do at the tavern. But why him? He was nothing so eye-catching as to warrant being called the captain's "special one."

Look at yourself! Thinking that being bedded by the captain might be enjoyable. He's a man and so are you. What good can come of it? And yet Captain Rider's touch had aroused him in a way he'd never been aroused with a woman.

He brushed the thoughts from his mind. His empty stomach was far more demanding than his half-hard cock. He'd eat his fill and explore the cabin. Later, he could think about his predicament. What more could he do, anyhow? And would he really want to try to escape? Things aboard the ship could hardly be worse than at the inn.

He ran his hand over the soft sheets and wiggled his toes beneath the blankets. At least here he'd be fed and sleep in a real bed. Would it be so terrible to stay?

TAREN awoke to the sound of the cabin door closing. He'd left the comfort of the large bed and the smaller sleeping room to explore the cabin beyond. He'd only once stolen a look at the captain's quarters on a large vessel such as this, and it had not had a separate room in which to sleep. The main cabin was larger than the sleeping quarters at the inn, and the walls, floor, and ceiling were made of polished wood, no doubt lovingly tended.

Taren touched the smooth surface of the captain's wooden desk, sat in the captain's chair and imagined giving his crew orders to attack an enemy ship. He gawked at the shelves full of books, but he feared opening them without the captain's permission.

By the bank of aft windows was a long table covered with papers— maps Taren guessed represented the Luathan Islands, beautifully and painstakingly rendered in ink with colorful embellishments. Taren had never seen a map before, except for the crude renderings in Borstan's journal. He ran reverent fingers over the parchment, as though his fingers might take him along the island coasts and around treacherous reefs of coral.

As a young boy, Taren had loved to sit by the fire after his work on the ropes was finished, and listen to Borstan recount his days serving aboard merchant ships. "The Derryth Kingdom is wealthy, but not as wealthy as some of the Eastern Lands." Taren remembered the wistful gleam in Borstan's dimming eyes. "We made the month-long crossing only once when the trade winds were favorable," Borstan had told an openmouthed

Taren. "Even then, the seas were rough and many a man suffered with sickness."

Borstan went on to regale Taren with stories of animals never seen in Derryth—colorful six-limbed animals who were trained to fight in the stadiums that sat thousands of people. "They anger the beasts with spears until they set upon each other and tear each other limb from limb. Then the prince'd take their fur an' make a coat for 'is princess."

As Taren ate the food Fiall had left for him—cheese and bread that tasted good and filled his empty stomach better than it had been filled in months—he imagined making such a crossing. Once he'd devoured every crumb on the wooden plate, he settled into a large comfortable chair by the windows in the main cabin and spent several hours gazing out the aft windows at the water. Finally, he curled up in the chair and slept, his full belly and the gentle rocking of the boat better than any lullaby.

Taren woke to see Captain Rider lighting the oil lamps that hung from the rafters about the cabin. The sun had already set, but the lamplight cast a warm glow about the room. "Now that's a sight for sore eyes." His rumbling voice warmed Taren, as did his eyes as they took in Taren's naked body. "Makes me wish I hadn't left you alone for so long."

Taren swallowed hard and did his best to school his expression. He silently wished he had gone back to the bedroom. At least there, he might hide his nakedness beneath the sheets. He feared the captain's hungry gaze as much as he craved it.

No doubt Rider sensed Taren's fear, because he asked, "Do I frighten you, Taren?"

"I… I… yes, I suppose you do." Taren hadn't planned to admit this, but something in Rider's expression told him he'd not suffer for speaking the truth.

Rider smiled. "No need. I'll not be hurting you unless you disobey me."

"What do you want from me?" Taren knew he was in no position to ask the captain anything, but he couldn't help himself.

Rider only chuckled. "They said you speak your mind," he said. "I daresay they were right. So what is it you do?"

"Sir?"

"Do you read and write?"

"Yes, sir." Taren had never thought much of it. He knew the other servants at the inn could do neither, but his master there had never taken advantage of his skills.

"Anything else?"

"I can rig a ship," Taren said with pride.

"Indeed?" This appeared to surprise the captain.

"If you give me my clothes," Taren continued, "I can help out on deck."

This time Rider's laugh was deep and throaty. "In time, perhaps. For now, the ropes are well manned and none are in need of immediate repair. My plans for you are far more… urgent."

Taren inwardly cursed himself as his cheeks grew hot once again. He was even more embarrassed when his cock also responded to Rider's words.

"Stand up."

Taren hesitated, afraid to let Rider see his traitorous erection.

"I said 'stand up', boy. You'll not be making trouble so quickly with me, will you?" Rider wore a stern expression, but Taren thought he saw a spark of amusement in Rider's eyes.

Taren did as he was told.

Rider's expression was inscrutable. He neither smiled nor laughed, nor did he look at Taren with disgust. "There is no shame in your desire," he said after a moment.

"But I'm a man."

Taren immediately regretted having spoken so quickly. "One of these days, boy," Borstan had admonished on many an occasion, "I'll whip you for that lip." The old man never had whipped him, and for that Taren had been grateful.

"Aye. That you are. And a fine man, at that."

"But—"

"Who were your parents, boy? Are they why you fear the touch of another man?"

"I never knew my parents. Borstan Laxley took me in as a baby. Fed me, clothed me, taught me to read and write, and gave me my name."

"And the old fool sold you." Rider shook his head. "What faith do you put in the morals of such a man?"

"I was his property. What choice did I have but to put my faith in—"

Rider frowned and wrinkled his weathered brow. "A slave is free to choose in whom to place his trust, even if his body belongs to his master. A good man will not mistreat a slave or sell him to pay for his own stupidity."

Taren looked at the floor, unsure what to say. He had little reason to believe Rider's words—he'd never known a master such as the one Rider described—and yet for the first time since Borstan had sold him to the inn, he began to hope for more.

"You will be treated well here, Taren Laxley. If you obey me, I will care for you, feed you, and clothe you. You will pay me with three years of your life, and then your freedom is your own. If you choose to leave after that, I will not stop you."

Taren opened his mouth in shock. Three years and he'd have his freedom? He could barely believe it. He'd lived his entire life knowing he would be an old man before he'd be able to pay off his indenture. He was nothing more than a slave. And yet this man—this pirate—was offering him freedom in return for three years of his life?

"You would set me free, if I choose it?"

"Yes. I would. If you choose to leave." Rider studied Taren with a look of patient understanding.

"And if I refuse you?"

"If you refuse, I'll return you to the inn."

Taren guessed Rider was lying, but he didn't want to find out. What were three more years of servitude compared to his freedom? And would it be so terrible if the pirate used his body for pleasure instead of putting him to work on deck? His face grew warm at the thought of such service.

"I will submit to you. I won't fight you."

At this, Rider laughed and shook his head. "I told you, boy, I'll treat you well. But I'll not have your submission without your soul. Tell me what you want. If you wish me to touch you, you must say it."

Taren released a slow breath. His body had long ago betrayed him, but he instinctively understood that Rider wanted him to speak the words. He also needed to say them for himself.

"I… I wish for you to touch me. I *want* you to touch me, as you did before."

A gentle smile lit Rider's face. "Come, then." Taren's heart pounded against his ribs as Rider offered him his calloused hand.

"Where are we going?"

"You're not going to sleep out here tonight, are you? The floor is mighty cold."

Does he mean for me to sleep in his bed? The thought both thrilled and terrified Taren.

Rider led Taren through the doorway to the bedroom and back to the curtained bed, next to which a small oil lamp provided a warm orange light. Pulling back the drapes, Rider said, "Climb inside."

The bed was not empty. Taren guessed its current occupant was a few years older than he: a beautiful young man with shoulder-length red hair that reminded Taren of the sunset. His eyes were a bright green, his face dotted with freckles. He was completely naked and stretched out on the sheets like an exotic cat, every inch of his skin visible in the lamplight. Taren could not force himself to look away. Had he stolen into the bedroom while Taren slept? Had he seen Taren naked? The thought secretly thrilled him.

"This is Bastian," Rider said with a smirk, no doubt guessing at Taren's desire.

Without warning, Bastian reached for Taren and pulled him onto the bed. He wrapped his arms around Taren's waist and kissed him, his tongue snaking its way into Taren's mouth and exploring it with eagerness.

Taren grew dizzy with the contact. The heat of their bodies pressed together felt like a wonderful revelation. Bastian held Taren spellbound by the feel of his skin against Taren's own. Taren had never kissed anyone like this, even the girls who had offered themselves to him. He moaned as he felt Bastian's hard cock against his own.

Taren gasped as the kiss broke. He wanted more but wasn't sure if he should ask for it.

"You were right," Bastian said as he slid lithe fingers over Taren's smooth chest. "He's perfect."

"It was Bastian's idea to bring another man into our bed," Rider explained to the still speechless Taren. Taren knew he'd betrayed his surprise, because Rider laughed. "Bastian is not a slave, Taren."

"He's not? But—"

"He was once my slave, but he is now master of my heart and my body." Rider glanced at Bastian with a look of pure lust and obvious affection. "He is also the *Sea Witch*'s quartermaster."

"*Quartermaster?*" Taren knew enough of pirate ships to understand that the quartermaster was nearly as powerful as the captain aboard a ship. It was the quartermaster, not the captain, who maintained peace amongst the crew.

"I gave him his freedom, just as I promised you yours. He chose to stay and I rewarded his loyalty. He is also a fine crew member. The other men obey him as they would me."

"Oh." Taren wasn't sure which of Rider's revelations surprised him more—that Bastian had chosen to stay aboard the ship when given his freedom, or that the ship's quartermaster willingly and gladly shared the captain's bed. *And they want me to join them?*

"You will watch and learn," Rider said, bringing Taren back to the here and now. "If you wish, you may join us, but I will not rush you." He winked at Bastian before adding, "Not yet, at least." He pulled his shirt over his head and tossed it onto the floor, then waited patiently as Bastian crawled over Taren and began to unfasten the large buckle on Rider's belt.

Taren's erection, which had begun to soften, reasserted itself as Bastian pulled Rider's trousers down to reveal a substantial cock, thick and hard. Taren had never seen anything as large, not amongst the other servants or even the guests at the inn when he had bathed them. Heavily veined, its tip broad and smooth, it both frightened Taren to behold and held great interest for him. He imagined how he might take it between his hands and how Rider's balls, now hidden in shadow, might feel as he rolled them about with his fingers.

Rider, noticing Taren's unabashed stare, caught Bastian's gaze and murmured, "Show him how it's done, love."

Bastian laughed and wet his lips as he watched Taren intently. Taren realized he too was licking his lips in anticipation—that he wanted to taste Bastian's seductive mouth again and explore Bastian's sleek body.

Bastian took Rider's cock into his mouth, swallowing him down so deeply that his nose brushed the curls at the base. Slowly, deliberately, he released Rider's cock, then sucked it down again, repeating the movement with obvious relish. Bastian sucked and moaned as though Rider's cock were the most heavenly of delicacies.

Rider slid his thick fingers through Bastian's silken hair, pulling on it until Bastian cried out. At first Taren feared Rider had hurt Bastian, but the corners of Bastian's mouth as they turned upward and the light in his eyes told Taren otherwise.

"Come closer and touch yourself," Rider commanded Taren. "I know you want to."

Taren swallowed his fear before doing as he was bidden. He moved beside Bastian on the edge of the bed, then took his cock in his hand and fisted it as he often had when he thought no one would see. The sensations he had felt in the darkness of the tavern's sleeping quarters were nothing compared to this. He mimicked Bastian's movements, matching the rhythm of his hand to Bastian's sucking. He imagined Bastian's mouth on him, imagined the softness of Bastian's hair, and watched Rider watching him with obvious desire.

It took only a moment before he came with a stifled cry. He spilled onto his hand and splashed the sheets. Ashamed at his lack of control, he looked away, only to feel Rider's hand on his shoulder.

"You're young. There will be time for more later, if you wish it."

From his position at Bastian's side, Taren watched Bastian roll Rider's sac in his hand as he continued to suck. From time to time, Bastian released Rider's erection and licked the puckered skin of his balls, wetting it until it glistened. Taren's cock swelled again as Bastian ran his teeth over Rider's hard member, teasing and nipping at the edge of the swollen tip. Taren imagined the feel of Bastian's mouth on his body, biting at him, taking him deep inside.

"You may touch him if you want," Rider told Taren as Taren watched the smooth, honeyed skin of Bastian's back.

For all that he was beginning to believe Rider's promises, Taren could not immediately comprehend what the captain had offered. *Why would he, my master, invite me to pleasure myself?*

"Go on, boy. Touch him." Perhaps noting Taren's hesitation, he added, "Do you not understand that seeing your pleasure increases my own?" With a shaking hand, Taren touch Bastian's skin. It was as soft as he'd imagined it would be—softer, even—and he explored the smooth surface of it with reverent awe.

"May I... taste him?" Taren asked.

Rider nodded his approval, so Taren leaned over and kissed Bastian's back, then licked it. Bastian tasted slightly salty, warm to the touch, enticing. Taren pressed the pads of his fingers into Bastian's shoulder blades, transfixed to see the muscles move beneath the silky skin. Tentatively at first, Taren nipped at Bastian's back as he had seen Bastian nip at Rider's cock. Bastian's breathing became ragged, his panted exhalations reassurance that Taren was pleasuring him. In spite of their obvious differences, Taren found both Rider and Bastian appealing. He imagined himself naked between the two men, and his body ached to be used.

Rider's groan of satisfaction as he came awoke Taren from his reverie. Bastian licked his lips and turned to look at Taren over his shoulder. "I want to fuck you, Taren."

The coarse language rekindled Taren's yearning. "Y-you want...?" Taren stammered, painfully aware of his lack of experience.

"Lean back," Bastian instructed. "Let me pleasure you."

Taren reclined on the pillows, and the next thing he knew, Bastian's hands were skating over his sensitive skin. Every fiber of Taren's being wanted this, *needed* this. He could not speak, so overcome was he by the feeling of those fingers. Then Bastian leaned over and took one of Taren's nipples between his lips and sucked on it until the flesh pebbled in reply. Bastian pressed the sensitive bud between his tongue and his teeth. The sensation was both painful and satisfying.

"Oh," Taren whispered. He did not realize the voice was his own until Bastian's gentle laughter filled the air.

By now Rider had climbed into the bed and was lying on one side, watching them. A vague thought flitted through Taren's mind: Rider *wanted* to watch them. The thrill of understanding coursed through Taren's blood like fire, and this time, he moaned louder. The thought of Rider's gaze on his naked body, of Rider watching as Bastian continued to suck and pull at his nipples, was heavenly.

"Turn over and spread your legs," Bastian murmured. Taren complied without a second thought. "Now lift your hips." Bastian pressed one of the pillows beneath Taren's belly to keep his hips raised. "Are you comfortable?"

Taren nodded, too enthralled to speak. Bastian reached for Taren's cock before exploring the place Taren had never dared touch. Instinctively, he moved to close himself, but Bastian stroked him gently and leaned forward so Taren could see his face. Like a falconer might calm an anxious bird, Bastian's touch was a balm to Taren.

"Close your eyes. Relax. Open yourself to me." Bastian's voice was husky with lust as he parted the cheeks of Taren's ass.

Taren didn't hesitate.

"Beautiful." Bastian traced a line from Taren's sac to the secret place between his buttocks with the wet warmth of his tongue. When Taren tensed once more, Bastian muttered, "I won't hurt you. Let me show you what you have waited to feel."

Taren breathed deeply and willed himself to relax. Bastian found the tight ring of muscle and probed at it with his tongue, coaxing Taren to release the tension there.

"Oh yes...," Taren moaned, unable to contain himself.

Bastian's tongue breached his opening.

"Gods!"

"Relax, boy," Rider said, his voice a soothing rumble to Taren's ears. The wetness from Bastian's mouth dripped between Taren's cheeks. "That's it," Rider said. "He won't hurt you."

Bastian probed Taren's tight opening with a finger, gently caressing it, then pressed inward so that the very tip of his finger breached Taren's hole. Taren keened beneath the touch, lifting his hips and tucking his knees underneath to allow Bastian easy access.

"That's it. Have I hurt you?"

"No." Taren's voice sounded as though it were someone else's, coming from far away. "Please. Oh please. I want... I need... more."

Rider stroked Taren's hair as Bastian pressed his wet finger inside. It was slick, but the feeling was different from before, and as the scent of rosemary and lavender filled his nostrils, Taren realized Bastian had covered his hands in fragrant oil.

"Just breathe, Taren. I promise you, this will feel good."

Taren did not protest as Bastian slid his finger past the tight muscles. It felt so good that Taren whimpered in response. "Oh... yes... oh...."

Rider looked on in pleasure as Taren's body yielded to a second finger, then a third. Each time, Bastian pulled and stretched the muscles to open Taren wider, his fingers slick with oil. Then, without warning, Bastian rubbed against something inside that made Taren shudder—something so wonderful he could do nothing but pant.

"Like that, do you?" Rider said with a smile for Bastian.

"Yes. Oh yes."

"Do you want me?" Bastian's lips nearly touched Taren's ear.

"Yes." Taren could barely breathe, his fear was so great. But he knew he could not resist. The siren call was too strong. He needed to *know*. To feel this.

"I want to feel your warmth, feel myself fill you. Show you what you've longed for."

"Ahhh... gods.... I.... Please... fuck me!"

It felt strange, crouching like a dog, his ass splayed so both men could see his most private of places, and yet he did not object. More than anything, he wanted this. He wanted to understand. He had not expected Bastian's fingers to thrill him so, and the thought of Bastian's cock in their place sent shivers through his body.

Rider lay watching them with an intensity that surprised Taren. He no longer felt shame beneath that lustful gaze. He knew only his desire, his hunger, and his aching need.

"Please. Oh please...," Taren begged.

Bastian pushed his hard cock against Taren's opening. "Relax. Just let me in." Bastian's voice soothed him, and Rider once again caressed Taren's head.

The moan that issued from Taren's lips as Bastian breached him was tinged with pain, but as Bastian seated himself inside, the heat from within erased all but the heady sensation of being filled.

The sensation of being impaled was at once glorious and frightening. With each increasingly powerful thrust, Taren moved to meet Bastian, drawn by invisible strings.

Taren looked to Rider for approval. Rider moved toward Taren and got to his knees to offer Taren his own cock. Taren understood. Although he had never tasted another man's cock, he put his lips to the tip and licked. Rider roughly pulled Taren's head down to match each of Bastian's thrusts, matching the same delicious rhythm.

"Close your lips around me."

Taren was too enthralled to think about his lack of experience. He tightened his lips around the captain's cock and allowed his mouth to be filled just as Bastian now filled his ass.

Taren gagged and spluttered, instinctively turning his head so Rider's large cock slid against the inside of his cheek and he no longer choked on it. Rider rumbled his approval and reached underneath Taren to pinch a pink nipple and twist it about. Taren knew nothing but the burning heat in his ass,

Rider's musky scent, and the salty taste of Rider's cock on his tongue. Never before had he felt so wanted.

Bastian cried out his fierce orgasm with abandon. At nearly the same moment, Rider emptied himself into Taren's mouth and Taren spurted onto the sheets beneath them. This time he did not hold back his cries, and the captain's warm release dribbled over his chin.

Clasped tightly in Bastian's arms a moment later, Taren gasped for breath, his body still shaking with the aftershocks. He saw the look the other two men exchanged and knew he had done well, that he had served them as they had hoped. The thought warmed him as he lay awake long after Rider extinguished the small lamp.

THREE

Two years later

THE island of Lurat was a frequent stop on the *Sea Witch*'s travels and one Taren loved. Hundreds of vividly painted clapboard houses dotted the green hillsides surrounding Newtown Harbor like flowers blooming on a vine. Vendors selling fruits and vegetables alongside exotic treasures from the farthest reaches of the seas filled the bustling market near the town's main square. Lurat's economy thrived upon trade, and the *Witch*'s crew always felt welcomed.

"We will sail for the mainland in less than a month," Bastian said casually as he and Taren strolled through the marketplace in the bright morning sun. He regarded Taren with quiet interest, clearly hoping to glean his reaction. "Does this please you? To be going home?"

Taren just smiled and ran his palm over his mouth and chin. "My home is aboard the *Witch*. I have no need to revisit my far-from-blissful childhood."

Bastian's expression told Taren this was just the reaction he had sought. The realization that the other man had been concerned that he might feel differently about returning to his childhood home warmed him. Bastian needn't have been worried—Taren wanted nothing more than to stay aboard the *Witch*, and he intended to make that clear to Rider when his three years were paid.

Bastian clapped Taren on the shoulder. "Good man."

They walked onward, stopping when they smelled meat cooking over open flame. How long had it been since Taren had eaten anything but fish?

His mouth watered. Bastian must have noticed, for he gave the vendor a few coins and handed Taren one of two small skewers. The meat was spicy and sweet, with a hint of coconut and tomato that was heavenly. Taren finished his share in a scant minute, then licked each of his fingers in turn. This garnered a lecherous look from Bastian. It thrilled Taren to know he was the cause.

"Later," Bastian said as they walked once more, "you will have to lick my fingers as well."

"I heard Rider say he'd bought more honey. He said he wants to watch me lick it off of you." Taren chewed his lip and smiled at the memory.

More often than not, Rider liked to watch him with Bastian before joining in, although sometimes Rider sent him up on deck and Rider and Bastian spent the evening in bed. Taren didn't mind; he was happy with his place aboard the *Sea Witch*. He had no need to possess either man's heart—his only wish was to serve them faithfully and bask in the warmth of their affection.

"Aye. He does like that." Bastian's eyes glittered. Taren could see his love for Rider as clearly as he could the ship in the harbor. He wondered if someday he too might look the same.

"I heard the men talking at the docks," Taren said, changing the subject. "Seems we nearly had company. The *Phantom*. Do you know her?"

Bastian's expression changed markedly, becoming quite serious. "I know her only too well. And her captain, Ian Dunaidh." He spoke the name in something approaching a hiss. "A rat bastard who would sell his own mother to the devil. He and the captain knew each other. Went to school together when they were boys. Captain won't abide his name spoken aboard the *Witch*."

"Oh. What did he do?" Taren knew little about Rider, but he'd never known Rider to hold a grudge.

"No one knows." Bastian spoke in a low voice. "Some say Ian betrayed him and left him to die. Others say they were lovers and Ian ripped out the captain's heart and spat upon it. Me, if I ever see the dog, I'll make him pay."

Taren didn't know what to say so he held his tongue. Taren could not imagine Rider with anyone but Bastian in his bed. He knew it was childish and even naïve, but he couldn't imagine anyone else in Rider's arms. Except perhaps himself, although he knew well enough that Rider's heart belonged only to Bastian.

A few minutes later, they arrived at the edge of the square, where Bastian stopped and handed Taren a small bundle of coins. "Run along and find something for our master's birthday next week while I arrange payment for our cargo."

"Me? But I—"

"You are more than capable of finding something the old man will enjoy," Bastian said with a laugh and a wink.

Taren nodded, brightening. He had seen something that had caught his fancy in one of the stalls hidden behind the fish vendor. "I have an idea," he admitted as he pocketed the silver. "Shall we meet back at the docks?"

"Aye. Captain'll be wanting to leave before noon. He'll not want to weather the coming storm in port."

Taren had felt the storm's approach two days before—a distant rumbling in his bones that grew more urgent the closer it came—so Rider had adjusted their course to avoid the brunt of it. Taren could sense changes in the weather long before the other men aboard the *Sea Witch*, and Rider had come to rely on Taren's instincts to keep the ship out of harm's way. They would not be able to outrun this particular storm. The best they could hope for was to catch only the leading edge and seek safe harbor to ride out the rest.

In spite of this, the storm excited Taren. The *Sea Witch* had only seen a few tempests since Taren had come to the ship, but he enjoyed the excitement of the wind and the waves.

Bastian left Taren with a quick wave of his hand. Taren watched him for a moment, then turned and walked back to the stalls, his step light. It took him only a few minutes to locate the vendor he'd seen before.

"Back, are ye?" The small man sat behind a wooden crate, his goods set out on pale-yellow silk. The smell of fish was strong here, but it didn't bother Taren. He found the familiar scent comforting. All around them, people chattered and did their marketing. Taren had spent many an hour at the market by the inn as a boy, although he had been there at Cook's behest and had never shopped for his own pleasure. How much had changed in the two years he'd spent aboard the *Sea Witch*.

He smiled and picked up a delicate carving made from smooth green stone. A horse, judging by its tail and broad muzzle. "From the Eastern Sea," the old man said with a glint of pleasure on his narrow face. "They say it takes months to sail there, and few ships return. Perhaps they never reach those shores. Perhaps they stay."

Taren set the figure down and picked up another, rubbing his thumb over the cool surface of it. He held it up to the light, trying to make it out but without success.

"A dragon." The vendor smiled broadly. "They say they are as plentiful as deer and that villages must sacrifice their most beautiful maiden each year to appease their angry spirits."

Taren grinned and shook his head. He'd heard of the fire-breathing creatures, although he doubted that they or their sea-dwelling brethren ever existed. He eyed the dragon once more, then set it back down on the silk. He had not come here for the carvings, but had it been a gift for Bastian, he might have taken one—the dragon's fire reminded him of Bastian's hair.

He brought his fingers to his lips and eyed the object he'd spotted before, set in a small box lined in velvet. Taren tried not to smile as he reached for it and lifted it from its container: a large ring carved from the same cool stone. He held it between his thumb and forefinger, studying it as his cheeks warmed. He was not ashamed—far from it—he was imagining how Rider might use it on him or Bastian. The thought also heated his loins.

"I see you know of its uses." The old man's smile was broader still.

"I… have heard of such a thing."

"In the East," the old man explained, lowering his voice, "there are slaves who wear such jewelry and nothing else. Their masters might parade them through a market much like this one for all to see their—" The old man grinned, pausing for effect. "—charms."

"How much?" Taren asked far too quickly. The thought of Rider parading him naked through the market, his manhood visible to all who passed by, aroused Taren. Two years before, he might have been ashamed to imagine this, but now it excited his passions.

The old man told him the price, which Taren paid with shaking hands. He headed back toward the port a few minutes later, his body thrumming, wishing Rider's birthday were tonight so he or Bastian could demonstrate Rider's gift.

He had almost reached the outer edge of the marketplace when he nearly tripped on one of the uneven flagstones. He caught himself before he fell, pausing with his hands on his knees, laughing at himself that he was acting just like a giddy child with a secret he couldn't wait to share.

When he stood straight once more, he noticed a withered old woman sitting on a blanket in the shade of a tree. Her eyes were milky, unseeing, her hair white and thinning so that Taren could see her scalp beneath. By her side lay a small metal plate with several coins.

Taren reached into his pocket and retrieved a copper coin—far more than she'd expect, but he had nothing smaller. Rider had often teased him for his overly generous heart, but Taren knew Rider approved of it as well. The copper coin clattered against the metal, making the old woman turn her face toward her benefactor. Taren wondered for a moment if he'd misjudged her, if she could see. But her gaze focused on a place beyond where he stood, and he realized he'd correctly guessed that she was blind.

"You are kind," she said in a voice that quavered and rasped. He wondered how old she was. Life on these islands was difficult. He'd seen few people as old. "Your kindness will serve you well."

"May I get you some water?" he asked, noting the empty cup behind her. She nodded, so he reached for the cup. As he did, she grabbed his wrist with surprising strength, pulling him toward her.

"You will be tested," she rasped in his ear. This close, she smelled of the ocean, salty and bright.

"What did you say?" He was sure he'd heard her clearly, but he did not wish to offend her. He knew that sometimes age clouded the mind as well as the eyes.

"The call is strong. Soon, it will claim you."

He pulled away from her so abruptly that he collided with a woman doing her shopping. He apologized for his rudeness, then turned back to the old woman. She was gone. He looked around, but she was nowhere to be seen. How had such a frail woman moved with such speed? The blanket and plate were gone as well. For a moment Taren just stared at the stones.

"Taren!"

Taren turned to see one of his shipmates waving toward him. He rubbed his chin and shook his head. *How strange.*

"Taren!" Charlie called once more. This time Taren shrugged, then went to join Charlie and the others as they made their way back to the ship.

TAREN swung down off the ropes from the foremast and made a surefooted landing on the deck. The sun had just begun to rise at the edge of the horizon. He inhaled a deep breath of salty air.

"The new halyard's secured, sir," he called to Rider.

"Just in time too," Rider replied with a nod. "With a little luck, we'll outsail the worst of the storm."

The growing moisture in the air and the cool fingers of wind intertwining with the warmer breeze spoke of the coming storm.

"Get yourself some rest," Rider told Taren. "We'll need to take shifts on this one. Bastian will relieve me at nightfall, and I'll want you by his side."

"Aye, sir."

Taren's body ached from his work high atop the mast. He had spent nearly six hours checking the ropes and replacing those too worn to weather the storm. Though the work had been exhausting, Taren loved nothing more than climbing to the top of the mastheads and looking out over the ocean.

Taren had become an indispensable part of the crew in the two years he had been aboard the *Witch*, working the lines, helping man the deck, even learning to chart the ship's course. As promised, Rider had treated him well. Rider had rewarded Taren for his loyalty with more and more freedom. With enough food to fill his stomach, Taren had grown from a lanky boy to a powerful man, taller even than Rider, with shoulders nearly as broad. His dark hair was now long and knotted at the nape of his neck with a leather tie, his skin a honeyed caramel from his time in the sun.

After taking the steps down to the aft cabin two at a time, he closed the door behind him and shed his damp clothing. He washed away the salt from his face and hands in the small basin, toweling himself off before heading to the bedroom. Later, he would straighten the cabin and see to Rider's laundry. It pleased Taren to serve Rider in this way—it pleased him to serve him in *every* way.

"Lazing around as usual?" he asked as he drew the curtains aside and climbed between the sheets. Bastian opened one eye, then closed it again with a soft huffing sound. "I can think of better ways to pass the time."

Bastian drew his arms over his head and stretched. "Indeed. But I have orders from the captain to rest."

"Then I will make sure you sleep well," Taren said with a chuckle as he dived under the sheets and took Bastian's awakening cock in his mouth.

"Tempting me from my duty, are you?" Bastian pulled Taren's hair free of its tie and ran his fingers through the dark silky strands.

Taren said nothing but put his hands underneath Bastian, cupping the muscles of his buttocks and letting out a low rumble. Bastian canted his hips forward to greet Taren's mouth, which made Taren smile with pleasure.

Two years, and Taren wasn't sure which he loved more—the feel of Bastian's smooth skin beneath his fingers or Rider's huge cock in his ass. He spent his days above decks, climbing high on the masts, and his nights enjoying the warmth of his two companions. Taren no longer thought of his servitude, he only wondered how he might live without the joys Bastian and Rider had shown him.

"Ah," Bastian shouted as he spilled himself into Taren's willing mouth, "what happened to the little whelp we brought aboard all those months ago? Your mouth is sinful and your body insatiable."

Taren laughed. He loved Bastian's sleek body and the way he felt buried inside of him, while Bastian seemed to enjoy letting Taren dictate the course of their lovemaking. On deck, Bastian was far from subservient—no doubt he enjoyed the respite from the strain of the command. It warmed Taren to know that Bastian trusted him with his secret.

"Shall I take you from behind?" Taren wondered aloud, knowing it would drive Bastian to distraction to hear him speak of his intentions without acting upon them. "Or perhaps I should have you sit upon me so I can feel your chest and watch the way your face contorts as I impale your body on mine. Or perhaps—"

"Stop your babbling and fuck me, you rascal, or I shall have you kissing the gunner's daughter while I take the cat to your haunches!"

"For as often as you've spoken of it," Taren said with a broad grin, "you might need to try it sometime. I hear tell there are whips that can bring a man pleasure as well as pain. But unless you mean to make good on your threat, I will fuck you." He laughed as he forced Bastian onto his belly. "From behind, since you beg like a dog for it."

Bastian threw his head back, sending his hair flying about his face and shoulders, then pushed back until Taren was seated deep within.

"Beautiful dog," Taren whispered into Bastian's ear. Then, thrusting so as to leave Bastian nearly breathless, he said, "I have tamed you."

"Perhaps," Bastian said as he shuddered with each movement, "*I* am the one who has tamed *you*?"

Taren tugged hard on his hair until Bastian cried out with desire. "We shall see about that, won't we?"

A gust of salty air blew through the room, causing the curtains of the bed to sway. *If this is servitude*, Taren thought as he climaxed with a satisfied growl, *then let me die a slave!*

BY NIGHTFALL the ship bucked like a filly in the waves. Lightning flashed in the distance as the sails snapped and filled with each howling gust of wind. Water slicked the deck, so Taren shed his shoes in favor of bare feet. He'd always preferred the feel of his skin against the wood to the slippery leather. He and the other men had also shed the waterlogged jackets that sapped the warmth of their bodies. The cold spray stung Taren's face, but the salt water was oddly reassuring.

Rider had gone belowdecks to rest. Taren knew soon enough he'd be back up top if the swells continued to grow. Bastian had steered the ship on a course to avoid the worst of the storm and give them the best speed, but the vessel now took each wave nearly head-on. They'd made a devil's choice, but the crew was well seasoned and the *Witch* soundly built; they would rely on the strength of her sails as well as the fortitude of the men to pull her through.

"Fiall!" Bastian shouted over the caterwauling winds and the crashing of the waves. "Why aren't you belowdecks?"

The gangly teenager forced a smile, but he appeared ghostly pale. Taren guessed he was seasick. Soaked to the bone, hair plastered to his cheeks and jaw. Taren saw him shiver as the wind rose once more and wrapped its icy fingers around them.

"I wanted to help, sir." Fiall stood straight, and Taren guessed he was doing his best to keep his balance without holding on to the rails.

"Stay away from the rails, you fool." Bastian shook his head and nodded to Taren, who grabbed a rope and made his way toward the railing. If the boy were going to stay up on deck, Taren would make sure he didn't tumble into the waves. Fiall would, Taren knew, make a good hand when he put a little more meat on his bones, but he had been growing so fast of late that he was awkward, and his coordination left a lot to be desired.

Fiall shot Taren a pained smile as a clap of thunder rent the air. "I'm sorry," he moaned. "I tried to stay below."

"Even the best of us feel ill when the swells are this high." Taren knew he was one of the few aboard who had never experienced the slightest sickness, even in the roughest of seas. "You need not fear. I'll just wrap a line around you so that if you stumble—"

The ship pitched and Fiall turned back to the rails, vomiting overboard. Taren moved forward to secure the line around the boy's waist, but at that moment an especially monstrous wave tossed the ship to starboard. In the blink of an eye, Fiall disappeared into the inky waters.

"Man overboard!" Taren shouted over another thunderclap that shook the ship. It was useless to shout; he doubted Bastian or the others could hear him over the wailing wind. Taren could run over to Bastian, but by the time they dropped the sails and circled back to find him, Fiall would drown. Without a second thought, Taren wrapped the rope around his wrist and dove over the side of the ship. Bastian and Rider would have his head later for his foolhardy rescue attempt, but they would forgive him his folly when he made it back to the ship with Fiall in tow.

Taren sliced through the surface of the waves. The icy water clawed at his bones, but he ignored it. The cold would be far worse for the boy; he had no time to bemoan his own discomfort when Fiall would succumb far sooner. He struggled upward to fill his lungs, then dove once more.

Taren could see nothing beneath the waves, but he became aware of movement on the surface. He could almost hear Fiall's struggle to stay afloat and feel the vibrations of his flailing arms and legs. The boy was close, perhaps only a few yards from where Taren had surfaced. He swam with all his strength against the force of the wind and the waves, clutching the rope in his hand. He knew Bastian had brought the ship about when the rope did not go taut in his grip. It was a testament to Bastian's skill as a sailor that he could turn the ship so quickly in the midst of the tempest.

As he drew nearer to the place where he guessed Fiall to be, Taren heard screams over the sound of the waves and the wind. His heart pounding against his ribs, he swam harder, surfacing only once to breathe. A flash of lightning illuminated the darkness and gave him a glimpse of Fiall as he slipped beneath the waves, his strength giving out at last.

No! Taren took in a breath so deep it hurt his lungs before diving beneath the water with all his strength. He saw nothing in the darkness, yet he could almost hear the beat of Fiall's heart and the last of his breaths as water filled his lungs. For an instant, Taren thought he could even smell the boy. With renewed determination, Taren swam deeper still to where the storm no longer buffeted him. He reached out, certain Fiall was close. A moment later, his hand touched Fiall's belt. He tied the rope around Fiall's waist, struggling to secure it. It was difficult to tie the knot as he held the boy and kicked to propel them to the surface.

There was no time for Taren to secure himself to the same rope that held Fiall. Instead, he hung on tightly, yanked hard on the rope and prayed someone on the ship would feel the tug. When the rope began to lift them both, he smiled in relief and continued to kick his way upward to ease their ascent. He had no air left in his lungs as they broke the surface.

Taren was too distracted by Fiall, who was no longer breathing. He didn't see the dark bulkhead of the *Sea* Witch as it approached. Just as the crew hauled Fiall free of the waves, Taren's head hit the wooden keel and the rope slipped from his hands. He fell into the water and sank down into the blackness of the waves.

HE DREAMED he was swimming beneath the water, breathing it in like air, his limbs cutting through the current and driving him forward with ease like those of a powerful animal. He wanted to laugh, so powerful was the feeling of the water on his body. He knew he had never truly lived before; he was reborn in the moment he surrendered himself to the darkness of the sea.

He was going home! Home to the place he had always known existed in his heart. It called to him. He did not need to see it to know it was there. He only needed to follow that call to find it.

TAREN floated on the surface of the waves, the cool seawater caressing his back, the warm sunshine on his face. Surely he was dreaming, or perhaps this was death? In the distance he heard the faint sound of voices. He struggled to open his eyes but was too weak.

The next thing he knew, he was being hauled out of the water by his arms.

"I told you we should have left him." The voice was rough, unfamiliar.

"Is he dead?" asked a second voice, more distant than the first.

He was dropped unceremoniously onto a hard surface. Every muscle and bone in his body protested at the rough treatment. A foot connected with his gut, rolling him onto his belly. He coughed and vomited salt water, gagging on the foul taste. He didn't have the strength to lift his head.

"Nah. But he looks pretty bad. Tell Captain Ian. He'll want to know how this one got past the island's defenses."

A vague memory stirred at the sound of the name Ian. Taren tried to protest as the men bound his hands and tossed him over a hard shoulder. He slipped back into the warmth of the darkness, and the pain faded.

FOUR

THE men who dragged Taren from the ship's hold shoved him so hard into the captain's quarters that he nearly fell face-first on the floor. His hands were tied behind his back. He'd been given water, although his throat was still parched. His belly growled. How long had it been since he'd awoken on the deck of the ship? He'd been locked away since he'd regained consciousness. He feared for the *Sea Witch* and her crew more than for his own safety. He prayed his shipmates had made it through the tempest unharmed.

In spite of his pathetic state, the ship and the men who manned her felt oddly familiar to Taren. He knew he hadn't met them before, of course, but the sensation was strong. Regardless, the sense of familiarity had not improved the conditions in which he'd been kept since his capture. He felt relieved to be freed from the darkness of the ship's hold, if only temporarily.

Through the large windows at the back of the room, Taren could see it was nighttime. He'd lost track of the days in the darkness. A nearly full moon illuminated the room, enabling Taren to make out a desk of carved wood, a simple table covered with maps, and several chairs. In the corner of the room was a large bed, also carved. The quarters were spartan, immaculate, and revealed nothing about their occupant.

"Leave us. And unbind him." By the dim light, Taren struggled to make out the features of the man to whom the rough, commanding voice belonged.

"But Captain," one of Taren's captors protested. "The Council will want to know why he's—"

"Leave us, Seria," the captain snapped with obvious irritation. "The Council has no jurisdiction here. My men and I can handle him without your help."

"As you wish." From the tone of his voice, Taren judged the man none too pleased to be dismissed.

The leather strap around his wrists removed, Taren brought his numb hands together and massaged them as the men left. "Do not think that you can run," the captain warned, perhaps sensing Taren's thoughts. "My men are stationed outside the door, and I am more than capable of killing you without their help."

The captain drew closer, and Taren could make out his features at last. What he saw surprised him. He had thought the man far older, when in fact he appeared to be only a few years Taren's senior. The same age, perhaps, as Bastian, although his body was far broader and he stood even taller than Taren himself. Taren could not help but marvel at the bright green of the man's eyes and the handsome edge of his strong jaw. For a moment he wondered if he'd seen Ian before. There was something familiar in the intensity of his gaze, something that stirred not only Taren's loins but also his heart.

Fool! He holds the power to kill you, and yet all you can do is admire his appearance? Bastian was right. You're a wanton, insatiable creature.

"What is your name, man, and how do you come to be here?" the captain demanded, his expression hard with impatience.

"I am Taren. Taren Laxley. I know not how I came to be here." He still remembered nothing after he had lashed the rope about Fiall's waist.

The edge of the captain's mouth turned upward in a sneer. "Taren?"

Taren said nothing but met the other man's gaze and held it, unafraid.

"I am Ian Dunaidh, captain of the *Phantom*." He spoke the words with little emotion, but Taren thought he saw a flash of pride in Ian's eyes.

Ian Dunaidh? Again that name. Taren struggled to remember where he'd heard it before. Then it came back to him—the conversation he'd had with Bastian, not long before Taren had been lost at sea. He remembered the hatred in Bastian's eyes when he'd spoken of Ian. What had Bastian said? Rider and this man had been schoolboys together, but Ian had betrayed Rider or perhaps broken his heart? But how could that be? Rider was a man well into his forties, but this man appeared far younger. Still, knowing they were bitter rivals, Taren became even more determined to keep secret his connection to the *Witch* and her crew.

"Where did you come from?" Ian asked when Taren did not speak.

"I... I don't know." Taren knew Ian wouldn't believe it. He didn't care. He would not endanger the crew of the *Sea Witch*, even if it meant his life.

Ian laughed. "You lie."

The ship lurched with a strong gust of wind and Taren, weakened from lack of food and thirst, stumbled back against the bulkhead and slipped down. Ian moved to steady Taren, pulling him up with a strong arm around Taren's waist. This close, Taren could smell the captain's musk and feel his breath upon his cheek. He responded to the rough contact in spite of himself, his cock filling and pressing against Ian's muscled thigh.

Their eyes met. Ian appeared momentarily at a loss, Taren's touch seeming to burn him. Taren knew he should attempt to free himself from Ian's grasp, but—to his shame and dismay—he didn't want the contact to end.

Ian turned to Taren and parted his lips but seemed unable to speak.

Without thinking, Taren leaned into Ian until their mouths touched. For an instant Ian seemed to hesitate, then took Taren's lips with obvious hunger, kissing Taren hard as he probed the warmth of Taren's mouth with his tongue. Ian's breaths came in stutters and Taren moaned. His tongue danced around Ian's with equal fervor. Gods, how he wanted this man!

When Ian finally pulled away, Taren was left gasping for breath, dizzy. Even Bastian had not aroused him thus. Ian seemed to hold some power over him that he was incapable of fighting. He couldn't understand it—Ian Dunaidh was his captor and Rider's enemy. Even so, Taren felt naked before him. The remnants of his tattered clothes did nothing to cover his body from Ian's piercing gaze. He also felt a sudden pang of guilt at the thought of Rider and Bastian. Not that they'd ever spoken of what might happen if Taren stayed with them after his three years of service were complete, but didn't he owe them his body, for at least that long?

Ian too appeared taken aback by what had transpired between them. His face appeared flushed, his brow dotted with sweat. "What...?" He stepped backward, leaving Taren barely able to stand but for the cabin wall supporting him.

"Who are you?" This time Ian's voice was softer, any anger seemingly replaced by something approaching wonder.

"I-I told you who I am." Taren wished he sounded more confident, but Ian left him ill at ease. In spite of the venom he'd heard in Bastian's words when he'd spoken of the *Phantom*'s captain, Taren wanted to tell Ian everything, if only to feel his body once more pressed against his own and taste his mouth again.

"Who were your parents?" Ian appeared to have regained his self-control. He straightened up to his full height and did not move to touch Taren again.

"I don't know. I never knew them." Taren touched his lips, which still felt warm from Ian's kiss. Then Taren added, almost without thinking, "What do you care?"

Ian appeared to consider the question. "Just curious," he said at last, his tone dismissive.

Someone knocked on the door and one of the men peered inside. "Everything all right, Captain?"

"Everything's fine." Ian barely looked at the man.

"Shall I return the prisoner to the hold?"

"No." Ian did not hesitate. "He will stay here with me."

"Sir?" The sailor appeared shocked.

"He will stay with me. Have the cabin boy prepare a bed for him. Post a guard at my door."

"Yes, sir!" The man turned and left, sparing a frown for Taren.

"Do you intend to keep me here as your slave?" In truth, the idea of submitting to Ian held more than a little appeal for Taren, although he was far too proud to admit it.

"No." It was not the answer Taren had expected. "You will sleep here. That is all."

Taren felt shame to realize this answer disappointed him. On the other hand, being in the captain's cabin might prove useful. Here, he'd have better access to the upper decks of the ship. With a little luck, he might be able to escape.

Ian narrowed his eyes as he said, "If you attempt to escape, I will lock you in the hold once more."

Taren averted his gaze. *Can he read my thoughts?*

Several men entered a few moments later with a bedroll and a few extra blankets.

"Bind him. See that he's bathed," Ian said. "If he fights you, return him to the hold."

"Yes, sir."

"And see that he gets some food. Nothing too heavy. Gruel or soup."

"Aye, sir."

Ian nodded, then quickly left the cabin and a very surprised Taren behind.

IAN stood at the bow of the ship, focused on the water. The moon had set and taken with it the last traces of purple and red that had colored the clouds. He had been standing here for nearly an hour, lost in thought. Only now did he take heed of his surroundings.

Taren. The name was foreign to his lips. Not a name given to those of his people. And yet he'd repeated it now more times than he cared to admit. He couldn't deny what he had sensed when they'd kissed. *He is one of us.* Was it possible Taren did not know? Ian had sensed no lie when he'd claimed not to know his parents, although Ian sensed deceit when Taren claimed not to know where he'd come from.

He doesn't remember how he got here. That was also the truth. The nearest ship had been days away—they had received no reports of other vessels in the area—and if by some chance Taren had survived a shipwreck as a result of the great storm, surely there would have been debris to accompany him. The crew said he'd been found on the surface of the waves. With nothing to keep him afloat. A normal man would have perished. Much as Ian wished there were another explanation, there wasn't. Taren was no normal man. But why had he sensed the truth of Taren's birthright only when he'd touched him?

Ian also couldn't deny the way his body responded to the boy, couldn't deny that for a moment he'd been tempted to do more than kiss him. What the devil was wrong with him? All Ea were dual-natured, animal and man, but only adolescents new to their Ea form lacked self-control.

Why did you kiss him? Ian stroked his hand over his lips, recalling the feel of Taren's mouth, his taste. Like the ocean, wild and vast. Something in

Taren's kiss had stirred Ian's other nature. Even now, Ian felt the need to dominate the boy. And yet, along with the primal hunger, there was something more—something strange and equally as wonderful as the powerful attraction. Familiarity.

FIVE

"SIR?"

The cabin boy's voice brought Ian back to his senses. "What is it, Aine?"

"Cook says your dinner is getting cold."

"He does, does he?" Ian chuckled. "Old goat. He wants his sleep. If he had any concern for my stomach, he'd cook something other than salt fish."

Aine blinked but said nothing.

"Do I frighten you, child?" The expression on the boy's face was all he needed to know. Ian sighed. The boy was new, the son of a good friend. No doubt he had seen the prisoner and heard the crew's stories—some true, others myths meant to instill fear in the child.

"N-no, sir," Aine replied, clearly doing his best not to betray his lie.

Ian sighed. "Barra has told you about your predecessor and how I threw him overboard in a fit of rage."

Aine's eyes widened.

"I suppose he neglected to tell you that *he* is your predecessor." Ian waited as his words sank in. Aine's mouth dropped open and Ian laughed outright. "Yes. Ask the others. And if Barra causes you any grief, you may tell him that I *shall* toss him overboard if he doesn't cease his endless prattle."

The corners of Aine's mouth turned upward, and Ian ruffled the boy's hair. "Aye, sir!" His face was bright with barely disguised glee.

"Now run along and tell Cook to set my dinner in my cabin. I'll be there shortly."

"Aye, sir."

"Oh, and Aine?"

"Sir?"

"The prisoner. Has he eaten?"

"Aye, sir. Cook made him some soup. He's been washed and has been given new clothing."

"Did he give the men any trouble?"

"No, sir."

Ian wasn't too surprised to hear this, but it did relieve some of his concerns. He didn't want to have to send the prisoner back to the hold. "Excellent."

"Sir? May I speak freely?"

Ian schooled his expression, doing his utmost not to smile at the formality of the boy's words. No doubt Aine had overheard the other men address him in this manner. "Of course."

"Why have you moved me out of your cabin? Am I not performing my duties to your satisfaction?"

Damn. He'd hurt the boy and he hadn't even realized it. "Not at all. In fact, I'm very pleased with your service to me." He rubbed his hand over his jaw. "But this prisoner is not to be trusted. Not yet, at least. And until I know it's safe for you to return to your place at my side, you will stay with the rest of the men."

"Aye, sir. Of course, sir." Aine appeared relieved.

"Good."

"But this prisoner... if he is so dangerous, then why do you keep him by your side?"

Ian smiled. "A good question, boy, and one that doesn't concern the likes of you. Now run along and tell Cook I'll be expecting my dinner soon." He could hardly tell the boy he feared what Seria might do to the prisoner. The thought of Seria aboard his ship still made his anger burn hot—twenty years in their service, and the Council doubted his loyalty.

"Aye, sir!" Aine trotted down the deck and disappeared down the stairs a moment later.

"Why indeed?" Ian asked the wind.

"A WORD, Captain."

Ian had not expected to encounter Seria on his way back to the cabin, or rather he'd hoped to steer clear of him. He'd done his best to avoid the man since he'd taken Taren from the hold, but he was hardly surprised that Seria had sought him out. "Of course."

"The captive. Surely you know what folly it is to keep him in your quarters?"

Ian heard the smug underpinning in Seria's measured words. Ian tolerated Seria as the Council's minder aboard the *Phantom*, but he nevertheless despised the Council for the fear its constant supervision instilled in his people.

"Surely the Council has better things to do than question my every action?" Ian met Seria's eyes unflinchingly.

"The Council does only that which is necessary to protect the safety of our people. No doubt even *you* understand the threat to our people if the boy is a sympathizer—"

"The Council can make its own decisions about the prisoner," Ian countered. "Or do you doubt they are capable?"

Seria narrowed his eyes and his breath quickened. "I would never question the Council's abilities. They have kept us safe. Without them, we'd have long ago perished."

"No doubt." Ian nodded and hoped he looked convinced. "But if I choose to make good use of a prisoner for my own purposes, what concern is it to the Council?"

Seria laughed. "He is a pretty thing. If it were my prerogative, I'd have fucked—"

"What else can I help you with, Seria?" Ian could only imagine what might have become of Taren had Seria been the *Phantom*'s captain. No matter what indulgences the Council offered its loyal followers, Ian would never abide such treatment of a prisoner.

No doubt Seria did not appreciate being dismissed, because he curled his upper lip and said in a voice that was barely audible over the sound of the waves striking the bow of the ship, "One day, the Council will see you for what you are."

Ian smiled and shook his head, releasing a slow breath for good measure. It would do him no good to strangle the man and heave him overboard, regardless of the temptation. "I have no doubt you'll be watching me."

"The Council has kept our people safe." Seria's demeanor changed markedly with these words. He stood straighter and thrust his chin forward with the look of a man who was utterly convinced of his rectitude. "They have sacrificed much."

No doubt those imprisoned upon the Council's orders would disagree, Ian thought wryly. He said only, "The Council serves the people."

"Aye," Seria said, his voice trembling with the fervor of a true believer, "that they do." His expression made it clear he knew Ian believed nothing of the sort.

"If there's nothing more," Ian said as he turned to descend the stairs, "my dinner awaits me. And after that—" Ian offered Seria a lecherous grin. "—the prisoner."

TAREN looked to the door as Ian entered the cabin. His long, wavy hair was windblown, his face ruddy from the breeze. He smelled of the ocean, tangy and sweet. The thought of the open air made Taren long to climb the ropes once more, and his heart ached anew for Rider and Bastian, and the crew of the *Witch*.

"Did you eat?"

"Yes." Taren met Ian's eyes without fear.

"Good." Ian unbuttoned his jacket and tossed it on one of the nearby chairs, then untied the high collar of his shirt. Taren noticed the smooth skin of Ian's chest where the fabric parted. Other than his own body, Taren had never seen a man of Ian's obvious strength without a dusting of hair on his skin. Even now Taren couldn't help but admire that powerful body.

The cabin boy entered with a knock, then set down a tray of food and several plates. Salt fish and potatoes. A goblet of wine. Taren's stomach rumbled its approval, despite the fact that he'd eaten only a few hours before.

"May I get you anything else, sir?" the boy asked.

"You may retire for the evening, Aine."

"Aye, sir."

When they were alone once more, Ian studied Taren with apparent interest. "There's plenty enough for two," he said. "Have a seat." He motioned to the table, then sat down and picked up the wine.

Taren considered the offer, deciding there was no harm in it.

"Take what you like."

"It would be easier to eat if I could use my hands." Taren guessed Ian had ordered the straps that bound Taren's wrists to be replaced by the metal cuffs after Taren bathed. At least the metal was lined in fabric and didn't cut into his skin the way the leather had.

Ian said nothing. He filled Taren's plate, then pulled his chair next to Taren's. "Open your mouth."

"You can't mean to feed me like a swaddled babe!"

Ian held out a piece of fish between two large fingers. Taren's mouth watered at the smell of the food as his stomach growled its response, but he said only, "I'd rather starve." He wished his hands were free so he could wipe the smug look off Ian's face. How dare he? And with his fingers, no less!

"Suit yourself." Ian picked up his knife and fork and proceeded to make quick work of the food on his own plate, pausing from time to time— intentionally, no doubt—to comment on how tasty it was. Taren thought he saw the hint of a smile on Ian's lips.

Infuriating bastard.

"Sure you won't have some?"

Taren considered leaning over the plate and eating like a dog, but he wouldn't give Ian the satisfaction. Before, he'd almost believed Bastian had been mistaken about Ian, that there was kindness in him. Now his gut clenched with anger. He would not give Ian the satisfaction of reveling in his humiliation.

"What is your specialty?" Ian asked a few minutes later.

Taren met Ian's gaze but did not reply.

Ian merely laughed. "If you do as you're told and work hard—" Ian speared another piece of the fish. "—I may decide to let you go."

This time Taren laughed. "I may be young, *Captain*, but I'm hardly naïve. What reason would you have to trust me?"

Ian raised an eyebrow. "You tell me."

"I've told you the truth."

"Part of the truth, yes." Taren thought he saw the corner of Ian's mouth move upward at this acknowledgment. Was it possible Ian believed him? Fine. He would throw the man a bone.

"Rigger." Taren watched for Ian's reaction. Perhaps if Ian let him up on deck, he might find a way to escape.

"Indeed. Borstan the rigger gave you his name, then?"

"You know Borstan?" Taren asked.

"Aye. Anyone who's sailed to Raice Harbor knows the man. Best rigger around."

"My parents sold me to him as a baby." Taren didn't explain why he'd kept Borstan's name even after he'd been sold to the inn. He knew he shouldn't have, but there'd been a time when he thought of Borstan as a father, and Lord Grell hadn't insisted he change it.

"I'm surprised he let you go." Taren thought he saw amusement flash through Ian's eyes. "Gambling debts?"

Taren nodded.

"Stupid fool. But the bastard's one of the best." Ian chortled, then added, "Rigger, that is. As a gambler, he leaves much to be desired."

Taren remained silent.

"Were you born on the mainland?"

Taren saw no harm in sharing what little he knew of his origins. "Aye. At least that's what I was told."

"And your parents?" Ian spoke the question as if it mattered little, although Taren guessed otherwise. Certainly a man like Ian would not have forgotten he'd asked the question before.

"You've asked me that twice. Why do you care to hear the answer?"

Ian scowled and speared another piece of fish. "I am merely curious."

Taren shrugged. He'd not press the issue now. Perhaps later. "I remember nothing of my parents. I doubt they cared much what happened to me after they sold me. I'm told they died not long after that."

Ian appeared to consider this, then shrugged.

The rest of the meal passed in silence, Ian apparently uninterested in learning more about Taren. After he'd finished, Ian stood and walked to his bed. When Taren made no move to follow, he turned around and pointed to the bedroll. "Make yourself comfortable. Should you have thoughts about wandering the ship, think no further than the guard outside the door."

Taren thought of how easily he might cut Ian's throat with one of the knives on the table, even with his hands shackled, and of how unconcerned Ian seemed to be for his own safety. Then again, even if he could overpower Ian, what then? A ship this size would have at least three dozen men aboard. He was wily, but not so wily that he could hope to defeat an entire crew by himself. No, his best hope for escape was when they pulled into port. He would bide his time and wait for the right moment to flee.

Ian dimmed the lamps in the cabin and pulled off his shirt before tossing it on a chair. The sinews of his back caught the light from the moon outside and seemed to ripple as he moved. Taren couldn't look away. His cock, too, seemed unconcerned that the object of its attention was an enemy and captor. Gooseflesh rose on the back of Taren's neck as he contemplated Ian's powerful build. He even forgot his rumbling belly.

Taren forced himself to turn his attention to the bedroll and set it out on the ground by the door, using his feet to position it. The breeze was stronger here, so he would sleep more soundly. The location also afforded him a clear view of the large four-poster.

When Taren looked up again, Ian was completely and comfortably naked, or so he appeared to be, judging by the slow pace of his ablutions. How long did it take to wash one's face in a bowl of cold water? The ache in Taren's groin became an uncomfortable pain. He began to wonder if, after their brief kiss hours before, Ian had shed his clothing in an effort to achieve just such a response. But when the captain made no move to approach him or even speak, Taren decided Ian was simply unconcerned by his nakedness. Next thing he knew, Ian had climbed into his bed and pulled the blankets over himself.

IAN lay in his bed, unable to sleep. Perhaps he should wear a nightshirt as long as Taren slept nearby. He wondered why he'd undressed in front of Taren if knowing that the boy's eyes were upon him aroused him so. The feel of the sheets against his naked skin had never caused his body to respond in such a way before. He considered visiting Barra's cabin to find his release. Barra had never complained. Quite the contrary—he'd always welcomed Ian to his bed.

Tonight, however, the thought of bedding Barra did nothing for Ian. Tonight Ian's more animal nature craved the coupling and sought a mate. The need to dominate was as ancient as his people, yet Ian despised it. From the moment he'd seen Taren, he'd wanted to possess him and make him his own. Tame him to his hand, even feed him like a pet just to relish that feeling of control. And then that kiss…. When he'd kissed Taren, he'd sensed Taren's need to submit. What was it about Taren that had awakened his other nature with such intensity?

Enough of this. It's none of your concern. Your duty is clear. He must face the Council.

Minutes passed, then hours. He slept fitfully, only to awaken to the call of the sea. He would transform. Better that than give in to his physical need. He would not take his prisoner by force, even if it was his right.

No. Tonight, he would embrace the water and his baser nature. He would release his less human self, but he would do so where he would not risk harming the boy.

He slipped out of bed and walked through the cabin to the large aft windows, where he climbed up onto the sill, shivering as the cool night air caressed his naked skin. He breathed deeply of the ocean, filling his lungs, the tang of salt on his lips. With one graceful movement, he leaned over and plunged into the waves.

TAREN shifted in his sleep, opening his dream-laden eyes. He gazed up at the man teetering at the window with his bare skin reflecting the starlight. A moment later, the man seemed to soar into the air. Then he was gone.

Taren smiled as he closed his eyes again. He dreamed of the ocean and Ian, of their bodies tangled beneath the surface, and of finding Ian's mouth with his own.

"*Come,*" Ian called silently as he swam away, his voice an echo in Taren's dreams. "*Follow me. Your life awaits.*"

Taren watched as Ian's lean body cut through the water faster than any sea creature Taren had ever seen. He marveled at the way Ian moved, at the sinews that rippled with each thrust of his arms, at the powerful tail where his legs used to be. Taren knew he should be surprised to see Ian's transformation, but he was not. It seemed as natural as breathing in air or feeling the warmth of the sunlight on his skin.

Please. I want to follow, but I don't know how.

SIX

TAREN awoke alone in Ian's cabin. The bedroll was far more comfortable than the floor of the hold, and he felt better rested than he had in days. Still, his stomach complained of lack of food. His arms ached from his restraints. His mood was black, his mind plagued with his desire for Ian and his shame for how he thought more about Ian than he did Bastian and Rider.

The door to the cabin opened with a rattle and Ian strode inside, followed by the young boy who had brought them dinner the night before. The boy set down a tray of food and waited.

"Will you be wanting anything else, sir?" the boy asked.

"That'll be all for now. Thank you, Aine."

The boy nodded and regarded Taren with obvious distrust. "Aye, sir." He turned on his heel and left them alone.

"Morning," Ian said with a quick glance in Taren's direction. He sat down at the table and tore off a piece of bread. "Care to join me?"

Taren boldly met Ian's eyes. "Will you unbind me?"

Ian raised an eyebrow. "No."

"Then I'll not be joining you." He *wanted* Ian to feed him, although he pretended otherwise. He wanted to take Ian's fingers into his mouth and taste them. He wondered if Ian sensed this as well.

Ian laughed, a deep and throaty sound. "You're but a boy, despite the man's body."

"Yet you treat me like a dog." Taren knew full well he was pressing his luck, addressing his captor in such a manner. If he was to be treated no better than an animal, he would at least learn the limits of his cage.

Ian said nothing, instead digging into his breakfast with far more relish than the dried fish and hardtack deserved. He was clearly enjoying Taren's predicament. Taren's mouth watered and his belly ached, yet he schooled his features so as not to show his weakness.

Once finished, Ian called for Aine again, who removed what was left of the breakfast—enough to feed several other men—and left without comment. Taren guessed that Ian had requested an abundance of food for the sole purpose of tempting Taren into submission.

"Behave yourself, boy," Ian told Taren as he made his way to the door. His eyes twinkled with mischief.

Taren did not respond, making clear his displeasure at his treatment. Ian merely smiled and walked out of the cabin a moment later, leaving Taren alone once again.

Taren slept most of the day, lulled by the steady rocking of the waves and the smell of the ocean. He dreamed of swimming through vast forests of underwater trees, dreams that began with joyful exploration and ended with him drowning as he became entangled in the trees' tentacled branches.

He tried to surface as he panted and gasped for air, unsure of where he was, fearful for those he'd left behind on the *Sea Witch*, craving the company of his bedmates but knowing he'd had no choice but to leave them. He imagined he heard Ian's deep voice through the veil of his sleep. He tried to return to himself and leave the dreams behind, but he could not find his way. He called out for someone to help him, but no sound issued from his lips. He ceased his struggle and allowed himself to sink down into the warmth of the water as he watched the sunlight above become darkness.

"DAMN him." Ian charged down the stairs and flung open the cabin doors, causing them to bang against the bulkhead. Aine knelt on the floor, bent over Taren. He moved quickly away to reveal a shivering figure on the bedroll. "How long has he been like this?"

"I came to set your dinner out a few minutes ago. I didn't see him at first, so I brought the lantern." Aine's gaze darted about the cabin, resting everywhere but upon Ian.

"Help me move him to the bed." He reached under Taren and drew him into his arms. He felt the heat of Taren's body and the dampness of his skin. *Fever.*

Aine pulled back the sheets of the four-poster and Ian set Taren down, covering him with the blankets. "Bring the healer."

"But he's not one of us. The healer—"

"Bring him now, boy!" Ian gingerly unlocked the metal cuffs around Taren's wrists to free his arms.

Aine trotted off without another word as Ian turned back to Taren. The fever had come on so suddenly.

"Damn you," Ian growled, knowing full well Taren couldn't hear him. "If you'd just eaten…." He shook his head, then began to smooth the blankets over Taren's body. *Less than a day without food, and he's this weak?* No, the boy was obviously ill. This was not his doing. Perhaps he'd caught a chill from his time in the water. Ian's anger waned and guilt settled into his gut in its place as Taren moaned and rolled onto his side, trembling as though he would die of cold. But apart from the red stain in his cheeks, Taren was deathly pale.

Ian should have done more for the boy instead of attempting to force his submission. Perhaps if he had, the illness wouldn't have come on so suddenly. But Goddess, he'd wanted Taren's submission!

He brushed these thoughts aside and poured a glass of water from the bedside table before lifting Taren with an arm beneath his shoulders. "Drink," he said as he brought the glass to Taren's lips. Taren's eyelids fluttered open, then closed once more, but he swallowed a bit of the liquid.

What the devil is taking them so long? "Aine!" Ian shouted.

Aine raced into the cabin. He was not alone. "Aye, Captain. I've brought the healer, sir." Aine's voice shook.

Ian nodded at the man standing in the doorway. "Leave us, boy."

Aine nodded quickly and shut the door behind him. Damn, but he'd frightened the boy again.

"Made a mess of things, have you?"

"I'm counting on you to fix it." Ian didn't need to look at Renda to know that his face was set in a scowl.

Renda stalked over to the bed. "Move," he commanded, pushing Ian aside and placing one hand on Taren's forehead. He shook his head and glared at Ian. "Twenty years as your friend, and you still keep things from me. I should have left you to rot in that cell instead of convincing the Council that you'd be of better use at sea."

Renda's black hair and equally dark eyes reminded Ian of a devil. And right now, he was tempted to call him just that. "Well?"

"When were you going to tell me about him?"

"You know what he is?" Of course Renda would sense the truth of Taren's existence; he'd been a healer long before he'd served as the *Phantom*'s quartermaster. Ian wondered what more Renda might sense, then pushed the thought from his mind.

Renda snorted like a horse. "Do you place such little faith in me?"

"No, of course not. I—"

"He's feverish. Weak."

"I hardly need a healer to tell me that."

Renda laid a hand on Taren's cheek and chuckled. "You'll be pleased to know he'll survive."

Ian looked up to see Renda's knowing expression. *Damn him and his patronizing manner!*

Renda smiled wryly before turning his attentions back to Taren. He closed his eyes and placed his palms on Taren's chest. Ian felt the slight zest of power in the air as Taren's chest glowed blue with Renda's touch, casting an odd pallor over Taren's already pale face. Renda muttered a few guttural, barely comprehensible words in the ancient tongue. Taren moaned and stirred, then stilled once more. A moment later Renda removed his hands and stepped away from the bed.

"Is that all?" Ian demanded.

"What? Perhaps you'd like to see me sweat?"

Blast the man! "No. But I thought—"

"He will survive. For now, at least."

"Explain." Ian gritted his teeth.

"Much as it would please me to tell you that your poor treatment of him is to blame for his current condition, I cannot." Renda paused. No doubt he knew full well how infuriating it was for Ian to wait for a complete answer. Ian, however, did not take the bait. "It is the transformation sickness. He must transform or this will only happen again," Renda said at last.

"Transformation sickness?" Only adolescents suffered with the transformation sickness, and even then it was rare that they experienced much more than slight discomfort. "But he's far too old—"

"He has been altered. No doubt hidden to prevent him from transforming when he was a boy. Only a trained healer would sense his true nature. Or"—Renda looked directly at Ian and raised an eyebrow—"someone who has forged a strong connection to him."

"I haven't—"

"You can deny the truth as long as you wish, but it is still the truth. You and he seem to share some deeper bond."

"I have no idea what you're talking about." An outright lie. Ian felt that bond grow stronger with each passing day.

Renda shook his head. "Half the ship can sense the claim you've staked. You're like a boy after his first transformation. I doubt there's a man aboard who hasn't caught the scent of your attraction, even in your human form—"

"How has he been altered?" Ian fought the urge to throttle Renda.

"I do not know, but whatever mage did this must have been powerful. The urge to transform is imprinted upon our hearts and minds."

"A mage?" Ian rubbed his hand over his mouth. Why would a mage have hidden one of their own kind among the humans? Mages on the island were tightly controlled, no doubt because the Council feared them. But Ian knew the mainland Ea embraced the old ways. With practice, a mage could grow strong enough to have masked Taren's true nature. "Still, Taren had to have transformed, or he'd have drowned before we found him."

"Indeed. Or at least he partially transformed." Renda nodded his approval, a condescending gesture that made Ian's anger flare once more. "Perhaps that initial transformation triggered his illness. I would venture that he has no conscious memory of it, though. Not surprising, since from what we know of him, he grew up on the mainland amongst humans, did he not?"

"So he says."

"How would the world of men explain such a transformation at all, let alone in a child? How would that child be treated? Humankind nearly exterminated our people. What would they have done to him if they'd discovered his true nature? At least you had your parents to protect you until you were old enough to control the need to transform."

Ian could well imagine what might happen to such a child. He himself had never shared his secret, even with his closest friends.

Renda frowned at Ian's lack of response. "What will you tell the Council about him?"

Ian shook his head. "I don't know. I must learn more about him before I can answer that." He dreaded to think what might become of Taren at the Council's hands. "I can hardly imagine the Council will care what I have to say about it. If Seria weren't aboard to keep a watchful eye on their behalf, I'd be tempted to let him go."

"Interesting." Renda gave him a look of smug understanding.

"It's none of your concern."

Renda rubbed the back of his neck and chuckled. "Then unless you have further need of me, I'll be going."

"That's all? Doesn't he need—?"

"Feed him well. Care for him. And when he's stronger, tell him what he is. If he doesn't fully transform and soon, this will only happen again. From what I can tell, the spell was meant to be broken when he found his people. Perhaps if you show him—"

"Thank you." Ian knew his tone was harsh, but he'd had enough of Renda's well-intentioned advice.

Renda inclined his head and left without another word. Ian doubted it was the last he had to say on the subject of Taren, but for now he seemed content to leave Ian be.

Ian settled onto the bed. Taren had stopped shaking and his breathing was slower, less labored. "More water, boy," he said as he propped Taren up and put the glass to Taren's dry and cracked lips. Taren's fever had broken, his skin now cool to the touch.

"Not... boy...." Taren's eyes remained closed, his words barely audible. "Name's... Taren."

"Shut up and drink, boy." Ian smiled as Taren drank, so relieved was he to see Taren already much improved. Even more so, he felt a strange sense of comfort and usefulness as he cared for Taren.

"Not—"

"Sleep, boy. There'll be time to argue with me come morning." Ian set Taren back down and pulled the covers up to his chin.

Taren exhaled audibly as Ian touched his forehead. A minute later he was asleep, judging by his soft breaths and relaxed features. Ian, his back to the hard wood of the headboard, just watched the rise and fall of Taren's chest for a while, deep in thought.

Taren was undeniably beautiful, with his full lips and smooth skin. Ian's sense of familiarity when he looked at Taren grew. Perhaps he'd seen Taren on one of the neighboring islands when they'd resupplied. Then again, he'd have remembered seeing Taren on the few occasions he'd visited a tavern or marketplace. He was sure of it.

He brushed his thumb over Taren's cheek. Taren sighed, a soft and endearing sound that made Ian imagine what sounds Taren might make if he traced his tongue over the silky skin of Taren's chest. How might Taren respond if he took one of those pink nipples between his teeth? Ian shifted slightly as his cock made its interest known. Not a surprise. The urge to mate was still strong. But there was something else, something other than the purely physical response. Ian felt strangely possessive of his prisoner.

He stroked Taren's soft hair and closed his eyes. Laughter from far away echoed through his mind. Taren's laughter? Ian relaxed as he allowed himself to follow the sound until his mind faded into sleep.

THE first rays of sun roused Taren, who was surprised to find himself asleep in Ian's large bed. More surprising, perhaps, was that his head was cradled in Ian's lap. Ian's soft snores told Taren the man was fast asleep. A vague memory—or was it a dream?—flashed through his mind. Ian, holding him. Telling him to drink. Giving him water.

Not a dream. His body ached as if he'd been with fever. His empty stomach growled in protest, and he realized his wrists were no longer bound. He struggled to move his arms but with little success. He was weaker than he'd been when they'd taken him from the hold.

Ian stirred. "Awake at last."

Taren couldn't think of anything to say in response, so he held his tongue. Besides, he found he liked the way it felt when Ian held him. He was tempted to press further into Ian's arms and feel the warmth of Ian's body.

"Good." Ian's voice sounded hoarse. Had he spent the entire night at Taren's side? Ian gently laid Taren's head on the pillow, then slipped out of the bed. His clothes were rumpled, his hair wild. He stepped out of the cabin and called to someone, then came back inside, rinsed his face in the basin by the bed, and toweled dry.

As Ian pulled a clean shirt over his head a few minutes later, Aine appeared in the doorway to the cabin with a tray of food. Taren's stomach rumbled in response.

"Do you wish me to feed him?" Aine asked.

"No. You may leave the food on the table." When the boy looked at Ian with obvious disappointment, Ian added, "Thank you, Aine. You've been very helpful."

Aine's face lit up. "Thank you, sir." He scurried out of the cabin and closed the door behind him.

For the first time that morning, Ian looked directly at Taren. Dark circles ringed his green eyes, and his skin was paler than Taren remembered. He looked exhausted. Worried, perhaps?

Hardly. Still, Taren couldn't remember how he'd come to be in the big bed, or how he came by the memory of Ian giving him water.

Without a word, Ian propped Taren up on some pillows, tucking a blanket around Taren's waist and putting a second blanket over his shoulders when he began to shiver. Taren tried to mumble his thanks, but his throat was so dry, the sound was far more like the croak of a frog.

"Gruel." Ian placed the wooden bowl unceremoniously on Taren's lap and waited.

Taren reached for the spoon and scooped up a bit of the cereal, but his hand shook so violently that he couldn't manage to lift the spoon to his lips. The gruel spilled over his chest in sticky lumps.

Taren half expected Ian to laugh or point out his obvious weakness. Ian did neither, instead taking a cloth from the tray and wiping Taren with it. Taren caught a whiff of Ian's masculine scent as he bent over to attend to the mess. Ian's powerful hands were surprisingly gentle, his touch arousing Taren's body in spite of Taren's pathetic state.

Ian's gaze met Taren's, a question in his eyes as he lifted the spoon. "Please," Taren said as his cheeks heated. Just a day before, he'd refused Ian's offer to feed him. Now he begged for it! The irony was hardly lost on him. No doubt Ian too found the entire situation amusing. Still, Ian's expression remained calm, almost sympathetic, as he filled the spoon and held it up to Taren's mouth. Taren took the food without protest and swallowed with some difficulty. The gruel was bland, but from Ian's hands it tasted warm and pleasing.

Before Taren could ask for water, Ian filled a cup and brought it to Taren's lips, waiting patiently for him to drink. Ian was so close, Taren felt his slow, stuttered breaths on his cheek.

"Thank you." Taren heard the weakness in his own voice.

Ian nodded but said nothing, instead continuing to feed Taren the gruel until the bowl was empty. He then dipped a piece of bread in water to soften it and set it gingerly on Taren's tongue, his fingers brushing Taren's lips as he withdrew. Taren shivered with the delicate contact. And gods, but he leaned into that touch as sure as he had when Ian had kissed him days before.

Taren noticed the muscles of Ian's jaw tense as he held another piece of bread to his lips, and Taren saw that Ian was aroused. He caught Ian's gaze, which caused Taren's pulse to quicken. Ian brushed a crumb from Taren's cheek and Taren gasped. Damn his body and his weak self-control!

Ian finished feeding him the bread, then offered him more water. For the first time, Taren realized that Ian could easily have asked the cabin boy to feed him. Taren had no strength to harm anyone in his current state, pathetic creature that he now was, nor had he threatened any of Ian's crew. Had Ian *wanted* to care for him? Taren pushed the thought from his mind.

"You will rest now," Ian said at last, having wiped Taren's face with the cloth. He removed the pillows and pulled the blankets over Taren's upper body. Without another word, he strode out of the cabin. He did not look back.

Taren closed his eyes and took several long breaths, hoping to quell the thrum of arousal from Ian's gentle ministrations. His body still ached for Ian's touch. Had it been so long since he'd left the *Sea Witch* that his body craved *any* man? He resolved never to let Ian know of his weakness. He would focus his efforts on escaping and returning to his place—his home—aboard the *Witch*. He missed the simplicity of his place in Rider and Bastian's bed.

IAN returned at nightfall to find Taren in bed, reading a book of poetry. Aine had left dinner—such as it was—on the table. Their stores were low, the only food left to the crew hardtack and dried fish. Again. He'd caught two men fishing in broad daylight, which would have been perfectly fine if they hadn't transformed to do it. He'd confined them both to the brig for the night—there were few rules governing transformation on the island, but here, outside protected waters and close to human civilization, the risk of detection was far too great. The day had left Ian tired and irritable.

"Are you hungry, boy?" He repressed a smile at seeing Taren's face light with pleasure. He guessed Taren was feeling better. Or was it that he craved Ian's touch?

"Yes" was all Taren said.

Ian schooled his features to hide his surprise at Taren's docile response. He wasn't sure he liked it much, but he guessed Taren was still weak. "Good." He filled one of the plates and carried it over to the bed on a tray, set it down on Taren's lap, and unlocked the cuffs that held Taren's arms together over his chest.

"I... thank you." Taren did not disguise his shock.

"Something wrong?" Ian raised an eyebrow and waited patiently for Taren's reply.

"No." Taren gave his response a bit too quickly, and something in his gaze made Ian wonder if Taren was disappointed that he had not offered to feed him again. As much as he wanted to feed Taren again, Ian feared if he touched Taren, he might lose control as he'd done when they'd first met.

"Enjoying the poetry, are you?" Ian asked as he sat on the bed near Taren's feet. This far away, he'd be less tempted to do anything untoward. Taren's pale cheeks had finally begun to pink again, an endearing look—too endearing, for much to Ian's dismay, his cock once again asserted itself. Trapped in his britches, it ached for attention. Ian ignored it.

"Yes. I haven't read much before. A few bawdy poems. Nothing like this."

"My mother gave me that book," Ian said, surprising himself with the response. "She would read them to me when I was little. We lived not far from the harbor, and she knew I loved the sea. I remember looking out at the water as she read the poems, imagining my father in some exotic land."

"Was your father a sailor?"

"Aye. But after his father died, he worked as a blacksmith." Ian smiled at the memory of watching his father work the smithy. He hadn't thought about his parents much recently, except to revisit his own pain at losing them.

Taren ate a few bites of the dry fish, then looked up at Ian as if considering something. "How long have you captained the *Phantom*?"

"Why do you ask?" Ian hadn't meant to sound suspicious. What harm could it do, anyhow, to humor his captive? If anything, Taren might be inclined to share more of his own story if Ian did the same.

"I'm curious. Bad habit of mine, I'm told. Got me into more trouble than I care to remember."

"I don't doubt it." Ian chuckled. "I've captained this ship longer than you've been alive, I reckon." He'd expected the look of surprise on Taren's face. "I appear far younger than I am."

"Where are we headed?" Taren chewed thoughtfully on a piece of bread and gazed out the aft windows.

"We spend two more nights patrolling. Then we return to the island."

"Island?" asked Taren.

"My home." Better Taren learn of what he might face now.

"Does it have a name, this island?" Taren regarded him with obvious interest.

"Ea'nu." When Taren raised a quizzical eyebrow, Ian said, "It's an ancient tongue. There are none alive who speak it now."

Taren lifted a small piece of fish to his lips and chewed it thoughtfully. "What will you do with me there?"

Ian breathed deeply, then said, "You will face the governors of the island. The Ea'ta. We call them the Council."

"I've done nothing wrong. You could just release me."

"You were found within the island's territorial waters. I can't just release you." He might have released Taren if he'd been human—the Council gave him at least some discretion in how to deal with outsiders. But Taren was not human, and he needed to learn of his true nature.

You lie to yourself. Part of his decision to keep Taren captive was purely selfish. He wasn't willing to let Taren leave. He wanted Taren. He wanted to touch him, possess him.

Ian stood up and stalked over to the window, gazing out to avoid looking at Taren. Goddess, when would his body heed his mind? His physical need was becoming more than he could tolerate—his mind seemed perpetually filled with thoughts of Taren. Sexual, to be sure, but more than that: Ian wanted to learn about Taren and understand him. He wanted to keep Taren close.

Ian had always lived alone and he'd never wanted it any differently. But now....

Romantic fool!

When he was a boy, he'd loved to hear his parents tell the ancient stories of his people—stories of sea monsters, lost cities beneath the water, and souls paired by the spirits—ancient myths from the days of the priests and priestesses, handed down from generation to generation. Thinking about Taren, Ian remembered the stories of souls whose fates were inextricably bound together and whom death could not part. His people had a word for it, although he'd rarely heard it used: soulbound. More than just the primal call of lust, such a pairing awakened both man and beast. He was drawn to Taren much like he was drawn to the sea. Was this the hunger of souls? He shook off the thought and focused once more on his duty.

Taren looked resigned. Tired as well.

"Rest now," Ian said as he stood and pulled on his jacket. "I will leave the food." This time, he refastened the metal cuffs in front of Taren so that he might eat some more. He would do no harm without a knife or fork. He left the cabin and locked the door behind him.

SEVEN

IAN took the helm and gazed out over the ocean. They had spent the better part of the day following the island's outermost line of defense in a large arc. This far away from land, Ian could almost imagine himself on the open sea. How long had it been since he'd sailed anything but the patrol route? He missed the vast expanses of blue water and the freedom to be found there amidst the towering waves. Ian felt an enormous sense of relief to be returning home in two days. Still, the knowledge that he must turn Taren over to the Council upon their return weighed heavily upon him.

With Taren's health on the mend, Ian had done his best to avoid his cabin except to sleep, instead taking his meals with the crew as he had done before Taren's arrival aboard. He'd told himself that Taren needed to rest and that he could hardly share his bed with a prisoner, but the truth was that he feared what he might do if he lost control of his more primal urges. It had become more and more difficult to ignore the steady thrumming of his physical hunger for his young captive. That, and the turmoil in his heart left him anxious and confused.

"How is your prisoner?" Renda said from behind him.

"Better, thanks to you." Taren's strength had returned quite quickly. After all, Taren was one of them.

"You're welcome." Renda touched Ian's hand. "Bit tense today, aren't you? I'd think you'd be happy to be going home."

"It's none of your concern."

"Barra told me you haven't come to his bed since we picked up the prisoner. Is this true?" From Renda's tone, Ian was quite sure he already had his answer.

"Barra will survive. I doubt his bed has been empty."

"I am not concerned about Barra."

"I will survive, as well."

"If you will not attend to your need, more than just your body will suffer the consequences. If you do not heed your other nature...."

"Whatever I choose to do"—Ian met Renda's eyes and held his gaze—"it will not interfere with my duty."

Renda huffed loudly enough to be heard over the sound of the wind and the waves. Ian shoved Renda aside. "Take the helm." He stalked aft and descended the steps to the cabins below without looking back. A moment later he stood in front of the door to Barra's quarters.

Barra took a moment to answer. Judging by the blond hair sticking up in odd places and the flush on his cheeks, Ian guessed he'd been sleeping after taking the night watch. He leaned against the door, grinned, and rubbed a hand over his bare chest. "Captain. So good of you to come see me."

"I've never known you to complain when I've come calling." Ian couldn't mask his irritation. Perhaps he should just transform and hope his physical need would be satisfied without the solid heat of another body.

"Please, Ian," Barra said, gesturing to the cabin. "Come inside."

WHEN the door to the cabin opened as dusk fell, a man whom Taren had not met before entered bearing a tray full of food. He was blond and blue-eyed, with a day's worth of beard. Handsome too.

"Where's Aine?" Taren asked as he sat straighter in the bed. He didn't like the way the man's gaze seemed to rake over his body, assessing him as one might assess a horse at an auction.

"I told him I'd take his place tonight. Poor boy's been working far too hard," the newcomer replied as he set Taren's dinner down on the table, then proceeded to unlock Taren's wrists from the cuffs.

"Oh." Taren hoped he didn't sound as disappointed as he felt. With Ian practically ignoring him, he'd come to look forward to Aine's regular visits.

"Name's Barra. Sailing master."

The *sailing master* was feeding him dinner? Sailing masters were nearly as powerful as the captain and quartermaster—on most ships, they were often the only men capable of reading a chart. Certainly Ian wouldn't have asked such a high-ranking member of his crew to tend to a prisoner.

"I'm Taren. But you already know that." Taren chewed his food—salt fish and hardtack again. He didn't mind. The food was familiar, even comforting, and reminded him of the *Sea Witch*.

"I hope your stay has been a comfortable one." A strange thing to say. The words, coupled with the look on Barra's face, made Taren guess Barra cared little that it had been comfortable. *He's casting for information.* Even more interesting. There was no denying that Barra wanted something from him.

"Fine." Let the man draw it out of him. Perhaps Barra would tip his hand if he was forced to ask more questions. In the meantime, Taren would tread carefully.

"I'm glad." Barra's smile held no warmth. "We will make port tomorrow."

"Oh? I thought we were headed somewhere." Taren wiped his face on the cloth and waited for Barra's response.

"We rarely head anywhere. This is a patrol ship." Taren believed Barra's sentiment to be heartfelt based on his wistful tone. He understood it too. Part of the joy he'd experienced aboard the *Sea Witch* had been when they'd put in to new ports of call.

"I see. Then I am to face this Council when we return?" Taren tried to sound nonchalant when in truth he feared what the Council might do to him. Ian's reaction when he'd brought up the topic had done little to assuage his fears.

"Aye. I wouldn't want to be in your position. As an outsider found within the island's bulwarks, you'll be branded a spy. You'll be fortunate to escape with your life."

"I'm no spy." Barra's words disturbed him; Ian's assessment of his predicament had been far less dire. Then again, Ian had never mentioned he believed him a spy. Did he? Or was it simply in Ian's best interests to keep him placated and docile before Ian tossed him to the dogs?

"I could be wrong," Barra continued after a pause. His expression, however, told otherwise. "Then again, many on the Council hold no great love for the captain, seeing as he grew up on the mainland." He paused for a moment, then laughed. "You have much in common, it seems."

Taren wondered why the islanders distrusted the mainlanders enough that they viewed them all as potential spies. What were they hiding on this island that its defenses were so important to its people? Pirates? Treasure? Taren decided it best to let the subject drop. He'd press the issue with Ian, but first he'd learn more about the Council. At least on the island, the opportunity for escape might present itself and Taren could flee. Aboard the ship and shackled, he had little hope of an escape.

Barra, perhaps sensing Taren's unease, did not discuss the issue further but waited for him to finish his meal. Taren had expected Barra would ask him more questions, but instead he left without a word a moment later, taking the tray with him. Taren watched in silence as Barra left. On the bed, the metal cuffs lay open. On the table was the small knife Barra had used to cut Taren's food.

Taren grabbed the knife and stood by the door so as not to be seen if someone entered. He'd expected Barra to return. But when minute after minute passed and Barra did not, Taren's racing heart took off at a gallop, pounding against his chest with anticipation.

EIGHT

TAREN waited by the door, the knife in his hand. He guessed that Barra intended him to escape, although he had yet to understand why. Was it treason to release a prisoner? Regardless, Taren doubted Ian would fail to punish his subordinate for doing so. Perhaps Ian's pride had been too great, and he'd ordered the man to provide Taren with the tools to escape. No. If Ian had wanted to set him free, he'd have done the deed himself.

Since Taren's illness, no guard had been posted outside his door, although a guard had accompanied Aine when he had brought Taren food. Tonight was no exception. The guard whom Barra had dismissed when he'd brought Taren's dinner had not returned, judging from the silence outside the cabin door. Taren turned the handle of the door and found it locked. It took little effort to force the latch open with the knife, and a moment later, Taren waited at the bottom of the stairs to the deck, hidden in shadow.

It was late, and Taren suspected few men would be up on deck. Barra, perhaps, would be at the wheel in Ian's place, although even as large as the *Phantom* was, Taren doubted Ian would be far. Aine had let slip that Ian spent much of his time in the officers' quarters beneath the foredeck. In the end, no one noticed Taren as he stole further aft to where the small launches were lashed just forward of the keel. He made his way by sneaking around the various barrels and crates on deck, hiding when he thought Ian's men were near, thankful for the darkness from the late-rising moon. He hoped the low wail of the stiff wind would disguise the sound of the ropes as he lowered one of the small boats.

He had nearly reached the cleat to which the closest launch was tied when he heard Ian call from behind him. "Going somewhere?"

Damn him!

Before Taren could respond, Ian lunged for him and grabbed him around the neck. Taren struggled, then managed to slip from Ian's grip by elbowing him in the belly.

"You!" Taren growled as he thrust the knife toward Ian.

Ian's eyes widened in surprise when he saw the weapon. "What do you hope to accomplish by running?" he asked as he backed away to avoid the blade.

"Did you think I'd just wait for you to take me back to your island stronghold? And what then? I've heard your men speak of the Council and what they do to outsiders. Did you just expect me to let you take me to my death?" Taren's gut burned with anger. "I'd rather die here, by your hands if the fates wish it."

"They won't kill you."

Taren thought Ian sounded unconvinced. He laughed and held his ground. "What guarantee can you give me? From what I hear, you hold little sway with the Council."

"Who told you that?"

Taren hesitated. He wished Barra no harm, regardless of his motivations.

"Who told you that?" Ian demanded again. When Taren still did not answer, Ian asked, "Was it Aine? Barra?" Taren's expression betrayed him. "Barra, then. Just wait until I—"

"It matters not who told me. Will you tell me otherwise?" When Ian did not answer, he continued, "If you value my life, why not just let me go? What good am I to you if I'm dead? Why did you spare my life when I was ill if you knew what fate awaits me?"

"Where will you go? That boat is no match for the open sea."

Taren backed toward the railing, glancing over at the small boat hanging from the side and judging the distance down. "I'm stronger than you think, Captain. I've survived far worse."

"The Council will not kill you. There's more here than meets the eye. I can explain—"

But before Ian could finish, Taren jumped over the railing to the launch. Taren had no time to loosen the ropes that held the launch to the side of the *Phantom*. He'd need to cut them before Ian could climb onto the small boat. He'd hoist the sails as soon as he could—for now, he just needed to put some distance between the ships. Ian would be hard-pressed to follow him in the larger ship, even more so to justify turning back for the life of a single prisoner who was already as good as condemned to death.

He didn't count on Ian launching himself over the railing in pursuit. He only realized his mistake when he saw Ian jump down from the deck. The rope he'd nearly cut through snapped, and the boat fell as Ian landed in the launch. Knocked off-balance, Taren tumbled onto Ian as they hit the water.

Ian groaned, clutched his belly, and fell face-first into the water before he began to sink. Only then did Taren realize his knife was no longer in his hand.

"No!" Whatever he'd wanted, Taren had never meant to harm Ian.

Ian disappeared beneath the waves as Taren struggled to find the oars. He spotted one a dozen yards away, floating on the surface. He couldn't find the other. The *Phantom* now blocked the moon.

Gods help me! Taren berated himself for once again being put in the position of having to rescue someone. Hadn't he learned his lesson with Fiall? Where had that foolishness got him? Rider had been right—he was too kindhearted for his own good. How often had the pirate reminded him that one day he would suffer the consequences for it?

He turned to look for the oar once more, trying to put Ian from his thoughts. It was no use. Try as he might, he couldn't simply let Ian drown, even if it was to save his own life. Taren had no other choice. If Ian was still alive—and Taren prayed to the gods he was—he had no time to waste. He jumped into the water and dove beneath the surface.

The water was warm, the waves far kinder than the last time he'd been foolhardy enough to leave a ship in hopes of rescuing a fellow sailor. Still, he could not see Ian. *He should be here.*

He rose to the surface and took a deep breath, then dove down once more. For a moment he thought he could smell Ian's blood on the water. But that was impossible, of course. Sharks could smell blood under the waves, but men?

Fear niggled at the back of his brain as he thought about sharks. He imagined he smelled them too. *I'm losing my mind.*

There was something else he imagined. Something he couldn't quite put into words. A feeling that something had happened to Ian. And then he saw them, two sharks swimming just beneath the surface of the water. Swimming directly at *him*.

Ian! He needed to find Ian before the sharks did.

"Get out of the water. I will handle this." He imagined he heard the voice in his mind. Ian's voice. But before he could react, one of the sharks was upon him, teeth sinking into the flesh of his right leg and tugging on it. The pain was excruciating, as if a thousand knives were slicing their way into his muscle and bone.

He saw movement amidst the blood. His own blood. Another creature—smaller than the shark but no less powerful—had the shark in its grasp and was prying its jaws open. The second shark made to attack the creature, but the creature's tail hit the shark so hard, it shook, then swam away.

By now, Taren had no air left to breathe. He felt light-headed, his body heavy. The pain subsided, his mind now filled with a dreamlike sense of calm.

"No!" Again the voice. Ian's voice. Even in death, was he consigned to always hear that voice?

Go away.

"Look at me!"

Taren opened his eyes and looked into Ian's face. Another dream. Taren's eyes drifted closed once more. Hands gently cradled his face. He leaned into those hands, allowing himself to drift toward sleep. He imagined his lungs filling with water, although he was breathing as though it were air.

"Taren. Open your eyes!"

Taren forced his eyes open again. The water was dark with blood. The smell was powerful and disturbing. He was dying. He wanted only to leave the pain behind.

Let me die.

"No. Take my hand, Taren. Let me show you the secret your body has hidden from you."

Taren reached out, knowing this was all a dream. Was he dead already? Then he felt it: a hand, solid and warm in his own cold one. *Ian?*

"Yes."

I had a dream about you like this. Beneath the waves. Taren took a long breath and smiled. He liked this dream. It was warm here, as if he were wrapped in blankets and seated before a fire. *I tried to follow you, but—*

"*You're breathing, Taren.*"

Hmmm? Why was Ian speaking to him? He only wanted to sleep.

"*Taren! Wake up! Look at me.*"

Taren forced his eyes open once more and smiled at Ian. He liked seeing Ian here, in his dream. He liked the feel of Ian's hands on his face. *Dreaming....*

"*Taren, listen to me! You're not dreaming.*"

Why couldn't Ian just enjoy this dream with him? Did he always have to be so contrary?

"*Taren! Look at me! You're breathing.*"

Ian was right. He *was* breathing. The water filled his lungs. *What the devil?* Was this part of the dream?

"*Listen to me, Taren.*" Ian's voice again, in his mind. "*This isn't a dream. You've lost a lot of blood. I can't stop it. But you can. If you follow me, you can stop it.*"

Follow you?

"*Look at me, Taren. All of me.*"

Ian pulled away, but Taren clutched his hand tightly. "*It's all right, Taren. I won't let go. Just look at me.*"

Taren nodded, then looked down at Ian's broad shoulders. His skin seemed to shimmer in the moonlight. Ian floated upward, still holding Taren's hand. That's when Taren saw the markings at Ian's waist. No. Not markings. Scales? And lower down, he saw a tail where Ian's legs were supposed to be.

What?

"*Don't be afraid. We're the same.*"

I'm not—

"*We're the same, Taren. It's how you found our ship. It's why I....*"

Why you what?

"*Why I couldn't let you go.*"

I don't understand.

"Taren, you must let it happen. Let your body change. You know what you must do."

I'm not one of you. I... I don't even know what you are.

"We are your people, Taren."

You're not my—

"You feel it. I know you do. Come, Taren. Please."

I'm not dreaming. Taren suddenly knew this with certainty. With that realization came pain so devastating, Taren wondered if the shark was back and he really *had* dreamed the entire conversation with Ian. But Ian's reassuring squeeze of his hand told him otherwise. He was awake. Awake, and watching Ian... swim.

It hurts. Gods, it hurts!

"The first time is the worst. Don't be afraid." Ian pulled Taren against him and held him close. *"It will be over soon. Just focus on the feel of my body against yours."*

The pain that had begun in his feet now traveled the length of his body. Much like the shark teeth that nearly sank to his bone, the pain was deep, all encompassing. As if his skin had been splayed open to the salt water and was burning him, consuming him like flame from inside.

I can't—

"It's almost done."

Before, when he'd been dying, there had been no pain. Now was far worse. More than he could bear. Then, suddenly, the pain was gone. Taren opened his eyes. Ian squeezed his hand and smiled at him, letting him float at arm's length.

"How do you feel?"

Strange. His body vibrated as though his skin was alive with sensation, as though he could feel every drop of water around him as it danced over his body. Taren looked down at his legs, but where his legs once were, there was now a powerful tail. *Good gods! What am I?*

"We call ourselves Ea. Neither man nor beast. The humans call us mermen."

Mermen? Then do you live in the sea?

"No. But we must live near it or we perish. Our bodies must transform from time to time—the call is too powerful."

How can I hear you?

"When we are in this state, we can hear each other's thoughts."

All of my thoughts? That Ian might know his true feelings left Taren feeling uneasy. Naked, even.

"No." Taren imagined he heard Ian's warm laugh. Or had he really heard it? *"Only those thoughts you mean to share with me. Any other thoughts are yours alone."*

Oh. I see.

Ian pointed downward. *"Swim with me, Taren."*

But my wounds? And yours?

"See for yourself." Ian lifted his arms so Taren could see the smooth skin of his abdomen. *"The transformation heals our human bodies. More than that, it heals our hearts and souls."*

I don't understand.

"You will come to understand it, as we have. But for now, follow me. We have only a short time before sunrise. We cannot risk being seen in this form, not this far away from the island." He released Taren's hand and swam a few feet away. For the first time, Taren realized he could see clearly beneath the water. His eyes no longer burned from the salt, and it was brighter than he remembered.

Taren didn't have to wonder how to move, his body knew what to do. He flicked his tail without thinking, slipping by Ian, his hands resting lightly on what would have been his thighs had he still been human. He didn't need his arms to propel himself forward; his tail was more than powerful enough. He laughed to feel the water rush by him, enfolding him in its blanket of warmth. As he often did when he swam, he heard tiny popping sounds by his ears. For the first time, he realized that it was not the sand he heard but millions of tiny creatures moving through the water. He didn't understand how, but he sensed them, much as he'd sensed the sharks before.

Ian had taken the lead again, swimming downward. Now that Taren could see him more clearly, he realized that what he'd thought were scales were pale silver markings that began at Ian's waist and ran to the end of his tail. He felt his own skin with his fingers and found it smooth to the touch.

"Let me show you something, Taren."

Taren followed Ian over a flat reef covered with sparkling coral and tiny fish that appeared like an underwater rainbow of color. When he'd first entered the water, it had been dark and he'd seen nothing but the murky blackness of the waves. Now it was as though the sun penetrated the darkness. He saw the vibrant hues of coral and fish as though it were daytime. He had seen the reefs before—Bastian had loved to dive on them, looking for oysters or clams—but he had never seen them so beautiful. So alive.

My eyes....

"Are no longer human," Ian explained. *"In this form, we can see in the darkness of the water without the sunlight. Our sense of smell is more powerful as well."*

Where are we going?

"Take my hand," Ian said as he swam beside Taren. *"You'll see."*

Together, they swam a few more yards until the reef seemed to end. Just when Taren was about to ask Ian what they were looking at, he saw it: a cliff that dropped straight down, ending in darkness far beyond where Taren could see. Ian led Taren over the edge, then hovered. For a moment Taren saw nothing, but then his eyes adjusted to the darkness, and an entirely new reef appeared before him.

Thousands of tiny silver fish swam in zigzags across the surface of the reef, in and around delicate purple-and-red fan coral. Ian pointed at a small hole in the surface of the rock and Taren saw a spotted eel emerge. It hesitated as if it were trying to decide if they were friend or foe, then withdrew abruptly, stirring several creatures Taren didn't recognize, tiny tubes with what looked like feathery petals at the ends. Taren reached to touch the fluttering surface, but Ian pushed his hand away.

"They are quite beautiful, but their sting is painful."

What is this place?

"The great reef that runs nearly to our island," Ian explained. *"In the sunlight, it is even more beautiful. Perhaps the most beautiful place I've ever seen."*

At the mention of the island, Taren felt both fear and longing. But before he could ask Ian more about his people—Taren's people—Ian took his hand once more and led him to the surface.

"We must find the launch before sunrise and return it to the ship."

The boat was not far from where they surfaced, Taren spluttering as his lungs protested the air. *"Stay below the water for now,"* Ian told him. *"We will transform when we rejoin the* Phantom.*"*

Taren could sense the ship in the distance. They were fortunate the winds were calm, or she'd have put far more miles between them. Ian seemed unconcerned as he took the rope from the bow of the launch and, with a flick of his powerful tail, sped off to join her. Taren followed, marveling at the speed with which Ian swam, despite the weight of the small boat. He wondered what else the Ea were capable of and wished there were more time for him to discover it.

Renda was waiting for them when they broke the surface of the water. He said nothing as he handed down the ropes to secure the launch. Taren wondered if he'd been able to feel them when they transformed. No doubt their struggle in the launch had alerted Ian's crew to Taren's escape. And although Seria, who had been Taren's jailor when he'd been confined to the hold, watched them with obvious interest, he did not approach Ian, nor did he speak. The silence was far more disturbing.

NINE

IAN arrived back in the cabin, having reassured himself that the ship would make port shortly after sunrise. He'd sent Barra to the hold for allowing Taren to escape. Ian knew he could have Barra's head for his treachery, but he also knew he shared the blame for Barra's actions. He'd assumed Barra had wanted nothing but a physical relationship, but he'd misjudged Barra's feelings for him. A stupid mistake, and one he would never repeat. No matter what Taren's fate, Ian would no more seek release in Barra's bed.

Naked, his hair still wet from the sea, Taren sat on the bedroll with his legs drawn to his chest, shivering.

"Are you ill?" Ian asked as he kneeled and put his hand to Taren's forehead. "Shall I call for Renda?" Was there something more to the illness that had plagued Taren before? Renda had assured him that Taren would recover fully once he'd transformed. Or perhaps it was the shock of realizing his true nature after so many years spent believing he was human.

"I'm well. You needn't worry." Taren spoke the words in a tone full of reproach. He stood up and stalked over to the windows, apparently heedless of his state of undress.

Ian felt desire stir at the sight of Taren's bare skin in the warm lamplight—the smooth curve of his back where it met the tight muscles of his ass, the sinews of his broad shoulders that moved as he laid a hand on the sill. Damn, but it was becoming more and more difficult to resist his captive's beauty.

Ian reached out and touched Taren's shoulder in an effort to reassure him, but also because he couldn't help himself. In response, Taren spun about and grabbed his wrist, holding it between them, his eyes intent on Ian's. Already Taren was stronger—a side effect of the transformation.

"Don't patronize me, *Captain*." The harshness of Taren's words stung.

"I didn't intend—"

"You knew what I was all along, didn't you? Did you think you could control me if you withheld my true nature?" A bitter laugh escaped Taren's lips. "But of course you did. What was I but a prisoner to you?"

"I...." What could he say in the face of Taren's justified anger? He'd been afraid to share the truth, but had it been more than that? "Aye. I knew the first time we met."

"Did you think it easier to manipulate me if I didn't know what I was?"

"You wouldn't have believed me." A weak excuse, he knew, but the only explanation he could offer in response. He wondered if what Taren said was true, although he doubted Taren understood that whatever he'd done, he'd done it to protect Taren.

Taren laughed again. "What else didn't you want me to know?" Ian had been naïve to believe Taren wouldn't sense he'd been withholding more. He'd underestimated the man. To be sure, Taren was young, but he was far wiser than Ian had been willing to admit. "What aren't you telling me about the Council?"

Ian remained silent.

"Fine." Taren's shoulders fell, his demeanor once again submissive. To see this pained Ian, more so because he knew he was the cause. "Why don't you just take me now and be done with it?"

"What?" Ian fought the urge to do just that. The beast within clawed its way to the surface, trying to push all reason from his mind. He wanted Taren so badly, he ached. It had taken all his strength to resist Taren in his Ea form, but this was far worse.

"You've wanted me since the day you saw me." Taren opened his arms in invitation. "Fuck me. Satisfy yourself. And when you're through with me, you can toss me to the Council's dogs."

"No." Ian did his utmost to focus his attention on Taren's face. *Damn him.*

Taren reached out and pulled Ian's face to his own, then roughly claimed his lips. "Tell me you don't want this." Again Taren kissed him, a bruising kiss that aroused his primal hunger.

"No." He would not be goaded into this! Ian shoved Taren backward with such force that Taren had to grab hold of the desk to avoid falling.

Ian saw the pain of rejection in Taren's eyes. He knew Taren's physical need had pushed him to his limits. The goddess help them both— Taren wanted him just as keenly. Without thinking, Ian pushed Taren against the wall and pinned him there, plundering his mouth just as he knew Taren wanted him to. Taren tasted salty, with a masculine tang that drove Ian to crave more. Their teeth and tongues fought for dominance, Taren's acquiescence in the end driving Ian to the limit of his self-control.

"Please," Taren moaned as he pressed his body against Ian's, closing the space between them.

Ian knew what this was: the pull between them, the reason for Taren's change of heart. *There are too many things he must understand before this can happen.* Ian struggled back to sanity, forcing his animal nature back into its place, asserting his human dominance.

"No! This mustn't happen." *Not like this. I don't want either of us to regret it.* He released Taren's wrists and backed away, panting. Taren knew nothing of his other nature, and Ian would not take advantage of Taren's lack of control.

Taren slid down the bulkhead, shaking as he clutched his knees to his chest. It was all Ian could do not to go to Taren, to reassure him, but Ian feared that if he touched Taren again, he wouldn't be able to stop himself. Tomorrow, before he escorted Taren to the Council, he would tell him all he knew. For now, he would leave Taren in peace.

TAREN watched numbly as Ian left the cabin. *What just happened here?* He'd been angry—angrier than he ever remembered feeling. He'd also felt frightened, lost. Everything he knew about himself had been a lie!

Upon their return from the water, he had struggled to make sense of his new reality. He'd been numb. Almost ill with the shock of it. And then just as quickly, he'd thrown himself at Ian, forgetting everything but the thrumming lust that had overtaken his senses. He'd wanted Ian badly enough that his mind had fled, leaving behind something so like an animal that Taren might have believed himself possessed. Ian had felt it too, Taren was sure of it. There was one more thing of which Taren was equally sure:

he would not surrender to the Council without a fight. Rider was the only man to whom he would ever owe his freedom. From now on, he would fight to stay free… and Ian be damned!

TEN

TAREN wrapped a blanket around his naked body and walked over to the aft windows, gazing out at the harbor. Crias'u, as Ian had called the island's largest settlement, was a dreary little enclave of a few hundred crumbling stone houses and hastily built shacks that seemed to rise from the water in a disordered and chaotic manner. Best Taren could tell, there had once been a plan to the settlement—the houses hewn from the same white rock that was found on all the Luathan Islands were set in a simple grid that rose from the harbor. These stately homes had at some point fallen into disrepair, and rather than fixing them, the locals had built wooden shacks beside them.

Unlike the colorful houses on Lurat, the shacks were poorly cared for and lacking paint. A few hens pecked at the rutted dirt streets, hoping to find something to eat, but Taren saw none of the goats and sheep some of the other island peoples kept to supplement the fish they caught in the warm waters. Nor did the people seem to mill about the harbor in great number—there seemed little excitement upon the *Phantom*'s return.

From his vantage point at the *Phantom*'s windows, Taren watched as men carried wooden crates filled with what he guessed were wine, sweets, and other delicacies the *Phantom* had been carrying. Aine had explained that although everything they needed to survive could be found on the island or in its waters, the more affluent islanders still craved some of the luxuries imported from the mainland. Often, Aine said, the *Phantom* would stop in a nearby port before beginning their patrol. Taren wondered if these stops weren't more to appease Ian's need for the open sea than anything else, although he had not raised the issue with Aine.

The harbor was filled with nearly a dozen other vessels, including several that appeared to be military ships like the *Phantom*, although none were as large as she. The other boats were obviously fishing vessels, something Taren found quite strange. Why would the Ea need to fish by boat if they could catch their prey under the water in their Ea forms? He could only guess that the Ea Council permitted only certain people to leave the confines of the island. All the more reason to escape before the Council could detain him here. What chance would he have to leave Ea'nu and return to the *Sea Witch* if the Ea themselves could not freely move about?

Aine knocked on the door sometime later. Taren had expected Aine's visit, although he had been surprised to find that Aine was not bringing him breakfast but new clothing Ian had procured to replace the clothes Taren had lost when he'd transformed. Aine, somewhat red-faced, offered to help Taren dress. Taren considered taking the boy up on his offer, if only to watch him squirm in discomfort. In the end, though, he shooed Aine out of the cabin and told him he was quite capable of dressing himself. Aine appeared both relieved and embarrassed as he fled the room and said he'd speak to Ian about breakfast.

Taren studied the clothing, a pair of trousers and a linen shirt. There was also a rope belt and a pair of sandals woven from some sort of plant. Sturdy and utilitarian. Taren left the shoes but took the trousers and shirt and rolled them around the belt, making sure the clothing was securely attached. He then tied the belt loosely about his hips and climbed up on the window as he'd seen Ian do the first night he'd spent in the cabin.

It was a far way down to the water, although Taren had jumped from higher places when he'd been aboard the *Sea Witch*. He smiled sadly at the memory of a lazy afternoon spent in a secluded harbor when he, Fiall, and Bastian had dared each other to climb to the end of the bowsprit and dive into the water. For a brief time in Ian's company, when they'd swum together beneath the waves, he'd felt much the same joy. Taren had forgotten how much he'd missed Bastian and Fiall. Rider too. Would he feel the same about Ian when he was gone from here?

No. Ian had lied to him, yet Taren's entire body ached when he thought of Ian. For a moment, his eyes burned with a powerful sense of loss. Then the sensation lifted and he could think once more. What the hell was wrong with him that he desired the stubborn, irritating beast of a man so powerfully? It was enough that he was still half in shock to discover the truth his body had hidden from him for so many years—he needed to get away from Ian, get back to the *Sea Witch* before he ended up losing his sanity.

Good-bye, Ian.

He waited until Ian had left the ship and he was sure that none of the men on the docks were looking aft. It didn't take long since they were all busy greeting loved ones or hauling more of the *Phantom*'s cargo from the hold amidships. The bright sun called to him like a beacon, urging him onward. His last escape attempt had gotten him nowhere. This time, no one would see him. How ironic that Ian himself had given him the means to leave the island unnoticed by revealing his true nature.

Taren dove silently into the turquoise water and swam down to the bottom so he couldn't easily be seen from the surface. Ian was right. This transformation was far less painful than the last, although it was still far from pleasant. His bones felt as though they were being sculpted into his new form, his skin stretching to its limit. But the pain faded quickly, and the feel of the ocean on his skin and the freedom he felt as he sped through the water with a flick of his powerful tail were exhilarating.

IAN slung a small pack over his shoulder and boarded the ship. He'd spent the better part of the last hour trying to negotiate Taren's prospects with the Council. Not that Ian thought it would get him very far—they'd imprisoned men for far less. It helped little that Seria had made his way ashore to report to his handlers long before Ian had been able to leave the crew. He knew Seria would have already explained the situation to his advantage. Even the one Council member whom Ian counted among his friends did little to reassure him of Taren's fate.

"I spoke with the Sovereign," Councilwoman Zera had told him, her green eyes hard and unsympathetic. "Gurian says he was found within the island's protective barrier." In her human form, she looked positively ancient, her body showing every one of her nearly two hundred years. Ian wondered how long it had been since she'd last transformed. So many of the Ea now refused to venture into the waters surrounding the island, fearful of what lurked beyond. Fearful of the humans. "You yourself don't deny that his true nature was hidden. If he's not a spy, then he's one of Vurin's sympathizers."

"I know the war between Vurin's people and the island hasn't been forgotten," Ian told her, "but I don't understand why the Ea'ta has imprisoned so many of our own. What have the prisoners done but suggest you send a peace envoy to the mainland? They only want to see their loved ones again." He didn't mention the Ea who'd been imprisoned or killed because the Council's mages had been unable to suppress their natural abilities. Only Ea with less threatening abilities such as Renda's healing magic were permitted training, and only if the Council believed those abilities to be useful.

"You mean well, child. But you can't know what it was like when our people first came to this place." She looked at him with an expression of barely disguised pity. "The Council only means to protect our people from further harm. If the humans take our people as slaves—"

"You know those rumors are untrue." Ian hadn't meant to raise his voice, but he was more than frustrated that the Council had done nothing to dispel the rumors. "I travel beyond the island's enchantments. I see that the humans mean us no harm. And if Vurin and his followers wish to live amongst them—"

"You push me beyond the limits of our friendship," Zera interrupted. "Do you mean to suggest that the Council itself is responsible for the stories of the humans' mistreatment of our people?"

"No, of course not," Ian lied. The Council, Gurian in particular as the eldest of the Council's members, exploited the islanders' fears. Since the war ended, Gurian had insisted the Ea train more men as soldiers. Gurian had used the Council's mages to build the island's defenses so that only those who had sworn loyalty to the Council could pass through the enchantments. Buildings crumbled and the people grew restless, but the Council would not be dissuaded. This reason, among others, kept Ian at sea more often than not; he was far happier aboard the *Phantom* than he was listening to the Council's imagined conspiracies.

"You'd do well to mind your place, *Captain*." She glared at him and Ian knew he'd made a mistake to speak his mind so freely.

"I apologize," Ian said with a low bow.

"This prisoner—" She smiled at him and pursed her lips like a mother might look at a petulant child. "—you care for him."

Ian took a long breath. "Aye."

"If he cooperates and tells us what he knows about Vurin, perhaps he too can find his place among our people as you have." Ian knew this would likely never happen. He doubted she believed it either, although he knew she hoped to reassure him.

UNSURE what he would tell Taren, whom he already knew was loath to trust him after his performance the night before, Ian took his time returning to the ship. At least he had convinced the Council to permit him to escort Taren to the detention building to await the convening of the full Council. They could breakfast together and he would help Taren prepare his defense.

"Aine!" Ian shouted as he boarded the ship. "Have Cook make us some breakfast." He was about to head to his cabin when Aine charged back up the stairs to the deck, and nearly collided with him.

"Sir! Captain, sir!"

Ian chuckled. "Salt fish again?"

"No, Captain, sir," the boy spluttered as he struggled to catch his breath. "It's the prisoner, sir. Taren. H-he... he's gone, sir."

"Gone?"

"I gave him the clothes as you asked. He thanked me and insisted he was perfectly capable of dressing himself." Aine blushed. "But when I went to set out breakfast, he was gone."

"Renda!" Ian shouted across the deck.

"Captain?" Renda stalked over and eyed Ian warily.

"Taren. Have you seen him?"

Renda raised an eyebrow. "No. Should I have? I thought he was secured in your cabin."

"Take two of the men and search the ship." Had he really believed Taren wouldn't attempt to flee again if given the opportunity? Yes. Of course he had. His gut clenched with the realization that Taren had played him for a fool. He'd allowed himself to be seduced by Taren's reaction to his transformation. He'd believed Taren would want to stay, if only to learn more about his people.

You have only yourself to blame for his escape. What if the Council's men found him first? Surely he'd given Taren enough warning about the danger the Council presented. *And there's the rub. You gave him reason to flee.*

Had he wanted Taren to flee? After the night before, Ian wondered. He'd been lax with the guards. He should have known Taren would try again.

Renda returned a few minutes later. "The ship is secure. Your prisoner is not aboard. Any further orders?" The edge of Renda's mouth turned upward in a knowing grin.

"Finish unloading. I will return as soon as I can."

"And if the Council comes seeking the prisoner?"

"Handle them. I'll bring him back soon enough." Or so he hoped.

ONCE far enough away from the ship that he was sure he wouldn't be seen, Taren swam along the shore, hugging the sharp edges of the coral so his shadow would not be seen from land. He'd first attempted to swim out to sea in search of the island where the ship had docked the day before, but each time he reached a certain distance from the island, he found that no matter how hard he swam, he could make no progress. After more than an hour, he decided to swim further from the main docks, thinking that perhaps the island tides were more powerful than he'd experienced before. And yet even farther from the port, he could make no more progress. Perhaps the odd tides were related to the island defenses the men aboard the *Phantom* had mentioned.

After several hours of swimming around the island, he decided to give up. He would swim toward land and find a boat there. Then once he escaped the tide, he would transform and make his way to safety. By now, Ian and his men would have discovered his absence. He knew he should hasten his pace and locate a remote beach upon which to make landfall, but instead he took time to appreciate his surroundings.

The coral shone in the brilliant sunlight. Fans of deep purple and knobby stalks of orange and pink grew like oddly shaped flowers, protruding from the rocks and sand, waving in the gentle current. Fish glittered in the rays that breached the surface—they approached him, tiny mouths tickling as they nipped their greetings. He could smell them too, each with a different scent, mingling like flowers in spring to create layers of fragrance. Transfixed, he brushed his fingers over the bulbous protrusions from a coral and watched as the creature's tentacles retracted in response. Seeing this, Taren recalled Ian's words about the beauty of the reef in the light of day. Again he felt a pang of desire and longing, stronger still than the night before.

Had it only been the night before that he'd swam at Ian's side and explored the coral cliffs? It seemed a lifetime since he'd been rescued from the waves. Why had he been so eager to submit to Ian's touch? Even as a slave, he'd never sought submission. He couldn't explain it. Even now he shuddered at the thought of Ian's mouth on his, of Ian's taste, of his scent.

For just a moment, he wondered if he'd made a mistake in fleeing Ian and the *Phantom. Even you sensed his hesitation. He has yet to tell you the truth.*

No. Taren would not trust this Council of elders with his life. Barra had spoken the truth, even if his motives had been far from altruistic. The Council would not trust an outsider, let alone one from the mainland. Whatever Taren's brethren were, they were fiercely reclusive and fearful. This was Taren's opportunity to flee and rejoin his shipmates, if they had survived the storm.

He swam onward until he came to a place where trees and bushes grew thick along the water. Here, where the scattered houses he'd seen from the water seemed to end, he hoped to find shelter for the day. Later he'd explore the volcanic hills by moonlight. He guessed that more remote fishing villages hugged the rough coastline. Perhaps there he would steal a boat and head back toward the port where the *Phantom* had made its last stop before returning home.

The shallow water provided an easy place for him to return to his human form—deep enough to accommodate his powerful tail, yet shallow enough that he needn't swim far to shore. He lay on the bottom, pausing for a moment to explore his curious body.

He reached down and touched the skin of his tail, noting for the first time the webbing between his fingers. He held one hand up to the light, turning it over and back again and noting the finlike protrusions that began at his wrist and disappeared into each finger like a fan. The skin between each finger was translucent but strong. The fins ended with powerful tines, sharp to the touch, pointed toward his fingers. Weapons, much like the barbs of a lobster. He imagined swiping them at an enemy. Taren imagined they would easily cut skin.

Taren slid his hand over his chest, taking care to use only his palm so as not to cut himself. In the light his skin appeared human, although to the touch it felt slippery, like a fish's. His chest was broader in this form, the muscles of his belly taut and defined. Quite human. And yet as he explored further downward, he realized with some shock that the place where his manhood had been was now smooth, the only hint of more was an opening in the skin.

He laughed as he imagined what Bastian might say to see him now as he probed and found the sensitive member within. But his next thought was of Ian as he pressed his finger inward, imagining the feel of Ian's slippery body against his own. Ian. Taren could still see the haunted look in the captain's eyes as he'd left the night before. Taren was sure Ian desired him, and yet he had fled as he'd done so many times before, leaving Taren bereft and unsatisfied.

No! He must focus on the task at hand: escaping this gods-forsaken island and returning to his home aboard the *Sea Witch*. His place was by Rider and Bastian's side, at least until his contract was fulfilled. He forced Ian from his thoughts and imagined himself human once more. If he never saw the captain of the *Phantom* again, so much the better.

Once returned to his human form and reassured that there was no one around to see him, Taren walked naked through the gentle waves and onto the small beach. Soft black sand outlined the volcanic rocks of the shoreline. Beyond, the vegetation was thick and green, scattered with palms and larger trees with smooth bark and leaves that reflected the sunlight and shimmered like glass.

He dressed in the clothes he had strapped around him. They were wet, but they'd dry soon enough in the heat of the sun. He shivered as the breeze caressed his damp skin, and wished he could stay longer in the blanket-like warmth of the surf. Strange, how the transformation seemed so natural, although less than a day before he'd had no inkling this part of him existed. He'd wanted to ask Ian how he could have spent nearly his entire life not knowing his true nature. He'd wanted to understand more about the merfolk—their people. *His* people. There were so many things he'd wanted to ask Ian, and yet they'd only managed to argue.

Pushing Ian from his mind, he turned toward a small path that led from the beach when he heard a voice from behind him ask, "Running again?"

Taren turned, ready to fight and wishing he had a weapon. "What?"

An old woman sat cross-legged, mending an ancient net that lay across her lap and spilled onto the sand. The net was primitive, made perhaps of the vines he'd seen growing around the island. Her withered hands shook as she continued to weave the fibers and close the gaps. Her face was full of crags, her eyes a milky green, unseeing. Familiar.

"You!" This was the same woman he'd seen at the market not long before he'd been lost at sea. Taren sensed no enmity from her—in fact, she appeared quite kind. Taren relaxed his stance but kept his distance, wondering not only how she had come to be on this island but how he had managed not to see her before.

"You're running again, Treande," she said in a voice that trembled nearly as much as her hands.

"Who is Treande? And what are you doing here?"

She smiled knowingly but kept about her task, apparently unconcerned. "Nothing has changed in the end," she said as if she hadn't heard him. "He seeks to avoid that which is destined, and you are determined to run."

He'd already lingered too long. Even if the old woman meant him no harm, surely she'd be able to tell the others she'd spoken with him.

"You needn't fear me, Treande." Her soft laughter nearly faded on the breeze. "I will not tell them where to find you. But *he* will know, of course. The fates will not allow you to run far."

"I'm sorry." Taren started once more toward the path. "I think you've mistaken me for someone else."

"The fates will find you, Taren," she said. "They always will."

Taren froze where he stood. Had she called him by his name? He turned to ask how she knew it, but she was gone, as was the net. For a moment he wondered if he'd imagined the entire encounter. Then he saw something glint in the sunlight where she'd been seated only moments before: a silver dagger. He kneeled and picked up the weapon with his right hand before brushing off its smooth surface. Without really thinking, he shifted the blade to his left hand. The weight of the weapon felt familiar there, as if he'd held it before. He closed his fingers around the hilt and pointed the blade away from his body.

Treande. What a strange name. Perhaps it was an Ea name?

He gazed down at the knife, thinking it odd that he would hold the weapon thus—he had only ever fought with his right hand. He opened his fingers and realized there was writing on the hilt—strange writing he did not recognize. He traced a finger over the text and felt a brief sense of recognition. For an instant it was as if he could read the words there, but then the feeling was gone. The words appeared once again foreign. He slid the knife into the waist of his trousers and, with one last look around, hiked up the path to the hills beyond.

"The fates will find you, Taren. They always will."

ELEVEN

RELIEVED not to have encountered Seria as he left the ship, Ian stole quietly off the docks and hid behind one of the nearby storage buildings. He shed his clothing, gripped his blade in his teeth, and slipped into the water, transforming before he was entirely submerged.

How long had it been since Taren fled the ship? Hours, perhaps. He could only hope Taren had breached the island's outer defenses as he'd done before. He didn't want to lose Taren, but he knew if he hadn't yet escaped, he'd be duty-bound to bring Taren back.

No. He's still here. On land. Looking for a boat. A boat would get Taren no further away from the island—the enchantments were too powerful.

Ever since the civil war that had cleaved the Ea in two, the Council had fortified the island's defenses so that only those who had sworn loyalty to the island Ea could come and go at will. Yet Ian's men had plucked Taren from the water within the outermost island barrier as the *Phantom* had put to sea. How ironic that now, finally aware of his true nature, Taren was unable to escape. Ian knew what Renda might say about this; he'd as much as said it already. The goddess had willed this. Let Renda believe it—Ian had long ago ceased to believe in the goddess.

Ian stopped a few miles from the docks in a remote part of the island where few dwelled. Taren had come this way an hour or so before. Ian left the water and climbed onto the sand before leaving the beach and taking the path that led up the side of the mountain. He noticed for the first time the block of volcanic rock that rose out of the sand. There were many such monoliths scattered about the island, but he had never seen this particular one.

"The touchstone is our connection to those who came before," his mother had told him when they had visited the island. It was the first time he'd visited Ea, having been born on the mainland not far from Raice Harbor. His parents had told him stories of the island from a very early age, and he'd been young, newly aware of his dual nature, and quite curious. "Our ancestors raised the stones when they first made this island their home, wishing to recreate the stones they'd left behind at the temple. This is a gift from one generation to the next."

Ian had known some of the older Ea to pray to the touchstones, although he'd never understood the practice. Most of the Ea had forsaken the ancient ways of prayer and worship. The island temples lay abandoned and crumbling, the priests and priestesses were long dead, and few alive remembered the stories of the ancient temples on the mainland.

He pressed his hand to the rough surface. Blackened and covered with pale-green lichen, it warmed with his touch. The enticing heat traveled up his arm, and he imagined the scent of incense, fragrant and earthy. He took a deep breath and closed his eyes.

When had things become so complicated? He imagined Taren as he had been beneath the waves. Wide-eyed, curious. He imagined ghosting his fingers over the smooth skin of Taren's back and shoulders, imagined the feel of their bodies as they slid against each other. His chest tightened.

Enough. He started down the path without looking back at the stone. *Damn the goddess and screw the fates!*

THE day grew older, and Taren looked down to avoid the sun. Just low enough that it nearly blinded him, but at least its heat had abated somewhat. He'd left the ship without eating, and he hadn't eaten the night before. He had only himself to blame: if he hadn't been so enamored with himself in his Ea form, maybe he'd have had the good sense to catch himself a fish. To make matters worse, he'd brought along no water, and his mouth felt drier than the sand he'd trudged through hours before.

He stopped and eyed a large fruit at the top of one of the tall palms. It was no different than climbing the ropes, he reasoned, and the knife would come in handy to open the thick casing.

A half hour later, covered in sweat and exhausted, he sat under a shady pine after using the dagger to pierce the hard casing of the nut, and greedily emptied the fruit of its liquid. He didn't hear the two men until they were upon him.

Taren shot to his feet and backed away from the newcomers. Both men were armed. Before he could escape, one of the men put his sword to Taren's neck. The metal was hot enough to burn Taren's skin.

Taren didn't recognize them as members of Ian's crew. The men wore black sashes around their waists with the same embroidered insignia he had seen on Seria's arm. The Council's insignia and the Council's guards, Taren guessed. How could he have been so careless as to allow himself to be captured? He reached for the dagger, realizing with frustration that he'd left it on the ground as he'd drunk. *Another stupid mistake.*

"The Council is waiting for you," the man with his sword against Taren's neck said. "Seems the good captain wasn't able to keep you locked up."

"Or maybe he wanted you to escape? You're a pretty one," the second man said with a smirk for his companion. "The captain likes 'em pretty." He ran a hand over Taren's ass and squeezed.

Taren bucked at the touch and spat at one of the guards. The guard rewarded him with a swift blow across the face and a knee to the gut.

Taren coughed and tried to catch his breath before raising his hands in a gesture of surrender. The guard who'd held him, believing him subdued, relaxed his grip, allowing Taren to bat away the sword with his left arm. Taren ducked beneath the blade as it sliced through the air a moment later. His forearm stung where it caught the blade's edge. He backed away, catching the glint of the dagger at the edge of his vision. The second man stood in front of it, blocking the way.

Taren had little choice: he needed the weapon. He ran at the second guard and tried to knock him off his feet just as the first guard swung his weapon again. This time, the blade hit the tree and Taren lunged for his weapon, rolling onto his side to avoid hitting the trunk but tripping over one of the raised roots. He managed to grab the dagger and turn to face forward just as the second man pushed him bodily against the tree. The point of the man's sword pierced the skin of Taren's chest, and a single drop of blood blossomed there. If Taren moved, the guard would run him through.

"You reckon the Council will be disappointed if we bring him back dead?" the man with the sword asked the other as he pressed harder on his blade.

Taren gritted his teeth. He'd not beg for his life. Better to die fighting than like a dog in the Council's prison.

"Easier that way," said the second man.

"Stand down." The familiar voice came from behind Taren. A barked command.

"Captain!"

"Stand down, Raila." Taren heard the contempt in Ian's voice.

Raila kept his weapon pointed at Taren. "We have orders to kill him if he resists."

Ian stepped forward, his shoulders even with Taren's. "I'll be taking him back."

Raila hesitated but lowered his weapon a bit. The other guard had already sheathed his sword. "Seems you weren't able to keep him, Captain. Best we accompany you back to the harbor." He flicked his sword, indicating the path.

From the looks in their eyes and the tone of their voices, Taren could tell that neither man trusted Ian. He glanced at Ian, hoping to learn his motives, but Ian's face was hard as stone. Then a muscle in Ian's cheek twitched almost imperceptibly. Taren made up his mind.

The dagger was just a few feet away. Taren didn't hesitate but dove once more to retrieve the weapon to the sound of shouts from the men.

"Damn fool," Ian growled as he grabbed Taren's arm and twisted until the dagger fell to the ground. "Did you really think I could let you go?"

Ian punched Taren on the chin.

IAN carried the unconscious Taren over his shoulder, taking him back to the harbor in the small boat the guards had used to hunt for him. They, of course, insisted on accompanying Ian at the Council's orders.

Twenty years, and neither he nor the Council had forgotten that he hadn't been born on Ea'nu. He'd spent two years in the Council's hellish prison, sick and starving. The Council had branded him a traitor and a spy when he'd come from the mainland to live on the island. At least he hadn't been killed. His parents had been less fortunate. They were buried in an unmarked grave, forgotten by all but him, in spite of their loyalty.

At the far edge of the settlement, Dubra Prison was solid but old. Creeping plants climbed the rough walls and thrust their way through the mortar that held the blocks of graying stone together. He had not been here in more than a decade; he'd avoided this place whenever possible, not wanting to revisit his own captivity.

He told himself it was his duty—that he'd had little choice but to recapture Taren—but he found it far more difficult to leave Taren in the guards' custody than he'd expected. He watched as they took him to one of the cells and locked the heavy wood door. He had lied to Taren, reassuring him that the Council would treat him fairly. He hoped that at least he'd spoken the truth when he'd told Taren the Council would not kill him.

The sun had nearly vanished in the water by the time Ian returned to Crias'u from the prison. Smoke rose from the volcano in the center of the island. No trees grew at the top of the peak, the scarred land a stark reminder of the island's turbulent past. Ea children grew up listening to stories of the slumbering dragon within the mountain who blew fire when angered. Ian wondered vaguely if the volcano wasn't more of a threat to the safety of the Ea than the humans, since in the past decade it had hardly kept its silence. And yet the Council seemed to fear men far more.

Ian owned a small cottage high in the hills that ringed the town around the harbor, but he rarely stayed there. Tonight, as most nights, he climbed the gangplank and boarded the ship, preferring to stay close to the water. The ship was empty but for the cook's assistant, whom he paid to make his meals when they were in port. He didn't bother to tell the man to make his dinner. He knew he wouldn't eat; he had no appetite. Instead, he descended the stairs to his cabin. He would sleep. But the cabin felt far too large without Taren, and the bed he'd not slept in for nearly a week felt cold. He lay down on the sheets and tried to relax, Taren's scent upon the pillow strangely comforting. He woke the next morning to the vague recollection of a dream, but try as he might, he could not remember the details save for the fact he had dreamed of Taren.

TWELVE

THE stifling air in the tiny cell made it difficult for Taren to breathe. Sunlight pierced the small opening near the ceiling and tiny specks of dust floated in the air, illuminated by the ray of light. Taren stared up at the palm fronds that thatched the roof of the cell. There, too, points of light shone through the leaves. He imagined each as a star, imagined the night sky and the feel of the ocean breeze against his face. His body ached as he imagined the water on his skin, the feel of it on his face, comforting and familiar. The heavy leg irons cut into his flesh, the blood they drew caking there. He was filthy and weak, unable to think clearly.

How long had he been here now? Three days, perhaps four? He pushed himself up to a sitting position and winced as his elbow met the hard dirt floor. He'd fallen when they'd forced him back inside the last time. The beatings were bad, but the hunger to be under the water was worse. Ian had said that he'd crave the transformation, that all those newly aware of their dual nature would crave it like a drunk craved ale. Once, in a fit of rage, Taren had tried to transform without success. Without the water, his body refused to respond.

He'd had nothing to eat or drink since they'd brought him here. Days and nights seemed to run one into the other. They always asked the same questions. Who had sent him? Did he come from a ship, or had he swum from a nearby island? Who were his parents? What did he know of the mainland tribe? Was he a spy?

He finally told them the truth about the *Witch*. He despised himself for it. The pain had been too great, his will too weak. He'd snapped like a piece of dry tinder, all of his resolve failing him, and he'd told them about the storm and how he'd been lost at sea, only to awaken floating on the water and rescued by the men aboard the *Phantom*. It mattered little to him that they hadn't cared to believe him. He had betrayed his crewmates. His captain. His friend. He was pathetic, unworthy. Much as he longed to return to the ship, he wondered if they could ever forgive him. He feared the Ea would see the *Sea Witch* and her crew as a threat. Would they seek out the ship?

"Did you come from the mainland?" his interrogator had demanded when they'd first beaten him. Taren saw obvious hatred in his captor's eyes.

"Yes," Taren had answered, hoping his honesty would convince them he was no threat to them. "I didn't know I was one of you. I—"

"Don't ever compare yourself to us. That you'd admit to such a thing is only proof that you are here at Vurin's command. Twenty years, and they still insist on sending spies. As if it wasn't enough that they killed our people when they left."

As Taren suffered their beatings in silence, he cursed Ian for not having warned him. He had no one to blame but himself for having trusted the man. He would not make the same mistake twice.

Whereas before the weather had been pleasantly warm, now the wind outside howled, causing the fronds that thatched the roof to shudder and hiss. Water fell unimpeded onto the dirt floor, and Taren retreated to a small corner of the room to stay warm and dry. It surprised him that he hadn't sensed the storm this time, although perhaps his body was too weak. The wind and rain echoed the turmoil in his heart, the longing and the pain. It was well past dark, but no one came. He was thankful. At least he could rest before the next interrogation began. He closed his eyes and dreamed.

HE LEANED over a fire to set more fragrant branches upon the flames. Where was this place? A building. Stone, crumbling at the edges, with long tendrils of ivy that wound through the holes in the mortar that held the walls in place. The walls themselves were hewn from rough blocks of white stone that appeared to shimmer in the fading light of the sun. Taren realized the fire he was tending was set on what appeared to be an altar: simple, crudely fashioned from the same stone used for the walls. An ancient temple, perhaps?

"Daydreaming, as usual." Taren recognized the rough voice. "Perhaps the branches are too heavy for you and you need my help?"

Strange, thought Taren, that even in dreams, he could not escape the man. "I'm doing just fine on my own," he shot back without a glance at his companion. Looking at Ian never did him much good, at least in as much as thinking. Why did his brain always melt like rendered fat in Ian's presence?

He chuckled at the thought only to find himself enveloped by two powerful arms a moment later, the feel of Ian's full lips against his neck. Taren sighed mournfully. He wouldn't waste his strength fighting this man in a dream, no less. If Ian inhabited the netherworld of his dreams, Taren preferred the dreams be pleasant ones.

Ian nipped and licked at Taren's throat as Taren struggled to put the last of the boughs on the fire. "You distract me as ever. Perhaps you should focus your attentions on your own work?"

"My task was complete nearly an hour ago. I've just been watching you work." Another kiss. Taren struggled not to shiver. "Quite entertaining, you are, love."

"I cannot finish if you insist on—"

Ian turned Taren and crushed his lips against his. Taren had wanted more of Ian's lips ever since the first time Ian had kissed him. He would hardly resist now.

Ian laughed as the kiss broke and Taren pulled away. For the first time, Taren saw Ian's face in the light of the fire. But it was not Ian, although it was Ian's face—the same eyes, mouth, and jaw. This man was markedly different from Ian. He appeared slightly older, his face broader, with high cheekbones and full lips. His hair was far lighter than Ian's, the color of wheat when illuminated by the sun's rays. The silky strands of it cascaded over his shoulders like the waters of a stream. He was taller than Ian, although nearly as broad in the shoulders. More than anything else, what struck Taren was the loving expression on his face—an expression of love clearly intended for him.

"Much as I'd like to take you right here, my beautiful Treande, the goddess might not look as kindly upon our use of the altar." The man sighed, then continued, "But come the next full moon, I will be sure to take full advantage of the opportunity to ravish you here."

Treande. *That name again. Taren thought of the old woman who had twice appeared to him and who had also called him by that name.*

"Owyn! Treande!" A young woman stood at the entrance to the temple. "Your dinner is ready. I'll be back on the morrow with breakfast."

"Do not come too early." Ian—Owyn, was it?—pulled Taren closer. "We intend to spend the morning resting."

The woman laughed knowingly, then waved and disappeared into the deepening darkness outside.

"Much as I love her food," Owyn laughed, "there are times when food does not satisfy. I would gladly sacrifice a full belly for the cause of love." He embraced Taren once more. "Come. We will eat, and then I shall ravish you."

Taren found it difficult to argue. It was his dream, after all. A product of his own needs and desires. Too soon, he would awaken in his cell, hungry and alone.

Taren followed Owyn from the temple and out into the cool night. Beneath the bright moon, he saw that unlike the island, this place had few trees. Cattle dozed in groups in pastures, and softly waving fields of grain broke up the bare hills. Owyn led him toward the lights of a small village. As they grew closer, Taren saw the stone houses with thatched roofs that lined the dirt road they traveled. It reminded Taren of a farming town outside Raice Harbor. Borstan Laxley had often sent him to fetch milk from the farms there, and although the walk was long and the milk heavy upon his return, Taren had enjoyed that chore nearly as much as climbing the ropes of the tall ships in port and stringing the new ropes his master had fashioned.

They reached the first house on the road, then veered off on a small footpath that led up a gently sloping hill. Owyn squeezed Taren's hand, and Taren returned the gesture without even thinking. Everything felt so familiar, as if he'd had this particular dream before. And when they reached the top, Taren gasped audibly. There, perched on the sheer cliff face, was a small stone house, thatched like the others. Below, the waves pounded the rocks. Above, stars shimmered, dancing with the breeze off the water.

"I know this place." He hadn't meant to say the words aloud, but the realization was so intense that he forgot himself. Taren felt tears course down his cheeks without reason. I'm crying?

Owyn encircled his waist, pressing his head to Taren's back. "Of course you know it. Callaecia is our home."

"Callaecia," Taren repeated, drawing out the last two syllables as Owyn had done. "It's beautiful," Taren said as he brushed his tears away. "As ever." He spoke the truth. He couldn't imagine a more beautiful setting *for his home. He dreamed of this life and of a man like Owyn. Owyn turned him around and claimed his lips, the kiss sweet and loving.*

Such a beautiful dream....

"GET up!" Taren awoke to a sharp pain in his side. The point of a boot in his ribs chased all thoughts of Owyn and the village by the sea from his mind.

His face was pressed to the floor. He tasted dirt and his eyes were full of grit. He attempted to rub away the haze so he could see more clearly, but realized his hands were bound behind his back. They'd grown so numb, he hadn't noticed.

One of the guards pushed him onto his back with his foot. Taren coughed and gagged, rolling onto his side and retching. "Water. Please." His throat was so raw the words came out as pathetic rasps.

A second guard kicked him in the stomach, a reward, perhaps, for daring to ask. They didn't ask him to stand but pulled him to his feet by his arms. The room spun, but without the use of his hands, he stumbled and received a backhanded slap against his cheek in return. On his knees now, he tried to catch his breath, but they just dragged him out of the room. When he tried to walk, his knees buckled each time, so he finally just let them drag him where they would. He had no strength to resist.

The guards stopped moving a few minutes later, releasing him so that he fell to the ground. His knees met stone and he cried out in pain. He thought he heard one of the guards snigger, and he clenched his jaw with the effort of controlling his anger. It would do him no good to fight them. Best do as Ian had suggested and cooperate. They would see he posed them no threat soon enough, wouldn't they?

As Taren's vision began to clear, he saw the guards had brought him to a windowless room with chains hanging from the ceiling. The room was nearly dark, the only light from a few oil lamps and the fire that burned in one corner. On each wall of the room were shelves and iron hooks that held implements of torture. To his right waited a man Taren recognized as his first jailor aboard the *Phantom*: Seria. His expression was slightly hungry. Self-satisfied.

The guards hauled Taren to his feet, then locked his wrists into the metal restraints attached to the ends of the chains. They then hauled the chains higher until only the tips of Taren's bare feet met the stone floor. Taren struggled not to dangle from the chains, but when one of the men pushed him, he swung about and the cuffs cut into the skin of his wrists.

He expected Seria would question him—every other man who had beaten him had asked him the same questions. But Seria said nothing; he just smiled and landed a blow to Taren's back and neck. Hard, stinging at the edges, cutting his skin. Taren hadn't even noticed the cat-o'-nine-tails in Seria's hands.

Seria raised the whip again and struck him in the same place. The pain intensified as the lacerations on his back bled. He could feel the wetness there, almost imagine it as if he were observing himself rather than inhabiting his own skin. Another blow. Pain and then numbness. Taren thanked the gods for this. When he imagined the blood on his skin as rain, he heard the faint growl of thunder from outside the prison.

Seria stepped back and admired his handiwork. With a smile, he set the whip down on one of the shelves.

"Why haven't you asked me anything?" Taren whispered.

"I will," Seria replied as he reached out and touched Taren's chest, directly over his heart. "But first I want you to understand what your lies will buy you."

"But I'm not ly—"

Pain, all-encompassing and blinding, radiated through Taren's body from where Seria's fingertips met his skin. A pale purple light seemed to emanate from Seria's hand, casting eerie shadows on Seria's face. It was far worse than the whip Seria had used only moments before. The pain in Taren's body gathered and grew in the places where he'd been injured. Each bruise, each cut, each old injury hurt as if Seria had just inflicted the damage.

"No… please…." The effect of Seria's touch grew too much for Taren. His eyelids felt heavy; his mind floated. He heard nothing but the rain and the wind. He imagined the waves as they battered the docks, rocking the ships in the harbor as if to force them to submit to their will.

He allowed his eyes to close and he embraced the darkness.

THIRTEEN

IAN pulled the slip of paper from his pocket and read it over once more before tearing it into pieces. Orders. His life was a bevy of orders, some easy to follow and others more difficult than he cared to admit. A swift gust of wind picked them up and carried the bits of paper away. He wished the same wind would carry off his troubles. *If it were only so easy.*

From his perch atop the railing, Ian gazed out at the harbor and Crias'u beyond through the fog and rain. From here he could barely see the lights of the fort, the seat of power where the Council convened. Weeks later, he could still see the look on Taren's face as he saved him from the Council's guards—an expression of hope that he'd worn until he'd realized he'd receive no better treatment from Ian. After two weeks in that hell of a prison, Taren would certainly despise him.

Orders and duty. He drew a deep breath, as if it might make his task an easier one. At least the waiting was over.

The wind blew harder, the gust picking up his wet hair and painting it against his cheek. He didn't bother pushing it back. He was soaked to the skin, having spent the better part of an hour on deck, trying to clear his mind. It rarely rained this time of year on the island but for exceptional storms like the one that had brought Taren to him. This rain felt like penance.

Ian looked down at the dagger in his hand. Taren's dagger. Where the hell had he found it? Ian had asked his men if any of them recognized it. Unless they were lying—and he had no reason to believe they'd lie about this—none of them had seen it before. Ian was pretty sure it was old, ancient even. He recognized the writing on the handle, although he could not read it. Ea'nu. Without a doubt.

Renda's hand on his shoulder startled Ian back to himself.

"How long will you sit here and feel sorry for yourself?" Renda asked.

"Why are you still here? Luria will have my skin for keeping you."

"I came back. She's asleep. You should be as well."

"I wasn't tired."

Renda blew air from between his lips. Then, noticing the weapon in Ian's hands, he said, "Thinking of using that on the Council?"

"Hardly, although the thought is a tempting one. But I could use your help." Renda raised an eyebrow but said nothing. "Do you recognize it?"

Renda took the blade and ran a long finger over its length, then paused to turn it over and study the writing on the hilt. "No. But it's similar to the weapons the priests once used. Of course now, they're just displayed at festivals. This one is very old. Centuries, maybe more."

Ian schooled his expression to hide his surprise. "And the writing?"

"Ea'nu. The ancient tongue." He looked up at Ian with just the hint of a smile. "But you knew that already, didn't you?"

Ian ignored Renda's comment. "What does it say?"

Renda appeared to consider this. "It's a bit difficult to translate."

"Try."

Renda scowled at the obvious order but moved closer to the railing so that the blade was illuminated by the lamp Ian had set down there. "This"— he pointed to the second set of runes—"means 'water'."

Ian nodded.

"And this," he said, moving his finger to what Ian guessed must be another word, "means 'power'."

"And the other word?"

Renda tilted the blade back and forth to catch the light, then shrugged. "I don't know. I don't recognize it."

"I thought you could read Ea'nu."

"I do my best." Renda looked unconcerned. "You know full well there are none who still speak it fluently. What I know I learned from the sacred texts. But they're hardly comprehensive."

Ian grunted. "Any thoughts as to how it came to be in Taren's possession?"

"Taren?"

"I took it from him when I recaptured him on the island. Convinced the Council's dogs the boy had stolen it from me. He claims to have found it but wouldn't tell me anything more."

"Found it?" Renda paused. "How strange."

"I don't believe he found it." Ian crossed his arms and leaned back on the railing. "He must have stolen it. If not from my crew then from someone on the island."

"You're wrong. If that were true, I'd sense the previous owner's touch upon it."

"I didn't know you could sense things like that."

"There is much you don't know about me," Renda said with a coy smile.

As always, Ian ignored the jibe. "What do you sense, then?"

"Only his touch." Renda handed the weapon back to Ian. "And yours, of course." When Ian did not respond, Renda added, "You seem distracted. Has something happened?"

"I spoke with the Council. They're convinced Vurin sent him. They don't believe his story of growing up amongst the humans and of not transforming." Ian clasped the dagger so tightly in his hand that his hand shook.

"But you know he's no spy."

"I—" What the devil was he trying to imply? "—of course I know he's no spy. I told them he likely came from a nearby ship."

"The *Sea Witch*?" Renda fixed his gaze on Ian's with obvious meaning.

Ian ignored this as well. The last thing he wanted to revisit right now was his relationship with Jonat Rider. "It matters not what ship he came from—the Council will not listen. They won't release him, not when they can use him as proof that the islanders need their protection, regardless of their methods."

"You fear for him." Renda leaned on the railing and crossed his ankles, resting his elbows on the wood as the wind lifted his hair from his shoulders.

"Why do you insist on forcing him upon me? And what would you have me do about it that I haven't done already?"

Renda ignored the questions. "You were once a prisoner as he is. Did they treat *you* well?" There was sympathy in Renda's dark expression.

"No." Ian knew only too well what the Council was capable of. When he'd returned to the island before the war, he too had been the Council's prisoner. They'd beaten and tortured him. If it hadn't been for the war, he might still be rotting in Dubra prison. Or dead. He imagined Taren hurt and suffering. The stab of pain to his gut took him by surprise, even as he forced the image from his mind. "But what do you expect me to do about it?"

Renda said nothing.

"Go home to your wife. I have no need for your concern."

"At least see him for yourself. If you choose to abandon him then, so be it."

"Abandon him? He was my prisoner, I can hardly aband—"

"You can lie to yourself, Ian," Renda said, so close that Ian could feel his breath on his face. "But you cannot lie to me."

AN HOUR later Ian waited as the guard let him inside the dark cell and locked the door behind him. The sound of the door being bolted made him feel ill, and the cries from some of the other prisoners weighed heavily on his heart. Even now, the memories of his time in this place were powerful. Imagining himself in Taren's stead was far too easy.

The storm had abated, the clouds parting to uncover a nearly full moon, but the light barely illuminated the outline of the shape that lay huddled in the corner of the room. The floor was wet and riddled with indentations that had filled with water. The air was cold and damp. Ian kneeled on the muddy floor as he pulled off his jacket and gently laid it over Taren's nearly naked body.

Ian knew they'd beaten Taren even before he saw the bruises and cuts on his face and chest, but seeing the damage made him ache as if Taren's pain were his own. Taren's lips were chapped and split, his left eye so swollen that Ian doubted he would be able to see out of it. Taren's hair was caked with dirt and blood, his nose broken.

Ian reached out and brushed the dirt from Taren's lips. Taren shuddered but did not immediately wake. When had he become so thin and frail? He had just begun to regain his strength when the *Phantom* had returned to its home port. Being prevented from transforming when his body had required it had taken its toll.

Ian stayed at Taren's side until the sunrise, holding him as he slept, as if by doing so he might lend Taren his strength. But he was no healer, and he doubted it would do much good. The best he could offer was the warmth of his body.

"You must survive a while longer," he whispered in Taren's ear, knowing that his words were useless but wanting to assuage his own guilt. He knew from Zera that Taren had finally told them the truth about the *Sea Witch*. The Council had not believed him. They meant to break Taren, to force him to admit something Ian knew was untrue: that Taren was a spy.

"Sleep," he said as he stood up and waited for the guards to let him out. *And dream.*

FOURTEEN

TAREN awoke to the feel of water being dumped unceremoniously over his head. The cold wetness felt almost good. How desperate had he become that just the feel of water on his skin seemed to ease his body's craving to transform? He'd been tempted to sleep in the muddy pools on the cell floor just to feel the water upon his skin, but he'd been too cold. He had dreamed of Ian last night, not Owyn. At least he was pretty sure it had been Ian. He dreamed he slept as Ian stroked his hair.

Gods, he was so tired! He only wished to sleep. No doubt his captors understood this and afforded him little opportunity to do so. At least when he'd dreamed of Ian, he'd slept soundly. Ironic that he'd felt safe in his dream, protected and cared for, when in truth Ian had quite literally handed him to the Council.

He was hanging from the wall, suspended by metal cuffs, naked but for the tattered remnants of his trousers. His skin still burned from the whip, although the pain had dulled somewhat as he'd dozed. His arms were numb, his feet felt heavy and swollen. He had begun to wonder if he'd imagined the pain of Seria's touch. Everything felt so distant and surreal.

Outside, rain had started to fall again. He couldn't see it, but he could hear it dance on the roof of the interrogation cell, light and misting. Taren shivered as the door to the room opened. Seria entered, flanked by two guards.

"Leave," Seria told the men. "I have no need for your assistance." The guards nodded and left silently to wait outside the room for further orders.

"Taren Laxley. You're stronger than you appear." Seria smiled, but there was no kindness in the gesture. Taren shivered again. "Will you not make this easier and tell me the truth?"

"I've told your men the truth." This response earned Taren a backhanded slap across the cheek. Not hard enough to break the bone there, but the blow fell atop an old wound, breaking it open once more. Taren felt the warmth of his own blood as it ran over his skin.

"That tongue of yours will earn you far harsher punishment." Seria's measured words hinted at what was to come. Taren didn't care. He'd decided he would die here. How could he ever go back to Rider and Bastian knowing he'd betrayed them? It was better this way.

Taren remained silent and steeled himself for the next blow. It didn't come. Instead, he watched as Seria picked up a device and held it up so Taren could see. Not a thumbscrew, although Taren had heard of those instruments of torture. Larger. *Gods. What now?*

"Who sent you?" Seria asked in a low voice that might have been considered soothing but for the steel at its heart.

"I told your friends," Taren hissed, "I was lost at sea. I remember nothing until I was pulled from the water." He thanked the gods that Seria asked him questions this time. Not that he thought it would improve his lot, but at least he would have something more to think about than the pain. No doubt Seria had beaten him the last time solely to wear him down, hoping he'd be more willing to talk now. Seria was right. Taren wanted to tell the man anything if it meant the pain would end. *But it won't end, because there's nothing you can say that will stop this. If you tell him what he wants to hear, it will be the same.*

"Of course. And you never knew your true nature until Captain Dunaidh helped you transform." Seria smiled again. Of course he believed none of it. *Why would he?* None of the Ea seemed able to explain it either.

"Yes."

Seria did not respond, but unlocked the cuff on Taren's right ankle and slipped the implement over it, then tightened the screws so the metal casing hugged Taren's raw skin. "Vurin sent you, didn't he? He used his magic to help you through the barriers?"

Vurin. Taren had heard the name once before when the other guards had beaten him. The leader of the Ea settlement on the mainland. "No. I'd never even heard of him before your men asked me about him. But if he'd truly sent me here, why would I have let myself be captured so easily?"

Seria tightened the screws again. Taren winced as the metal broke the skin of his ankle.

"Gods! If I were his spy, why would I even admit I was from Raice Harbor? Wouldn't a spy have been more cunning?"

"Perhaps you are the humans' spy, then. One of their Ea slaves, taught to heed their commands." Another turn of the screws and tears ran from Taren's eyes.

"No. Please stop! I'm no one. A slave from a ship—a lowly rigger. I care nothing about Vurin and the mainland Ea or your petty fight." Taren knew even before the words had left his lips that he'd regret speaking his mind. Gods, the old rigger had been right—his mouth would get him into more trouble than he'd bargained for.

"Petty? You know nothing about how our people suffered. You only care for Vurin and his fanciful dreams. Dreams that will destroy our people." Seria tightened the screws again, causing the metal to press painfully against Taren's bone. Taren bit back a moan. He'd suffered through the beating before without showing Seria his weakness. He would do so again.

"Where is the village hidden?" Seria spoke the words next to Taren's ear, his voice an undertone.

"Village? What village?"

Seria reached for the press. How much could a bone take before it shattered from the pressure? Taren suspected he would discover the answer soon enough.

"Vurin's stronghold."

"I don't know what you're talking about. I don't know of this Vurin. I know of no village."

Taren felt his ankle crack. Taren wished he would lose consciousness so he might forget the agonizing pain.

Seria reached out and touched his fingers to Taren's chest.

Taren screamed.

"WAKE up, love. You were dreaming again."

"Ia—Owyn." Not a dream. It had been a nightmare. He remembered the feel of his ankle as it broke under the pressure of the vise and the way

the pain seemed to permeate every part of his body as Seria continued to turn the screws. "Gods."

Owyn drew him into his arms and brushed his lips over Taren's shoulder. The moan Taren heard was his own, pathetic and vulnerable. Even now, in Owyn's arms, he could feel the pain. "Tell me about the dream. You know it helps when you do."

Taren hesitated, more out of confusion than anything else. For a moment he had thought the dream real. But if that was real, what is this? He decided this was far better a reality than the dream.

"I was a prisoner." His voice shook with the effort to speak, as if by speaking, he would somehow revisit the pain of the dream. "They believed me a spy. They...." He shuddered and moaned once again, the pain still shimmering at the fringes of his mind like a ghost.

Owyn kissed his hair and held him, rocking him as a mother might rock her baby. Comforting him. He'd done this before—taken Taren in his arms when he'd been haunted by dreams—Taren was sure of it. Owyn's arms felt familiar, sturdy, like the branches of a powerful tree with roots that ran deep into the soil. Slowly, Taren's body ceased its shaking, molding itself to Owyn's.

"I don't want to dream again."

Owyn chuckled sympathetically. "Best tell the goddess." Taren was pretty sure he had, or at least that Treande had. "It was a mistake," he added, "telling you about my visit with the commander of the humans' army. I knew you would worry. But I'm sure he will see reason. We pose the humans no threat."

Taren considered Owyn's words, then asked, "What do they fear?"

"I'm not sure. They understand so little about us. I tried to explain that the myths of a weapon are exaggerated and that the rune stone poses them no harm. I don't know if he believed me. He asked so many questions... too many questions." Owyn shook his head.

"We can speak more of this later. You look tired."

"I want to swim," Taren said wistfully. His body ached for the water.

"Then we shall swim." Owyn smiled down at him. Owyn must have seen Taren's surprise, for he added, "We are not needed at the temple today. Remember? The acolytes will take the offering. If you wish, we can pay tribute later, but this day is ours alone."

Taren pulled gently out of Owyn's grasp and stood up.

"Now?" Owyn's smile had grown, the edges of his mouth reaching for the lines around his eyes.

"Can we?" Taren had never felt so impatient in his life. The call was powerful, his need great.

"Of course."

A few minutes later, they walked back toward the village, Owyn's hand clasping Taren's. It was still dark outside, but the sky had begun to lighten with the impending dawn. They turned away from the village as they reached the crossroads. The path was familiar, the scent of grass and trees enticing and fresh. The sound of his feet on the dirt and gravel comforted Taren, as did the sounds of the birds as they awakened with the morning and called to their kin.

When they reached the top of the hill that led down to the shore, Taren sighed audibly, the sound lost on the breeze as it blew up from the water and tickled his skin. He did not wait for Owyn but took off at a run down the slope, shedding his clothing as he ran, laughing. As he reached the edge of the water, he glanced back to see Owyn watching him with both surprise and happiness. His strong features, which before had been set in an expression of concern, now softened as he too undressed.

Taren found it difficult not to admire the broad chest that tapered to Owyn's waist. For a moment he imagined he was seeing another man. Ian. He rubbed his eyes, confused at the memory. If this was real, then Ian and the Phantom were the dream, right?

He pushed the thought away. This, Owyn and this beautiful land, these were real. Owyn's love for him was real.

"I'm waiting." Owyn stood with his hands on his hips in silent challenge.

To hell with dreams! Taren ran into the water, which felt icy cold against his human skin. No matter. In a moment it would be warm enough. He dove down and felt his body begin to change.

FIFTEEN

IAN swore under his breath as the rain pelted his face. The waves rocked the *Phantom* with such violence that he was relieved the crew had moved the ship away from the docks. At least here, anchored in the harbor, she wouldn't be damaged banging against the pylons.

When had the weather become so unpredictable? Nothing, it seemed, had been normal since they'd picked Taren up two weeks before. He laughed at the thought, but felt no joy in the sound. He was quite sure he'd forgotten the meaning of the word. Here he was, Ian Dunaidh, war hero and captain of the fastest of the Ea's ships, about to do something that might cost him his life.

Ian had gone before the Council to plead once again for Taren's release, but to no avail. "We know Vurin sent him," the Sovereign, Gurian, had told Ian from the dais of the Council chambers. "It is the only explanation for how he managed to defeat the island's enchantments. Vurin is a powerful enough mage. He's doubtless trained others."

"If the prisoner is so powerful," Ian argued, "why did he allow himself to be captured?"

None of the Council had answered. In the end, Ian had left, barely able to contain his anger. They would believe what they chose to believe; he'd been naïve enough to think they would come to their senses. He'd been faithful to them by turning Taren over. Now he would give up his comfortable circumstances and his ship and fulfill a promise far older than the one he'd made to the Council.

The goddess was toying with him. Or perhaps the human gods had decided to exact their revenge. They'd been dogging him for years now—

why should this be any different? "Child of two worlds, belonging to neither," the oracle had called him when his parents had taken him to be consecrated to the goddess. "You will suffer much before you find your home." She'd frightened him with her wild, unseeing gaze and her throaty voice.

He flung his pack into the launch and lowered the boat into the water. Before he untied the ropes, he ran his palm over the smooth wood of the ship. She'd been a good ship. He clenched his jaw and released the ropes.

For nearly an hour, he paddled past the main docks, past the beach, past where the mangroves grew thick, to the small dock by the prison. The current was powerful, the waves lashing the shoreline with the storm. If anything, the wind had grown stronger, making it difficult to see. In spite of the rain, one of the prison's guards met him at the docks. He knew them all, of course, although he was relieved to discover this particular guard had not once been part of his crew.

"Captain! What brings you out in such a storm?"

"I'm here to see the prisoner."

"I'm sorry, Captain, but he's with Seria now. If you'll come back in the morning, I'm sure—"

Ian punched the guard in the jaw and he crumpled onto the dock. He dragged the unconscious guard beneath one of the nearby trees, then pulled a set of keys from his belt. He climbed the stone steps that led up the side of the hill, unlocked the main entrance on his second attempt, and slipped inside.

The building was nearly as damp inside as out, the thatched roof little protection from the rain. The Council cared little for prisoners' comfort. Ian had nearly died when he'd become sick with fever that first winter. He wondered how many others hadn't been as fortunate as to survive. He pushed the thought from his mind. It had been easier to forget about the prison while he lived aboard the *Phantom.*

He turned down the hallway that led to Taren's cell, taking the shortest route to avoid rousing the suspicion of the jailors. The cell was empty. He sensed Taren's presence nearby. If Taren was still with Seria, Ian knew where he'd find them. His jaw tightened at the memory of the interrogation room. He ran back toward the large room in the center of the building. Fortunately, the Council posted few guards to the building at night, and he only needed to subdue one other man before he faced the guard posted to the interrogation room.

"Captain?"

The guard, clearly startled to see Ian so late at night, lowered his sword. Ian didn't wait but grabbed the man's wrist with his left hand and wrenched the weapon free. It landed with a thud on the dirt floor. The guard hit Ian across the face with the back of his hand and moved to recover his sword. Ian elbowed him as he bent over, then struck him on the chin with his fist.

The guard stumbled and collapsed against the door, blocking Ian's way. Ian quickly dragged the man a few feet, then, seeing no one else to challenge him, returned to the door.

This time Ian managed the lock on the first attempt—a lucky guess— and kicked the door hard. Seria had clearly heard the commotion outside, because the crack of a whip cut the air and landed on Ian's cheek as he charged into the room. He put his hand to his face and felt blood.

"Back here to retrieve your whore?" Seria offered Ian a feral grin. "Good. So you were the spy all along, not this pathetic creature." He gestured toward Taren, who hung limply on the wall, his face nearly unrecognizable, swollen and bloody. Worse, his legs were mangled, his feet protruding at odd angles. Ian felt ill to see the vise discarded on the floor. It was worse than he'd expected.

Ian didn't care to dignify Seria's bile with a response, although seeing Taren so broken made Ian's gut clench. To think Seria might be the next captain of the *Phantom*!

Ian drew his sword, doing his best to ignore the implements of torture scattered about the room. He knew them only too well; his body remembered them. Even so, the Council had not abused him as they had abused Taren.

Goddess! He'd had so much hope for the Council after the war. Hope that they'd establish a government that treated accused criminals fairly. But they'd rejected a more democratic governance, claiming a firm hand was necessary to protect the remaining islanders from harm.

Ian did not wait for Seria to attack. Seria might be a rat bastard, but he was a damned dangerous one and among the finest swordsmen on the island. Ian's sword met Seria's, the sound of metal against metal vibrating throughout the room, the sharp clanging almost painful.

For a moment each blade held the other at bay. Then Seria shouted something unintelligible and pushed Ian back with surprising force. Ian parried, meeting Seria's sword once more as Seria easily repelled the attack.

"I've been waiting for you to show your true colors," Seria said with a hungry expression. He obviously recognized Ian as the weaker man. "Twenty years. I told them you couldn't be trusted."

Ian said nothing but added his left hand to the hilt of his weapon and swung at Seria's waist even before Seria had finished speaking. Seria dropped his sword to his side, causing Ian's weapon to vibrate as it met the edge of Seria's blade.

"I know your kind," Seria continued with obvious amusement. "You believe you understand your people better than the Council. You would have them act as humans and coddle their people, leave them vulnerable. Our people do not need a parliament, they need protection."

"Protection?" Ian shook his head. "Is that how you explain this place? Or the beatings you seem to enjoy?" He'd told himself he wouldn't engage Seria, but if he got the man to speak, he might catch his breath.

"The people do not know how vulnerable they truly are. They don't know what they need."

"And the Council does?" Ian knew his situation was dire, or he might have laughed.

"The Council has our best interests at heart. Children need direction. They need discipline and sometimes they need to be punished."

Ian thought of the old man who lived under the crates at the docks. Had he needed to be punished because he had no home? And what of the young men who had refused to serve the Council, whose only crime was that they wished to travel from the island? No. He couldn't reason with someone whose heart was already inured to the pain of the Council's iron rule.

"Damn the Council to hell."

The look of shock on Seria's face was worth the blows his words provoked. Ian responded by beating back Seria's repeated attacks, but he was slow and out of practice. The last of Seria's thrusts caught Ian in his left arm and sliced through skin and muscle with stinging heat. Ian ignored the wound, despite the blood that ran unimpeded down his arm.

Ian shouted and ran at Seria, ducking to avoid yet another swing of Seria's sword. He had hoped to knock the other man off his feet but managed only to upset his balance enough that Ian was able to elbow Seria in the belly. Seria grunted, then laughed as he turned and managed to catch Ian's upper thigh with his blade. This time the wound was shallow, although the pain was enough that Ian had to catch his breath. Seria swung his weapon once more, causing Ian to back up against a table.

Metal devices clattered on the stone floor, causing Taren to stir and cry out in pain. The mournful sound pained Ian more than his own wounds. He was losing this fight. Seria knew it too. With both arms, Ian swung his weapon, aiming at Seria's arm. Seria, however, pivoted. Ian's sword hit the stone wall with such force that Ian's right wrist erupted into a blaze of pain.

"Surrender," Seria said with a smug expression, "and perhaps they'll spare your life."

Ian laughed. He was as good as dead if he remained on the island. The Council had slaughtered his parents with no proof of any wrongdoing. He'd given the Council every proof it needed to brand him a traitor. He would fight and die, if need be, before he surrendered.

Seria swung again and again, pushing Ian back toward the wall and forcing him to meet each blow. Seria knew Ian was tiring and that each time their weapons met, he became less of a threat, if he'd ever truly been one.

Goddess, Ian thought, *give me strength!*

The blow that struck him in the leg was hardly an answer to his prayers. He fell backward and his right shoulder hit the stones. He dropped his sword as the shock of the blow shuddered through his body. He slid down the wall and looked up at Seria, who now had his sword pointed at his throat.

Seria's next move surprised Ian: he reached out and touched Ian's chest. The pain in Ian's leg and shoulder was nothing compared to the pain that bloomed red hot in his body with Seria's touch. Seria was an empath, and a powerful one at that! Had Seria hidden his powers from the Council? Or had the Council sanctioned his gift? Ian had little time to ponder the question. He needed to do something fast, or he and Taren would both die by the Council's hands.

Time to reveal a secret of my own.

For twenty years Ian had hidden his birthright, suffering his captivity to gain the islanders' trust. The Council feared the gifts and the ancient ways. Had they known he possessed one of the most powerful of the ancient abilities and that he'd been trained to use it, they'd have killed him as surely as they'd killed his parents.

"The goddess has a plan for you," his mother once told him. He'd only wanted to be like the other Ea children, and yet he'd nearly killed one of them when he'd unknowingly called upon his gift. His father had taught him to master his skill, telling him the gift of protection had long been in his family's bloodline and that it was a gift from the goddess herself. He'd hidden his power, learning instead to fight with his fists and his sword.

You've known all along, haven't you? I asked you for strength and you laugh at my foolishness.

He repressed a sigh. He'd sealed his fate by freeing Taren. He'd known he'd have to use his gift and still he'd hesitated, telling himself continuing to hide it gave him the benefit of surprise. He knew he'd lied to himself. He detested his gift because it set him apart. More than that, he feared it. Enough that he'd stupidly risked Taren's life as well as his own.

"I surrender," he said.

Seria motioned Ian to his feet before retrieving a pair of metal cuffs from a nearby table. Ian focused his power on his right hand and felt the heat build until it threatened to burn him. As Seria moved to place the shackles on Ian's arms, Ian lifted his hand, palm facing outward, and released his power in a flash of blue-and-green fire. The flames engulfed Seria's chest but did not burn him. Seria's triumphant expression became one of stunned shock. Then he fell to the ground and remained still.

Ian turned Seria's limp body over, rummaged through his pockets, and retrieved the key for the metal cuffs that held Taren to the wall. Then he recovered his sword and sheathed it.

"Taren!" If anything, the damage to Taren's body was worse than he'd expected. He worked to unlock the cuffs, trying to focus on something other than Taren's mangled legs and the streaks of blood that ran from his shoulders down his back.

One of Taren's arms now freed, Ian struggled to balance Taren on his shoulder. His leg ached and his left arm stung from his wounds. It was nothing compared to the pain Taren would experience if Ian let him fall and Taren put his weight on his shattered ankles. Ian gritted his teeth and forced the pain from his mind.

"Taren!" he shouted again, hoping his voice would jar Taren back to consciousness. Taren did not stir. Ian freed Taren's other arm and caught him as he fell from his bonds. He cradled Taren, put a hand to Taren's throat, and caught the faint pulse of Taren's heart. *Thank the goddess!* Taren was alive, but barely. They'd not get far if Taren couldn't transform.

Ian heard shouts from outside the prison. No doubt one of the guards he'd subdued had been discovered. Ian had no time to think about it—he had to get to the water. He kicked the door to the room open wider and managed to get Taren through the doorway. He'd only gone a few more yards when he heard someone cry from a nearby cell, "Please! Take me with you!"

Goddess! He couldn't leave them all here, but he couldn't save them all either. He had to get Taren to safety.

He heard banging now, soft and pathetic. "Please! Take me with you!"

"Damn," he growled under his breath. Ian was compelled to act, even knowing he'd already been foolhardy in rescuing Taren. He set Taren down gently and rummaged through the keys he'd recovered from the guard. He tried several in the lock until he found one that worked. The cell's occupant appeared pathetic and emaciated, but he grabbed hold of Ian and embraced him, his thanks more of a babbled stream of pitiful sobs.

"Take this," Ian said as he backed away and shoved the keys in the man's shaking hands. "Let the others out as well."

The man just stared at him.

"Take my weapon." Ian handed the man his sword. "Free the others and have them help you."

The man nodded dumbly in acknowledgement. Ian prayed he'd understood. At least now, perhaps he had a chance to escape.

He didn't wait for the man to speak but ran back out to the corridor, picked Taren up, and hauled him over his shoulder. For the first time, Ian realized how light Taren was. He'd probably eaten next to nothing since he'd come here, and his body would have starved for the water. Without water, an Ea would eventually die. Whoever had cast the spell to hide Taren's true nature must have been a powerful mage, that his body had not suffered as it was suffering now.

Ian heard the sound of another cell opening, and his heart filled with hope that the other prisoners might soon be free.

And then what? It pained Ian to realize they probably wouldn't get far. For twenty years he'd justified his complacency. He'd told himself he could do nothing to help the prisoners, not by himself. He was just as helpless now as he'd been before. Where would they go? Guilt clawed at his belly like a vicious beast.

Taren moaned.

No. He'd get Taren safely to the mainland and he'd live with his guilt. Much as he'd done his best to deny the truth of it, he knew in his soul that Taren's freedom was the goddess's plan. If Taren died....

Resolved, Ian hurried back down the corridor toward the entrance. Carrying Taren slowed him down. By the time he reached the door leading to the outside, a half dozen guards waited for him in a semicircle, weapons drawn.

Ian had no choice. He couldn't fight them all, not and protect Taren. He held Taren tighter on his left shoulder, then lifted his right hand and released fire in an arc. One by one, the guards collapsed.

Ian ran until he reached the water's edge and grabbed the supplies he'd packed from the boat. He jumped into the water with Taren and, in his human form, swam down as far as he could toward the mangroves. He wedged Taren between several roots and pulled off his own clothing, keeping only his belt loosely wrapped about his hips to hold his weapons and supplies. He breathed the last of his air into Taren's mouth, then transformed; he could do little more for Taren in his human form. He'd grown weak from loss of blood, and he knew he'd be of no assistance to Taren if he lost consciousness as a result.

Taren! He pulled Taren from his place amongst the roots, shaking him. Taren wouldn't survive long beneath the surface; his human skin was damaged, and his frail frame gave him no protection. Tiny bubbles of air drifted up from Taren's mouth and nose, which were now filling with water.

Washed of blood, the cuts and bruises on Taren's face were now clearly visible. Taren's skin looked like death, his swollen face nearly unrecognizable. Seeing Taren's beautiful face so badly marred, Ian feared Taren would die before he transformed. The fear tempered his burning anger at Seria's cruel treatment.

Goddess, Taren! Breathe for me!

YOU'RE slow! *Taren shouted as he swam with all his strength away from the shore. He knew Owyn was right behind him; he could sense his presence. He laughed as he moved through the water, reveling in its smoothness against his skin, drinking in the scent of the sand, the kelp, and the tiny creatures that darted about him as he reached the ocean floor. He turned and waited for Owyn, then swam circles around him until he was dizzy from the effort.*

Owyn laughed and playfully grabbed Taren's dorsal fin, letting Taren pull him through the water. Taren had the feeling he and Owyn had done this many times before, although Taren had forgotten he had a fin between his shoulder blades. Taren rose and fell on the warm current he caught, halfway between the surface and the sea bottom. Finally he rolled onto his back, forcing Owyn to release him, before sprinting off toward the rocky outcropping a few dozen yards away. He watched the fish dance around the rock, coming close to him, then darting away as he moved to touch them.

Owyn caressed the back of his neck with his lips and Taren shivered, suddenly cold despite the warm current. He turned to offer Owyn a smile, then shivered once more, unable to shake the ice that settled into his bones.

"Something's wrong," *Owyn said, his eyes full of concern.*

It's nothing. Just a chill.

But Taren knew it was more than just a chill. It was becoming difficult to breathe. He tried to fill his lungs, but with each breath, he felt as though he were drowning. It was as if he were human again beneath the water, his lungs protesting the salt water.

"Taren!" *Owyn grabbed him by the shoulders, doubtless sensing Taren's panic.* "Gods, Taren! Breathe for me!"

What was happening to him? Was he returning to his human form? But he hadn't willed it, had he? Was that even possible?

"Taren!" *Owyn grabbed his arm and pulled him closer.*

Wait. What name had Owyn used? Taren? But—

"Treande. Beloved. You must go now." *Owyn smiled sadly.*

Taren tried to argue, but the world felt as though it were fading around him. He reached out and touched Owyn's cheek, knowing that if he stayed here, he would die. Go? But where? I'm happy here with you.

"He is waiting for you, love. You must go to him."

Taren shook his head. No. This was real. That—that *was the dream. There was nothing but pain to face if he returned.*

"I will be with you. Always. You only need to look for me, and you'll know."

No, I—

Owyn's lips met his and Taren inhaled....

TAREN. Please! Ian could sense the guards at the water's edge. He knew Taren would die if he stayed beneath the water, but he knew they risked death just as surely if they surfaced. More guards were on their way—he felt them approach. Some had already entered the water. How could he fight them off and tend to Taren?

"When I said you should see him, I didn't mean you should take him for your own."

Ian nearly jumped at Renda's voice, and he moved between Renda and Taren. *How did you know I was here?* Ian demanded. He tensed, ready to fight.

Renda smiled and tilted his head to one side, his long tail planted in the sandy bottom so that he swayed side to side with each push of the waves. *"I know much about you, old friend."*

Are you friend or foe?

Renda's smile faded, and he shook his head. *"I have only ever been your friend, Ian."* He put a hand on Ian's shoulder and moved past him to Taren, pushed back the roots, then pressed his palm to Taren's chest. Ian steadied Taren from behind as he shuddered in Ian's arms. Ian put his hand to Taren's chest, sure Taren was dead, but then he realized Taren was breathing.

Breathing without transforming? He'd only known young children to do so, but he had little time to consider the question.

"There is much we have to learn about him, I think," Renda said. *"Now take him away from here before the guards find you."*

But—

"Don't worry about me. I'll keep them at bay."

They'll hang you for it!

"They'll remember nothing. You aren't the only one who has hidden their gift."

How did you know…? Ian began, but before he could finish, Renda was gone. *May the goddess protect you,* he offered, knowing Renda could still hear him.

Then, without hesitation, Ian snaked his arms tightly around Taren's waist and moved away from shore, his tail beating the water with such power that he had to look downward to avoid the rocks and sand that battered his face. The storm had stirred the bottom, pulling sediment from the ocean floor. The bits of debris felt like tiny thorns as they stung his skin.

Ian swam for more than an hour before he realized the storm had passed. Slowly, the water cleared, making it easier to see. He continued to swim downward until he reached the base of a reef several miles offshore, just beyond the island's barriers. There he could shelter unseen and rest. He was exhausted, but at least this far away, the guards would no longer sense his presence. The island's fortifications were keyed to an individual Ea's touch, and Ian had worried that he, like Taren, might not be able to penetrate the barriers. But his touch had permitted them both a way through. Ian thanked the goddess that the Council hadn't had enough time to amend the enchantments around the island.

He released Taren, then pulled him by his arms into a large crevice in the coral where they could hide. Ian felt the slippery skin of a nurse shark as it swam beneath them—he'd disturbed the young shark's rest. The shark was harmless and would find another place to hide. For now, he and Taren needed the refuge more urgently.

As the sand settled around them, Ian tried to make Taren comfortable. He removed Taren's tattered trousers, then inspected his damaged legs. His gut clenched as he saw the bits of bone that protruded from Taren's ankles. The salt water would keep the wounds clean, but until Taren transformed, his body would heal slowly and painfully, as any human's. Taren's body appeared thinner than before. Had it not been for the rise and fall of Taren's chest and the steady beat of his heart, Ian would have despaired that his rescue had come too late.

How cold would Taren be in this half-human form? Thank the goddess the water was warmer this time of year. In the rainy season, it would have been far worse. In his Ea form, Ian could stay under the water indefinitely. Taren would not survive the night. Ian was just about to raise his hand and strike Taren to consciousness when Taren's eyes fluttered open.

"TAREN?"

Taren cried out as he came back to himself. The pain in his legs was more than he could bear. *Kill me. Please. I can't... I won't.... Just let me die!*

"Taren." Ian's voice again, in his mind. Another dream. He was tired of dreams. He wanted to return to Owyn. There had been no pain there.

This… this was too much. He forced his eyes shut and tried to imagine Owyn.

It was so cold. *Owyn. Please. Help me!* Strong arms encircled his chest. Owyn? Gods, why did it hurt so much?

"You must transform or the pain will remain. Please, Taren."

Transform? But hadn't he already transformed? He'd been swimming with Owyn. And then…. Through the pain, he managed to open his eyes once more. He turned his head, noticing the dark hair that moved about his companion's face with the current. This was not Owyn. How many times had he been surprised to find one or the other at his side, never sure which one until he took a moment to really look? They felt so similar, so familiar. Taren's thoughts seemed entangled in them both, as if the line between reality and dream blurred when it came to them.

"Taren," Ian said, his eyes full of fear, *"you mustn't stay in this form."*

Taren finally looked down, still unsure of where he was, surprised to see his legs. He noticed the strange angle of his feet and the pain flared with his own recognition. *I don't know if I have the strength.*

"You're nearly there. You're breathing, aren't you?"

Ian was right. He was breathing as he had when he'd transformed before, even though his body was still human. He shook his head at the thought—he knew so little about his body and of what it was capable. The pain surged once more and he nodded quickly, holding on to Ian, fearful of what might happen if his mangled legs touched the sand below.

He pressed his head into Ian's chest and allowed his body to change. The pain of transformation was almost pleasant, nothing like the pain in his legs and back. He saw palpable relief on Ian's face as he flexed the muscles of his tail. He tried to understand why Ian was with him and how he'd come to be here, but his mind felt strange—murky, like the water after a tempest.

The storm. He remembered a storm pounding the walls of the prison. Water raining down on him through the bars and thatch that made up the roof. He'd felt its power in his body, longed to drown himself in it….

"Can you swim?" Ian clasped his shoulder. *"We must make land soon, or we risk being captured."*

Captured? Why would they want to capture Ian?

"Come, Taren." Ian grasped Taren's hand. *"Follow me."*

SIXTEEN

THEY arrived near the port city of Newtown in the waning hours of the next evening, having stopped only to eat the fish they'd caught. Ian feared Taren might still be weak from his internment in the Ea prison, but he'd been able to swim nonetheless. More troubling, perhaps, was Taren's silence. He swam as if half-asleep. Ian hoped his dreams were more pleasant than reality.

Wait for me here, he told Taren as they stopped at the outskirts of the harbor, where just a few derelict fishing shacks dotted the shoreline. *I'll get us some clothing.* He was relieved when Taren didn't protest but just nodded. Partially relieved, at least. Taren would be safer here, although Ian feared Taren might wander away.

You must stay here, he reminded Taren, who nodded once more but still said nothing. Ian missed the Taren he'd come to know: spirited and stubborn. He knew only too well that it would take time before Taren recovered from the emotional scars of his confinement even though the physical scars were gone.

Ian returned an hour later with clothing he'd borrowed from a clothesline hanging behind a house at the edge of town. Well, *borrowed* wouldn't exactly be the word for it, but they could hardly walk around town naked. After dressing in the threadbare linen trousers and ragged shirt, he had rented them a room where they could wait until they found a way to escape to the mainland or other safe haven. He'd also bought some food at the market.

The building behind the inn was a hut that he guessed had once housed animals and still smelled of hay. It was, however, clean, and the straw mattress newly stuffed. Taren said nothing as they looked inside, but leaned on the doorframe.

"You will eat, then rest."

"Yes." Taren sat on the mattress. He was still gaunt, but his wounds had healed as expected. No scars marred his human form.

Ian ignored the tightness in his chest and the anger that still burned hot. Why did he care so much for this man he barely knew? He brushed the thought away and pulled a piece from the bread, then used his knife to cut a bit of cheese. He handed both to Taren, who put the cheese in his mouth and began to chew. A good sign, Ian reckoned.

Taren ate in silence, nearly falling asleep several times. Ian settled in behind him and supported him, encouraging him until he was satisfied that Taren could eat no more. He himself would eat later. For now, he was just relieved that Taren had not lost his appetite.

He wiped Taren's mouth after he'd finished, then helped him lie down and pulled the covers over his shoulders. Taren fell asleep a moment later, his soft breaths a sweet sound to Ian's ears. Ian undressed, then slipped under the covers and wrapped his arms around Taren's thin body, willing Taren to share his strength.

For the longest time, Ian watched Taren sleep. He would keep Taren safe, regardless of the cost, even if it meant giving him up.

THE sun was high in the sky when Taren awoke the next morning, arms curled around something solid and warm. *Owyn.* He always felt safe when Owyn was near.

He sat up and rubbed his face with his hand, squinting at the bright sunlight that lit the room. Where was this? The room was small, unfamiliar, and smelled a bit like the stables he'd sometimes mucked when he worked at the inn. It was a pleasant odor. Comforting. He remembered another room. Pain. Hunger. Without really thinking, he ran a hand over his chest. He remembered bruises and cuts that had bled, but now the skin was smooth even though his muscles ached as if he'd walked for days.

Owyn rolled over and mumbled something in his sleep. But it wasn't Owyn, it was Ian who slept beside him. He had a vague recollection of swimming with Owyn, then nothing more. Or had it been Ian? His mind felt fuzzy, as if he'd slept too long. He closed his eyes and tried to focus. He tried to recall what had happened before Owyn.

He remembered the name, Vurin, and the feel of the cat-o'-nine-tails on his shoulders and back. Seria and the others. The prison. They'd wanted to know if Vurin had sent him. He'd tried to tell them he knew no one by that name, but they hadn't believed him. In his mind, he felt pain when the bones in his ankles shattered. Then he remembered Seria's touch and heard himself scream. He shuddered and rolled onto his side, curling up as he had years before to stay warm in the sleeping quarters outside the inn. He needed to forget. *Please let me forget.* He heard a moan, then realized it had issued from his own lips.

"You're awake."

"I… yes." Taren realized he'd been holding Ian as he slept. He sat up abruptly and nearly tumbled off the bed.

"I'm glad to see you've recovered." Ian wore a kind and concerned expression.

"Glad?" The memory of the prison and of how Ian had delivered him to the Council flared white hot. "To think that I trusted you—that I believed you when you said they would treat me fairly." He'd been a fool.

Ian blanched at Taren's words, but he did not immediately reply.

Good. Let him stew. Bastard can go to the devil, for all I care! "Where are we?" Taren demanded, wishing to grasp whatever he could of his strange circumstances. Had the Council released him to Ian as some sort of reward for his faithful service? Was he Ian's slave?

"Lurat. The closest of the Luathan Islands to Ea." Ian did not shrink from Taren's ire.

"Closest?" Taren knew this island—he'd been here less than a month before with the *Sea Witch*—but Ian's answer confused him. "But how…?"

"I brought you here."

"You? Why? Did the Council—?"

"The Council had nothing to do with it."

Taren heard contempt in Ian's voice. Hatred, as well. *Hatred for the Council?*

"*You* were the one who freed me from the prison?"

"Yes." Ian's mouth tightened, and he looked away. Did Taren see a hint of guilt in his expression?

"But you were the one who…. Why?" Had he misjudged Ian after all? Surely the Council would have Ian's head for this.

Ian stretched his arms over his head and sighed, as if he cared little about what he'd done. Taren knew better. He sensed Ian's unease. "Because I'm a fool."

Taren sat up and glared at Ian. "That's hardly an answer."

"It's the only answer you'll get." Ian looked away once more, resolute.

"How did we come to be here?" Best change the subject for now, Taren reasoned. Later, he hoped to learn more. He didn't know what to make of Ian's apparent change of heart. It seemed far too improbable that Ian had rescued him out of concern or pity when he'd been the one to deliver him to the Council.

"We swam." Ian hesitated a moment, then continued, "Don't you remember?"

Taren shook his head. He remembered more than he wished, but he had no memory of transforming. He rubbed his face with his hands and willed away the tears that burned his eyes. "You should have let me die." Bad enough that he'd betrayed his friends—the only family he'd ever known—now Ian had risked his own life to help him.

Taren hadn't expected Ian's hand on his shoulder. He leaned into that gentle touch, the war between his conflicted emotions now tipping in favor of his need. As angry as he was, he still craved Ian's comfort. Ian did not push him away as he'd done before, but drew him closer and gently kissed his hair. Taren shuddered, then pulled away.

Ian took Taren's chin in his hand, turning his head so Taren had to look at him. For a moment, Taren imagined he was looking into Owyn's eyes—they were so similar. Warm, inviting. Ian wanted him. And yet just weeks before, Ian had pushed him away.

A sigh escaped Taren's lips as Ian held him there. "Please," Taren whispered. "I want. I need—"

Ian silenced him with a kiss, as if gentling an injured animal. He combed Taren's hair, stroking him as Taren parted his lips to allow him entry. Softly at first, Ian sought Taren's tongue with his own. A question. Taren answered by wrapping his arms around Ian's solid chest. Ian tasted of the sea and of memory, of the wind and of the waves.

Taren lay back on the mattress, Ian's hand in the small of his back, supporting him. He leaned over Taren and brushed the hair off his forehead, then kissed him again, more urgently than before. When the kiss broke, Taren asked, "Why did you push me away before? Aboard the ship?"

Ian's eyes grew dark with emotion, as if he were contemplating how to answer. "You were my prisoner. If I'd let myself take you then, I'd have always wondered if you'd offered yourself to me freely."

"I thought I displeased you."

"I feared I might do something rash." Ian laughed and shook his head. "Apparently I was right to fear it."

"Return me to the prison. Tell the Council you were wrong to help me escape. Perhaps they'll—"

"No." The fierceness of Ian's response took Taren by surprise. "Neither of us are going back."

"But—"

"I'll hear no more of this." Ian's tender expression belied the harsh words.

Taren reached out and touched Ian's cheek. Ian closed his eyes and inhaled a long, slow breath. Emboldened, Taren leaned in and kissed Ian, running his tongue over Ian's lips and parting them. At first Ian seemed to welcome the kiss, but after a few heartbeats, he pulled away.

"No," Taren said, refusing to release Ian. "I am not doing this out of gratitude. I do this because I desire you."

"How did you...?" Ian asked, obviously startled.

"How did I know that was your fear?" Taren shook his head and shrugged. "I'm not sure. I just knew it."

"We must get you some food, and then we will swim. Your body demands both."

Taren knew Ian was avoiding the subject, but he also knew Ian was right. His stomach protested the lack of food, and he longed to transform again. He also longed for Ian, but he would not press the other man. At least Ian had finally admitted he shared Taren's feelings.

"Come." He clasped Taren's hand. "I know a place that will be safe."

"Safe?" Weren't they safe here?

Ian's jaw tightened visibly. "We must be careful. The Council will seek to bring us back."

Taren shuddered, but Ian squeezed his hand.

"I can sense them. We will be safe, I promise. But we must also be vigilant."

IAN led Taren to a secluded cove about an hour's walk from the village, where they sat and ate the meager lunch Ian had purchased on their way. Taren knew they would fish later, but the small meal satisfied him like a feast, and the crisp scent of the salt water reawakened his spirit.

They undressed in silence under the shade of the palm trees. Taren admired Ian's beautiful skin as it shimmered and rippled with each of Ian's movements. Once beneath the waves, Taren swam against the current, his belly full, the water warm on his skin. How long had it been since he'd felt the sun on his back? It had rained nearly every day in the prison, the weather mirroring the bleakness of his future. He'd expected to die there. Worse, he'd *wanted* to die.

At this thought, the warmth of the sunshine seemed to fade, and Taren let himself sink to the sandy bottom. He wished the dreams would find him once more, but they did not. A wave of grief and the memory of pain washed over him as surely as the sun had only minutes before. His eyes burned. Could an Ea cry?

"Taren?"

Taren felt the reassuring pressure of Ian's hand clasping his own, willing him back from the depths of his despair. He forced a smile before taking off in the direction of the dark shadow of a reef in the distance. He didn't want to show Ian his weakness. Ian had done enough already. He didn't need a simpering fool for a companion.

"You're running from me."

I'm fine. He knew that would do little to assuage Ian's concern. *Just tired.*

"You lie. I can sense it as clearly as I hear your thoughts."

Taren swam away, slipping between two large protrusions of rock and coral and out of the sunlight. A parrot fish swam up to him, eyed him warily, then darted away. He turned to find Ian directly behind him, blocking his exit. *I thought you couldn't read my mind unless I wanted you to.*

"It's different with you." Ian did not move—a challenge, no doubt.

Taren was half-tempted to simply accept Ian's dominance. He wanted to go home to Rider and Bastian; he wanted to go back to his life aboard the *Sea Witch*. He knew he could do neither. How could he? He wasn't one of them and he never could be. Now that he understood what he was, he wished he could forget it and return to the simple life of a slave. What Ian asked of him—whatever it was—Taren feared it. He feared a future with choices and uncertainty.

Leave me be. Taren pushed past Ian, brushing his slippery skin and emerging on the other side only to feel Ian grab him around the waist. Still weak from his time in the prison, Taren struggled to escape Ian's grasp. He finally gave up and laid his head on Ian's shoulder. Ian stroked his hair, calming him. For the longest time, Taren allowed Ian to hold him.

"You've suffered." Taren sensed the guilt in Ian's words. He knew as surely as if it had been his own thought to share. *"And you fear the future."* Ian kissed Taren again, and Taren released a long, slow breath. Ian's tender embrace seemed to ease the painful turbulence in Taren's heart.

They continued to float, Taren's face pressed against Ian's chest. Taren could sense Ian's physical desire for him, but Ian waited patiently and held him close. The feeling of peaceful repose settled deep within Taren's heart, and Taren became slowly aware of how much he wanted Ian. Not a new feeling, but this time Taren's doubt had fled with the onslaught of Ian's embrace.

Taren reached up and kissed Ian. He wasn't sure what he'd expected of the kiss. He'd never kissed anyone under the water. Ian's mouth felt hotter than before. The saltwater caused Taren's mouth to vibrate with sensation, as if Taren could taste Ian's desire. Ian's scent was powerful and primal, more like those of the other creatures Taren had smelled beneath the waves. No longer human. Taren's body responded to the scent even more strongly than to Ian's touch. The stirring inside his body felt both strange and wonderful. They swam side by side a few feet above the sand.

Taren's heart beat a steady tattoo, and his body heated under Ian's intensely possessive gaze. Taren's need to submit was primal and demanding. Ian flicked his tail and moved to nuzzle Taren, brushing against

Taren's skin in a sensual and dizzying dance. Around and around they swam, spiraling, their bodies always in contact. Without thinking, Taren nipped at Ian's neck. Ian swam on his back, exposing his neck to Taren's mouth and teeth. Taren continued to bite and lick until Ian hissed in reply. The sound was like a soft whistle, audible through the water.

"Goddess!" Ian's voice in Taren's mind was a husky growl. *"Where did you learn to do that?"*

Taren had no answer except that his body knew this. He floated just above Ian, their bellies now pressed together, tails propelling them in unison. They moved in a slow, languid line above the sand. Taren nearly laughed to feel Ian's cock hard against his own, where before they'd been hidden inside their bodies. He stopped moving and reached down to clasp it, surprised at how human it felt, hard and veined. He wanted to taste it, to learn its secrets with his lips.

Ian gazed down at Taren and stilled so Taren might better explore his body. Taren wrapped his arms around Ian's tail and hooked his own tail around Ian's body so they floated as one, their bodies rocked on the gentle current. With a quick glance upward at Ian—Ian's expression was serene, even vulnerable—Taren took Ian in his mouth.

Ian's cock was long and thick. Taren licked around the tip, flicking his tongue in tiny circles until he felt Ian's body shudder with pleasure, then swallowed Ian's erection until it tickled the back of his throat.

Ian moved his tail just a bit, sending them spinning again as Taren continued to explore with his tongue, reveling in Ian's sweetness. How strange it felt to hear the surf as he coaxed Ian's body to the brink. Stranger still, Taren's mind filled with images from Ian's thoughts, as if by giving his body over to Taren's attentions, Ian had given all of himself to Taren.

Through Ian's eyes, Taren saw the waves buffet the *Phantom* and felt joy stir in his heart as the mighty ship rode the crest of a wave and fell, the spray cool on his face. He saw himself asleep on Ian's bed, his head in Ian's lap as Ian stroked his hair and spoke softly to him. He felt Ian's concern for his welfare, Ian's need to reassure himself of Taren's well-being. He felt the freedom of Ian's transformation, the power of Ian's body as it cut through the water and chased dolphins in the surf. He felt his own lips on Ian's member, his mouth hot and hungry, and Ian's climax as it exploded through Ian's body. When Ian finally spent himself in Taren's hungry mouth, Taren experienced Ian's climax as if it were his own. Taren's orgasm sent him over a cascade of emotion and physical sensation.

THEY drifted near the sandy bottom, and Ian held Taren as he dozed. *"Do you know how truly beautiful you are in this form?"* Taren had also been beautiful as a human, but there was something about him now, when his mind was open and his heart full, that Ian found particularly striking. To Ian, finding Taren felt like a homecoming after years spent at sea. Was this the connection of which Renda had spoken?

Taren awoke and stretched catlike, arms over his head. Ian secured Taren around the waist and sucked at a pale nipple. He flicked it between tongue and teeth, continuing to work the flesh until it pebbled. Taren arched his back to meet Ian's tongue, and Ian moved his hands over Taren's tail, cupping Taren's ass and squeezing it.

"What was that? Before, when you spent, so did I, as if I were the one...?"

It isn't just thoughts we share, Taren. When Ea mate in this form, they share sensation as well. Ian didn't need to hear Taren's thoughts to know this pleased Taren. He smiled, then went back to work, making sure to give Taren's other nipple its due.

Ian. Please don't make me wait.

Ian heard the unspoken question. Taren had never experienced any of this before; he didn't understand how, even if he understood his own need. Ian smiled at Taren, then wrapped his tail around Taren's and pulled him close. He grazed the skin of Taren's belly with his fingers, then skirted lower until he found Taren's hard cock. Ian found it difficult not to pause here, but for now he could wait—he would thoroughly explore Taren's body later, perhaps in his human form. Ian traced a line further downward to the opening at the base of Taren's tail.

He rubbed it with his thumb, feeling Taren keen beneath him and cry out. Taren couldn't have known that place was far more sensitive in this body than for a human. Thrilled to realize how much he could show Taren, he began to press at the edges of Taren's fold, noting with pleasure the way Taren's body rocked with every touch.

"You could have told me that the sensation was different," Taren said with playful indignation.

And deprive you of the glorious surprise of it? Ian laughed. *Hardly.* He maneuvered with his tail, pivoting until his mouth was pressed against Taren's second opening—the opening that he hoped someday to fill in Taren's human form. *Just wait.* He drew Taren's body against his mouth, grasping Taren's ass to pull him closer, and worked his tongue inside the fold to find the treasure beneath.

"Hellfire! What are you doing to me?"

Showing you that there is more than meets the eye. He pressed further inward, causing Taren to pant and moan. *Your body is not the same. It is at once more sensitive and more flexible. Less pain, more pleasure.*

"Ian. I don't know if I.... Gods!" Taren's cry was lost in a torrent of bubbles. They spun around, set adrift by Taren's movements. Ian clung fast to Taren, flicking his tail expertly to avoid colliding with a rocky outcropping. The animal within responded with pleasure for the hunt. Held tightly as he was, Taren could not escape Ian's embrace if he even cared to.

Ian withdrew his tongue but continued to lick and pull at the opening, stretching it easily. Later, he would give Taren an extended lesson in the pleasures of his Ea body. For now, he would satisfy them both.

Taren. Follow my lead. Ian released Taren and straightened up, swam toward the surface, and hovered there with his tail pointed down. Taren watched him and followed, his body upright to match Ian's. They floated together for a moment before Ian caught Taren's chin and their lips brushed. *Stay there,* Ian said as blood pounded in his ears. He allowed himself to sink a bit below Taren, their skin rubbing, Taren's cock hard again with need. Then he grasped Taren's hips and pulled himself up along Taren's body.

"Ahhh...," Taren moaned as Ian slipped inside his opening. One flick of his tail, and Ian was seated deep within Taren's body. *"Gods...!"* Taren dug his fingers into the muscles of his back until this time it was Ian who cried out with the delicious pain.

A strong flick of Ian's tail sent them spinning just beneath the surface of the waves. With each rise and fall of the water as it buffeted their bodies, Ian's cock found the sensitive place within. Taren opened his mouth, and his heartsong reached Ian's ears. The song was an ancient and instinctive one that blossomed from the depth of an Ea's joy. Haunting and beautiful, meant for Ea ears alone, the music could not be heard above the waves.

Ian joined in Taren's music, their voices carried upon the water, the vibrations causing the sand beneath them to move in circular patterns. Ian clasped the back of Taren's skull, forcing Taren to meet his gaze. An expression of joy and surprise lit Taren's beautiful face.

Good. Let him understand what pleasure our other nature can impart. Ian's thoughts fled as their bodies and song reached their climax.

SEVENTEEN

THEY returned to land a few hours later, having fished and eaten their fill. Ian waited until Taren fell asleep, then dressed quickly and headed into town. After dark, it was easier to navigate the narrow streets without fear that he'd be recognized. The Council's men were still here looking for them, but Ian knew these streets better than they and was able to avoid the main thoroughfares as he made his way to the docks.

The dockworkers had long ago stopped work, the docks now dark and silent. Oil lamps lit the sole ship there. The portholes glowed like tiny harvest moons, and the scent of the ocean filled Ian's nostrils. The *Sea Witch*. Judging by the light from the aft cabins, Ian guessed Rider would be working through the accounts now that they'd off-loaded their cargo— contraband, perhaps stolen from another vessel or smuggled from an enemy land.

From the edge of the docks, Ian spotted several crewmembers walking the decks, keeping guard. Pirate ships always garnered some curiosity from the locals, and sometimes a man might be daft enough to climb aboard. Ian had no intention of climbing the gangway to enter the ship. There was only one man he hoped to see tonight.

He tossed the rope expertly onto the aft deck, where it landed silently, the metal hook swinging about one of the ship's stays and taking hold there. He'd done this enough during the war to gain access to enemy ships. It was far easier when the ship he sought to enter was not underway.

The sound of the wind caused the ropes to flutter and bang against one of the masts, more than enough to cover the sound of his bare feet as he climbed the side of the hull. He swung back and forth on the rope until he managed to claim a foothold at the edge of one of the large windows. Fortunately, they were open to let in the cool breeze. It only took him a second to reach the ledge and release the rope. He jumped from the window into the cabin.

Rider sat at a table, mouth turned upward in a crooked grin, the lines around his eyes bespeaking his amusement. "You took your sweet time."

Ian took a deep breath, then sighed. "You knew I was here."

"Of course. Do you take me for a fool?"

"No."

Rider just laughed. "But of course you do. You always did, didn't you?"

Ian did not reply but waited to see what Rider would do next. He honestly didn't care that Rider had known all along—it would make the entire situation simpler. Less to explain. Fewer questions.

"The boy is mine."

Ian's jaw tensed. He'd expected this, but he hadn't expected his strong reaction to Rider's claim to Taren. "That's for him to decide."

Rider laughed. "Indeed. But you already know what his decision will be, don't you?"

Ian wouldn't lie—Rider knew him too well for that. It made little difference that they rarely saw each other. Rider could always read him. "Aye."

"Then why not hand him over and be done with it? He will be safe with me."

This *was* a surprise. Rider knew about Taren?

Rider ran a large hand over his beard and sighed. "You really do take me for a fool. I've known since I brought him aboard what he was. The woman they found dead by the water, half-transformed, the orphan left with the rigger, and you just having left to avenge your parents." Rider shook his head. "When you left, I had hoped.... So what is it you want?" His voice sounded flat, even dismissive.

"Safe passage to the mainland."

"And why shouldn't I demand the return of my property?" Rider leaned back in his chair, rubbing his neck, the lines that etched his handsome face pronounced. He looked older than Ian remembered. Tired, perhaps? No, not so much tired as wistful. Resigned.

Ian pushed the thought from his mind and replied, "He needs to be with his own kind. For now, at least. He needs guidance." He had few illusions that Taren would choose to stay with him if given the choice.

"And if I give you time, what then?"

"If he chooses to return to you, I will respect his wishes." Ian knew he'd regret this promise. Still, he had little choice in the matter. He would not keep Taren longer than needed. He would school Taren in the ways of the Ea and then set him free. He'd never expected more, much as he desired it.

Rider appeared to consider the bargain, although Ian was quite sure he'd already made up his mind. "You have a year. That should be plenty of time for you to guide him. After that, he is mine."

"Agreed." Ian bit back the urge to tell Rider that Taren belonged to no one. For now, he'd let Rider think what he wanted. First and foremost, he needed to get Taren away from the islanders. On the mainland, they would be safe—he doubted the Council would pursue them and risk recommencing hostilities.

"I am surprised, though." Rider leaned back in his chair and rubbed the back of his neck.

"It surprises you that I'd risk my life for him?" Ian laughed.

"No." Rider's eyes twinkled in the candlelight. "Not at all."

"Then what?" Ian had the distinct impression that Rider was toying with him. Then again, this much of their relationship was familiar territory.

"I'm merely surprised that you would be willing to return him."

Ian gritted his teeth. He'd taken a risk in coming to Rider. He wondered if Rider guessed at his attachment to Taren. Rider knew him too well. *Best tell the truth.* "My feelings for Taren are irrelevant. My only concern is for his safety."

Rider raised a quizzical eyebrow. "We leave at sunrise," he said. "I wish to speak with Taren alone before we get under way."

Ian nodded. Even now, he fought the low thrum of jealousy. He hoped it would fade in time. *Best get used to it now. Your time with him is short.*

Eighteen

TAREN looked down at the harbor and inhaled a slow breath. "*This* is the ship that will take us to the mainland?"

"Aye. Familiar, isn't she?"

"I don't know what you mean." Taren frowned, clearly indignant.

"Of course you do." Ian offered Taren a knowing grin. Taren, in turn, glared back at him. "Rider and I are old acquaintances. Our paths cross often. I knew the *Witch* was in the area when we picked you up." Ian could sense Taren's anger, but he reasoned it would abate quickly.

"You knew all along, didn't you?"

"I guessed." He watched Taren as they continued to walk toward the docks, doing his best not to smile.

"Might have shared that with me, you know."

"To what end? Besides, why not just tell me you served aboard the *Witch*? Why keep it a secret?"

Taren glanced down as if he were embarrassed to say it. "I… I heard tell that you and Rider were enemies. I feared you might do the *Witch* harm."

"You care for the crew, don't you?" It explained the conversation with Rider the night before. Rider clearly also cared for Taren, however much he denied his feelings.

Taren did not meet Ian's eyes. "Aye. Does that surprise you?"

Ian couldn't help but smile. "No. Not at all." He too cared for Rider, even though their relationship was long over.

Taren, perhaps disbelieving Ian's words, stopped and crossed his arms over his chest. "What else do you know about me that you haven't told me?" he demanded with a furrowed brow.

"Do you wish me to speak it?"

He didn't mean it as an affront, but he realized Taren had taken his words badly when Taren blushed and clenched his jaw. Ian hadn't wanted to embarrass him, but he knew it served no one to deny the truth.

"Your relationship with Rider and Bastian doesn't concern me." Ian spoke the partial truth, at least. There was no need to tell Taren of his jealousy.

THEY boarded the ship to little fanfare. A few of the men greeted Taren warmly, while others clearly recognized Ian and regarded them both with open hostility. They had nearly reached the top of the stairs that led down to the cabins when Taren heard a shout, and one of the crewmembers ran toward him and hugged him tightly.

"Fiall!" Taren exclaimed as he returned the embrace. "Thank the gods." He stepped back to appraise the boy. "No worse for wear, I see."

"Thanks to you." Tears streaked Fiall's cheeks as he said this. "Gods, I thought you dead. If I hadn't been such a stupid—"

"I'm none the worse for wear either, as you can see." Taren ruffled the boy's hair, then squeezed his shoulder.

Fiall eyed Ian warily. "Are ye who they says ye is?"

Ian's grin surprised Taren. "Who do they say I am?" he asked.

"Ian Dunaidh," Fiall replied. "Captain of the *Phantom*."

"Aye," Ian said. "That's me."

Fiall furrowed his brow, then turned to Taren and asked, "Has he hurt ye?"

"No." Taren offered Fiall a reassuring smile. "Saved my life, in fact." Taren glanced to Ian and met his gaze. "Twice."

Fiall formed an O with his lips, and his expression softened. "So it's true, then? Both of ye are sailing to the mainland with us?"

"Aye," Taren said.

"Will you stay with us?" Fiall asked with another glance in Ian's direction.

"I don't know." Taren felt his belly flutter at the thought. He wasn't sure which he feared more—leaving Ian or leaving the *Witch* and her crew behind.

"Your captain awaits us," Ian put in, perhaps noticing Taren's uneasiness.

"We'll speak later, Fiall," Taren said with a smile. "I promise."

A SHORT time later, Taren stood at the doorway to Rider's cabin. *My cabin*, he reminded himself. Or it had been until only a short time ago. Barely six weeks away from the *Witch* and he felt like a stranger. His stomach lurched and he wondered if seasickness felt something like this. He didn't much like the feeling. He knocked.

"Enter."

Rider's voice hadn't changed—why had he thought it might? The man seated at the table, eating his breakfast, hadn't changed either. "Captain, sir!"

Rider smiled, and gods if Taren's eyes didn't burn! Whatever his feelings for Ian, he'd missed Rider. Missed Bastian. Missed them all so much it had hurt. "Come here, boy. Let me look at you."

Taren approached and waited, his gaze set on the floor, his heart pounding against his ribs.

"Look at me."

Taren forced himself to meet Rider's eyes.

"Whatever sin you believe you've committed, you will now cease to berate yourself for it. That's an order."

"But sir, I—"

"I know about the prison. I know what you told them." Rider's expression of kindness did not waver.

"But I—"

"Always the same, aren't you? Talking too much. Challenging me." Rider pursed his lips and chuckled. This time Taren held his tongue.

"I've no secrets, boy," Rider continued. "You've betrayed nothing. I am only pleased that you're well. I despaired at first...." Rider's Adam's apple bobbed as he swallowed. "No matter. You're safe. Although I should tan your hide for your idiocy."

Taren's eyes filled with tears.

"I must ready the ship." Rider winked, then added in a low voice, "Bastian is still asleep." He motioned to the bedroom. "I reckon he will be pleased to see you as well."

Rider stood up and ruffled Taren's hair as he walked past him. He nodded to Taren, then left the cabin, shutting the door behind him.

Taren closed his eyes and sighed. He should have known Rider would say the things he needed to hear. He'd always said those things. Taren admired that about him.

He walked over to the bedroom and tapped on the door. He'd never knocked on that door before, but this time it felt almost strange not to. Bastian mumbled something incomprehensible, and Taren entered.

Bastian had indeed been asleep. But the moment he saw Taren in the doorway, he flew off the bed and launched himself at Taren, embracing him so powerfully it nearly knocked Taren off his feet. This time the tears did not wait. Taren didn't care that he might look the fool.

"Gods, Taren," Bastian said as he held Taren in his arms, "I thought you dead. We all did." His face, too, was wet. He wiped the tears away with the back of his hand, then stepped back and scowled at Taren. "How dare you do that to us? And just when I'd come to accept that I'd never see you again, you...." Bastian's tears began anew.

"I'm so sorry. I was a fool to act so rashly. Forgive me?"

"Always." Bastian reached out and traced a single finger over Taren's lips.

In spite of himself, Taren gasped, suddenly conscious that Bastian was naked and feeling his cock respond. For an instant he was tempted to run his hands over that enticingly familiar skin. He wanted to plunder Bastian's mouth, feel his body beneath his own. "Bastian, I want...."

"Shhh." Bastian offered Taren a wistful smile. "I know, love. I can feel it too." He kissed Taren tenderly on his cheek. "But you can't, can you? Not now, at least."

"I... no." Bastian had always understood him so well.

"You love him, don't you?"

"What? I...? No." Of course he didn't love Ian. He'd just met the man. But he'd agreed to go with him and learn about his people. Taren understood the need for that.

"We knew your time with us was short." Bastian clasped Taren's hand and brought it to his lips. "We wanted this for you—for you to find someone for yourself. Rider says Ian's a good man."

"But I thought—"

"The rumors," Bastian said. "Rider says they were just that. He vouched for Ian. Said he trusted him to take care of you."

"He... he said that?" Taren hadn't expected Rider to approve of Ian. Tolerate him, perhaps, but only because Taren guessed Ian had paid for their passage.

Bastian nodded, although he appeared wistful. "Aye."

"I'll be back aboard the *Witch* in a year. With you and Rider." Taren tried to sound more sure of himself than he truly was. So much had changed since he'd left the *Witch*. He wasn't sure what to believe.

Bastian did not respond, but changed the topic instead, his expression now one of eager anticipation. "Care to help me man the lines?" he asked as he turned and slipped into a pair of trousers and began to pull a shirt over his head.

"You know me too well." Taren's heart soared as he imagined himself up on the deck once more.

"Come, then. We've a ship to sail."

IAN stood on the bow of the ship, looking amidships, where Taren helped to raise the *Witch*'s sails. The joy in Taren's face reminded Ian of what he'd seen when Taren had first transformed.

As the ship turned upwind, Taren climbed the mast with surprising grace. Once atop, he freed one of the sails that had caught on a rope and set the sail free. A moment later Rider steered the vessel slightly off the wind and the sails filled. But Taren did not descend to the deck when his job was complete; he climbed higher still and wrapped his legs around the mast, his hair whipping about his face as the ship slowly picked up speed.

How could Ian not smile to see the joy on Taren's face? He imagined what it might have been like to have Taren at his side as they sailed the *Phantom*....

But she's no longer your ship. The reminder pained Ian. Whatever he'd thought of the Council and its backward ways, he'd loved his time aboard the ship. He'd had a good and loyal crew. He already missed them.

"I've never seen anyone who loved the sea more," said a gruff voice at his side. "Except perhaps you."

"I often wished you and I would sail together," Ian admitted. "I regret it never happened."

Rider shrugged. "A child's dream. We both know it could never have been."

"Aye."

"What will you do when we make port?"

"My parents' house will be safe enough. The Council would not be so bold as to send its men onto enemy soil." Ian felt wistful about returning after so long—he had not been back to his family's house in more than twenty years. He knew that the memories there would be both painful and happy.

"I still don't understand why they fight amongst themselves," Rider said as he turned to gaze out at the island, now just a tiny dot on the horizon. "Why wouldn't the islanders just let them leave?"

"Fear. Isn't that what drives us all to hate? When my people fled to the island centuries ago, the humans nearly exterminated them. Our ancestors survived. And although there are none still alive who remember the slaughter, the islanders feared those on the mainland might expose their island sanctuary." Ian shook his head. "Ironic, isn't it, that the war between my people took so many of the precious lives the Council wanted to save?"

Rider nodded.

"I see you're flying the mainland flag," Ian said. "Serving His Majesty this trip?"

"I serve whatever master pays best. And I do not bite the hand that puts gold in my pocket."

"A wise choice." Ian leaned back on the railing and let the wind caress his cheeks. "What cargo do you carry?"

"A valuable one."

"I see." Ian chuckled; he'd expected just such a response. Trust only went so far.

"We should make port in four days if the winds permit." Rider stood a bit straighter as he said this.

"You've done well with her."

"Your boy is partly to thank for the *Witch*'s speed. He's quite skilled with the ropes. Clever too."

"He's no boy," Ian retorted, knowing full well that he too had called Taren this once.

"He was a boy when I brought him aboard. Whether he's yet a man is to be seen." When Ian made his displeasure known by a deep scowl, Rider added, "But he will be a fine man someday."

NINETEEN

IAN lay back on the blankets and stared up at the ceiling planks. With the exception of the captain's cabin, the *Sea Witch* was smaller than the *Phantom*, so the only sleeping area not already occupied was in a small corner of the hold that was empty of cargo. Ian didn't mind—he didn't want to share the crew's quarters.

Taren had returned to the rooms he had shared while he'd lived aboard the *Witch*. Taren was a grown man, in spite of Rider's words, and could choose with whom he wished to share his bed. Rider's bed was more comfortable than the hard floor. *And far more interesting.* Ian imagined Taren naked in Rider's arms and his hands balled up in tight fists at his sides.

Enough of this! With this thought, Ian stood up and began to pace. Of course he'd known what Taren had been to Rider and Bastian. Rider himself had readily admitted it, perhaps for the sole purpose of demonstrating his control over Taren. Damn the man to hell! The sooner they got off this ship, the better.

Finally, having tired of the same four walls, Ian climbed onto the deck and settled down with his back against the foremast and tried to sleep.

TAREN gazed out the aft windows at the moon glittering over the water. He knew it was long past time to sleep, but he was restless. Rider, perhaps sensing his conflicted heart, had instructed Fiall to set a bedroll outside of the bedroom. Part of Taren longed to sleep beside Rider and Bastian, although it was Ian he desired. The thought made him feel guilty—Rider and Bastian had done so much for him, and yet he knew that nothing between them could ever be the same.

I've changed. He rubbed the bridge of his nose and let out a slow breath. His world had grown far larger since he'd left the *Witch*. More than just the obvious physical change, Taren hungered for something he couldn't quite fathom. The dreams had changed him, although he wasn't exactly sure how. All he knew was that he longed for something—elusive and deep.

Bastian threaded his arms through Taren's. "Are you disappointed not to be sleeping at his side?"

Taren nodded. How had Bastian so easily guessed his thoughts? Taren had wanted Ian to claim him, and yet Ian had not objected to him sleeping in Rider's quarters.

Bastian pressed his face against Taren's back. "Rider is on watch tonight. Come sleep by my side. I promise nothing more will come of it."

Taren nodded.

Later, as he lay with his head on Bastian's chest, Taren wondered where Ian slept. Taren loved Bastian, truly he did, but as the cool breeze caressed his bare shoulders, Taren fell asleep to thoughts of Ian.

TWENTY

"TAREN," Bastian called from the deck, "you've been up there nearly half the day! Captain says you must eat."

"Mother hen!" Taren laughed from atop his perch on the main, then climbed down the mast. He'd have stayed there all day, so happy was he to be back on the water, although his stomach would have protested mightily.

In the three days since he and Ian had joined the crew of the *Sea Witch*, Taren had resumed his duties as rigger with little fanfare. Taren saw so little of Ian he had begun to wonder if Ian was avoiding him. He'd seen Ian about the deck, often conferring with Rider, but he had spoken to Ian only once, on the first day of their voyage to the mainland.

Much as he hoped Ian would tell him more about the Ea, he decided it was best not to press him for now. They would have a year together—plenty of time for Taren to learn what he needed about his people. Or so he told himself. In truth, he wondered if he had done something to offend Ian. Or worse, perhaps Ian had decided their lovemaking had been a mistake. Taren wasn't a free man, after all. And although Rider had been kind, Taren didn't expect Rider to release him from their bargain.

"You look as though you're far away from here," Bastian said, bringing Taren back to himself.

"Just thinking." Taren offered Bastian a smile, hoping it would dissuade him from pressing him further.

"About him again."

"Am I that obvious?"

"I know you too well. I can sense the turmoil in your heart. You want him, and yet you hesitate. Why?"

"I'm not sure." Taren shook his head. "There is something more here. A feeling I have." How could he explain the strange dreams he'd had when he'd been imprisoned?

"Do you fear he will hurt you?" Bastian appeared deeply concerned.

"No. He would never hurt me. Not intentionally." Taren had no idea why he believed this. After all that had happened, he knew he should be wary. Ian had rescued him, but he'd also delivered him into pain and misery. And yet in spite of this, Taren knew the words he spoke were the truth. Ian would never seek to harm him. There was something more going on here than Ian was willing to tell him.

"Go to him, Taren. What can you learn by staying away?"

"But if I go to him…."

"Rider and I will always love you." Bastian smiled and touched Taren's cheek. "But you know it's time to fly the nest. You've known it all along, haven't you?"

"Aye."

"Go on, whelp. Get you some food, then find him and show him your heart." Bastian laughed, then kissed him on the lips.

AS HE had since they'd come aboard, Ian slept on deck. If the crew noticed, they said nothing, although he'd made sure to return to his improvised quarters before sunrise when most of the crew awoke. Tonight, however, the fog that had rolled in and the rain that began to fall in the early morning hours sent Ian retreating to the hold.

He climbed down the steep ladder, still groggy with sleep, then pulled off his shirt and trousers. He'd hoped he might read the book he'd borrowed from Rider the day before, but it was still too dark in the hold to see anything but shadows. With a sigh, he pulled back the blanket from the straw bedding that, in the darkness, seemed even lumpier than usual. Something—someone—in the bedding stirred, and Ian started.

Even in the dim light, he recognized Taren, half-naked and curled up, asleep, arms clasped around a bundled blanket. Ian kneeled at the edge of the bedroll and smiled at the peaceful expression on Taren's face. Taren murmured in his sleep, an endearing and vulnerable sound that made Ian's throat tighten.

Soulbound. The word seemed burnished in his mind since he'd first met Taren weeks before. He turned his hand over to examine his palm, remembering how he'd used his power to overcome Seria and the guards at the prison. Now, watching Taren sleep, Ian wondered if his mother had been right. Had he been given this gift to protect?

He slipped alongside Taren, who rolled over and wrapped his arms around him and pressed his face against his back. "I waited for you," he murmured in a voice thick with sleep.

Ian closed his eyes and reveled in the feel of Taren's body against his. Goddess, but he'd missed Taren. And yet now, with him once more by his side, Ian could not find the words to express this.

"Do you not want me?" Taren asked.

Ian felt Taren stiffen, as if he were steeling himself against Ian's response.

"Why do you say that?"

"You did not ask me to sleep here with you." Had Ian heard pain in Taren's voice?

"You are free to sleep where you wish. Do what you wish. At least until I must return you to Rider's care."

"No. I… I wished to sleep with you. I… wished to… share my bed with you." When Ian didn't answer, Taren sat up and looked down at Ian with a deep frown. "Did you believe that I… that I would… that I *could* just return to Rider's bed after all that has happened between us?"

"I did not know what to think." Ian knew it was bluster, even an outright lie, but he couldn't bring himself to admit he'd believed just that. Never had he felt such a fool. Never had he felt such jealousy burn as when he imagined Taren with Rider. What the devil was wrong with him? He'd never wanted for lovers, nor had his lovers expected his fidelity. Until Taren, sex had satisfied his physical need. Yet now he imagined Rider taking Taren, ravishing his body, and he felt both anger and envy.

"Stupid fool." Taren gazed down at him with surprising tenderness, his lips pursed. "You do so love to leave me to my own devices, don't you? Never asking me what I think?"

Had he done that? Yes. He supposed he had. "I don't intend to."

Taren stroked his cheek and said with a sigh, "If you wished me here in your bed, why didn't you just say so?"

It was a fair question, and one Ian struggled to answer. "I didn't want to force you—"

"I wish to be with you." Seeing Taren's questioning gaze, Ian began to understand that Taren looked to him to take the lead. Not surprising, given that he'd spent his entire life in servitude. He knew Taren spoke the truth but was simply not comfortable asking for what he wanted.

Someday, Ian would set Taren free of his bonds. For now, he would give Taren what he needed.

Ian lit the lamp near the bedroll, then pulled Taren down on the blankets and rolled him onto his back. He rubbed a thumb over Taren's lips, taking a moment to study Taren's face in the soft light. Unlike most Ea's, Taren's eyes were warm brown with flecks of gold that reminded Ian of the sunlight as it penetrated the surface of the water. Despite his stature, Taren's features were delicate—not a woman's features, but lovely nonetheless. His slim nose was set against high cheekbones, emphasizing his full lips and smooth jaw. Although Taren's skin had lost some of its sun-kissed color, it was still a warm tan. Now that the color of Taren's skin had become lighter, Ian noticed that tiny freckles dotted Taren's cheeks. But for the light, Ian wouldn't even have seen them. He leaned over Taren and kissed the tiny points of color, eliciting a long and happy sigh from Taren.

Working his way downward, Ian kissed and caressed Taren's supple skin. He tasted salt and inhaled the faint scent of musk. Ian's other self roared its pleasure, urging him to take what he knew was his. He held the animal need at bay—this time, it took little effort. He wanted to savor these delights as a man, know Taren's body as a man might, learn its subtle indulgences, and understand Taren's needs.

Taren's eyes fluttered closed as he arched his back to meet Ian's touch. Ian pressed his lips to a pink nipple and teased it until it hardened. Knowing what Taren wanted, for he instinctively understood, Ian released the hard bud and licked a line up to Taren's neck. "No. Please. More."

Ian laughed and ravished Taren's lips, pressing his way inside Taren's warm mouth to explore every bit of the moist heat. He ran the tip of his tongue over the smooth surface of Taren's teeth, catching the sharper edges, then plunging once more into Taren's softness. Much as he fought his own dual nature, he appreciated that duality in others: the softness of skin over hard muscle, the primal hunger and sweet affection. No doubt this was why

Ea mated in both human and animal forms—there was much to enjoy in each.

Having teased Taren as much as he wished, Ian now reclaimed the nipple he'd abandoned minutes before. This time he was not gentle, nipping at the flesh until Taren cried out. Ian flicked his tongue over the bud as he held it between his teeth until Taren keened once more with his ministrations. He knew Taren wanted this rougher contact, although he was at a loss to understand why he knew it. So much of Taren's body felt familiar, and yet he knew he had never explored it as carefully as he did now. He moved to the nipple's neglected twin, laving and teasing it to match the first.

Taren's hard cock pressed against Ian's thigh through the fabric of his britches. Ian sat back and untied the waist before pushing the thin linen fabric down to Taren's ankles. Taren kicked off the trousers.

Ian paused to study Taren's lithe body. Taren's cock, long and graceful, rose erect from the dark curls at its base. Ian didn't hesitate but took Taren's cock in his mouth, pushing back the foreskin to taste the reddened tip.

"Gods!" Taren gasped as he bucked into Ian's mouth.

Ian took the globes of Taren's ass in his hands. He squeezed them until Taren cried out again, then held Taren's body hostage as he swallowed Taren's cock nearly to the base. Once more Taren rose to meet his mouth in a silent plea.

Ian covered his teeth with his lips and worked his way upward along the shaft, stopping to look up at Taren's face. Ian grinned to see Taren's lips part to release a halting breath. Up and down Ian moved, pulling, scraping, driving Taren to the brink and then holding back until Taren begged him for more. With each of Taren's cries, Ian's body responded, his cock aching for release. Ian didn't care. He was claiming Taren as his own, satisfying his animal nature even as he held it at bay.

Ian released Taren's buttocks from his iron grip, slid his thumb and several fingers into his mouth, pressing against Taren's cock alongside his tongue. Taren was close now; Ian could feel his impending climax in the shudders that wracked Taren's body. He withdrew his wet fingers and sought Taren's entrance, making sure to rub his thumb over Taren's sac, then traced his way over the smooth skin behind.

The beast's growl echoed about the hold—Ian now let it free to enjoy the pleasure of the claiming. *Mine. You are mine alone. I will not share you.*

"Ahhh," cried Taren as Ian breached his opening with a slicked finger, pressing inside without delay.

I will not share you.

Taren exploded into Ian's mouth, hot and salty. Ian greedily swallowed his seed, then lifted Taren off the sheets so he could feel the heat of Taren's body and reassure himself that no one would take Taren from him. In that moment Ian surrendered to his other nature completely, digging his fingers into Taren's back, the pulsing in his groin driving him. He was possessed of one thought alone. "Mine," he growled in a voice that sounded nothing like his own. "Only mine."

"Yours alone." Taren gasped the words, clinging to him with nearly the same intensity.

"I must have you." *Mark you as my own. Take your body. Own your soul.*

"YES." Taren breathed quickly against Ian's neck as he came back to himself. For a moment he'd been so overcome with the sensations that he'd lost all ability to reason or speak.

He pulled a small bottle of oil from beneath the blankets. Bastian had given it to him; Bastian had understood before Taren. That Bastian was willing to let him go caused Taren's heart to swell and ache in equal measure.

"Lie back," Taren directed.

Ian stretched out on the blankets and watched as Taren climbed onto his thigh, slicked his fingers, and began to work the tight ring of muscle between his ass cheeks. Ian's gaze did not waver, his green eyes raking Taren's skin so that Taren felt himself the center of Ian's soul. Taren shivered as the familiar sense of memory once more washed over him.

Ian reached for Taren's thighs and stroked the skin, but he never took his eyes off Taren's face. Taren's cock began to reawaken with Ian's touch, and his face heated with the intensity of Ian's gaze. Taren pushed a second finger inside himself, hissing with pleasure and anticipation. Gods, but he wanted Ian inside him! Much as he'd loved their coupling beneath the water, he realized he'd been waiting for this moment. His entire life he'd been taught to please others, but that had all been in preparation for this. What a strange thought—that he'd waited for this man. And yet he believed it as surely as he believed that his fate was inextricably intertwined with Ian's.

He continued to work himself open, soft moans escaping his lips, each one causing Ian's breath to stop and start once more. The scents of the oil and the salt water were more powerful than the strongest ale. Taren felt dizzy, overcome, as if he were under a spell. He imagined himself impaled upon Ian, their bodies entwined beneath a full moon. What higher worship was there but the love he felt in that moment?

"Ian." He could not speak the words. Not yet, although he knew that he loved Ian. He'd loved him forever. He'd known him as long. He knew it was impossible, but as he withdrew his fingers and lowered himself onto Ian's hard member, he felt as though their spirits hovered over them, united as they were in body.

"Goddess, but I've wanted you, Taren." Ian's throaty rumble caused Taren to clench around Ian's cock. The ship rocked gently from side to side, reminding Taren that they were upon the water they loved.

Taren slid down until he had completely swallowed Ian inside of him, then waited a moment, allowing the sensation of being filled to wash over him like the waves. He closed his eyes and floated in the beauty of the moment, then sighed and looked once more upon Ian. Slowly, he began to move. He leaned forward to press a palm against Ian's chest, wanting to feel the beating of Ian's heart in the same way the rumble of the surf had so often soothed his troubled mind. He imagined their hearts beating in unison, their breaths mingling, drawing upon the same air.

A gentle breeze blew down from the deck, cooling their bodies, caressing them. Time stopped as if to acknowledge their coupling. Taren knew only the feel of Ian beneath him. The heat of their union burned his chest and spread to his shoulders, arms, and legs. Ian found Taren's cock and stroked it in rhythm with Taren's movements. The sensation was nearly too much for Taren, who whimpered and shook.

Taren moved faster now, wanting more of Ian's moans, wanting to bring Ian the pleasure he'd received and knowing he could not continue. He stroked Ian's nipples, finding the peaks and valleys of muscle as he explored Ian's chest. Ian cried out as his body tensed, lifting his thighs from the blankets to bring him closer to Taren. Taren felt the heat of Ian's release as it filled him.

I've found you! Taren's soul shouted as he too came, splashing Ian's chest and collapsing, boneless, as the last bit of strength fled from his limbs.

Ian encircled him, capturing his lips with his mouth and bruising them with kisses.

Taren heard Owyn's words in his mind: *"I will be with you. Always. You only need to look for me, and you'll know."*

TWENTY-ONE

IAN awakened from a deep sleep to the rocking of the ship. He smiled as he looked at Taren asleep on his chest. *Mine.* He stroked Taren's hair and thanked his goddess that Taren had sought him out. It pained him to admit to himself how afraid he'd been that, once aboard, Taren would seek comfort in Rider's bed. He knew now that he'd been a fool to give in to his jealousy. He'd avoided Taren when Taren had wanted nothing more than to be with him.

Mine. Not a possession, like a slave, but master of his heart.

Ian had nearly fallen back asleep when the ship heeled so suddenly that Taren nearly rolled on top of him. There was only one explanation for such a sudden change of course: they were no longer alone on the water.

"They've found us. You feel it too, don't you?"

Taren nodded, and Ian saw fear in Taren's eyes. "At least two dozen. Who are—?" he began, but the lurching of the ship cut short his words. The deafening sound of cannon fire rang from above.

"Damn." Ian grabbed his clothes and Taren followed suit. They ran barefoot to the ladder and began to climb. Halfway up, another blast shook the ship, this time from the *Sea Witch*'s own cannons. The ship lurched once more, causing Taren to lose his footing. Ian grabbed Taren's ankles and pulled him back onto the rung as Taren swung by his arms with the rocking of the ship. They scrambled on deck a moment later to the sound of shouts.

ALTHOUGH Taren had never been in a battle while aboard the *Witch*, he knew well the maneuvers she might employ. The *Sea Witch* possessed the weather gage, sailing upwind of the attacking vessel. Upwind as she was, the *Witch* forced the other vessel to maneuver a narrow course to avoid heading into the wind and losing speed. The enemy ship heeled with the sideward pressure of the wind, its cannons elevated so she could not aim at the *Witch.*

Why would the attacking ship leave herself so vulnerable? In the dim light of morning, with the steady rain beating down on the water and the fog that had only now begun to lift, she'd have had the advantage of surprise.

Ian grasped Taren's shoulder and squeezed. He pointed toward the other ship, his expression tense. Then the other ship came more clearly into view.

"It's the *Phantom!*" Taren exclaimed.

Ian nodded, then strode with purpose to where Rider steered the ship, Taren not far behind. "Hold your fire!" he shouted.

Rider looked at Ian and scowled. "And why should I do that?" Rider snapped. "They fired upon us first. I can hardly let such an insult go unanswered."

"You know full well if they'd wanted, they'd have hit you by now. They had the advantage, but they chose not to take it. They've allowed you to gain the upper hand."

"They want you and the boy. You may be foolish enough to give yourself up to them, but I won't let the slimy bastards take him as well." Rider met Taren's eyes for a split second before fixing his gaze on Ian.

Taren suddenly realized Rider knew not only about the Ea but about Taren's own dual nature. How long had he known? With this realization came the certainty that Rider also knew about Ian. Taren's thoughts raced as he struggled to understand the implications of this discovery.

"No. If that were the case, they'd have forced your hand. They have no love of humans. Why would they spare your vessel?"

"Sir!" Bastian shouted from where the gunners stood ready to fire again. "What are your orders?"

"Prepare to fire!"

"Jonat. Please. Give me a chance to speak with them," Ian pleaded. Taren had never seen Ian so desperate.

"I'll go with you," Taren told Ian.

"No." Rider's voice was rough. "I'll not risk your skin as well. You'll stay aboard the *Witch*."

Ian ignored Taren. "So you'll wait for me to board her? Speak with them?"

"Aye. But if they so much as go near a cannon, I'll sink her with you aboard." Rider gave Bastian the sign to stand down and head off the *Phantom*.

Ian nodded and strode to the aft steps with Taren at his heels.

"I'm perfectly capable of taking care of myself," Taren told Ian with growing anger. "I can help you."

Ian stopped and grabbed Taren by the shoulders. "You'll stay."

Taren stood his ground. He would say his piece now, even if it meant losing Ian. "I know you're a spy, Ian." How had it taken him so long to realize it? But the truth was too difficult to deny.

Ian's lips parted and his brow furrowed in obvious surprise. "You what?"

"It all makes sense. Seria believed I was a spy—thought Vurin sent me. You rescued me and secured us safe passage to the mainland, where you know Vurin and his followers to be. Barra told me the Council had no love for you. That they didn't trust you." Everything seemed so clear now. Why hadn't he seen it before? *You were too infatuated with him to think clearly.*

"I—"

"I'm not that naïve," Taren said as he pushed Ian's hands off his shoulders and stepped back. "Why did you lie to me? Did you think if you told me the truth I'd reject your advances?"

"You don't know what you're say—"

"I know damn well what I'm saying."

Ian's jaw tightened visibly.

"You were ordered to bring me back to the mainland. Vurin ordered it."

Ian took a deep breath. "There's no time to speak of this now."

Taren gritted his teeth. He knew Ian was right, but he was angry. When he'd given Ian his heart, he had expected Ian to guard it well. What other lies had Ian told him? What other truths remained unspoken? He didn't doubt Ian cared for him, but he had hoped for so much more.

Taren watched in silence as Ian pulled off his clothes and climbed up to the open windows. He turned to look at Taren for a moment. "We will speak of this later. I promise," he said, his expression unreadable. A moment later he disappeared into the waves.

TWENTY-TWO

IAN found the rope ladder waiting for him when he reached the *Phantom*. He climbed it quickly. If his instincts were wrong, he supposed his death would happen long before Rider could fire a shot. Should he have left Taren without answers? *There was no time to explain.* Ian feared Taren might not forgive him if he survived long enough to explain. He wondered if losing Taren now might be worse than death.

As he reached the top of the ladder, he grabbed the hand offered to him and climbed aboard. "Captain. We hoped you'd get our message." Renda offered Ian a crooked grin as he handed Ian a blanket to cover himself. Behind Renda stood Barra, Aine, and a dozen others from his crew. *Not your crew. Not anymore.*

"What message might that be?" Ian asked.

"That the *Phantom* needs her captain, sir." Aine's voice cracked as he spoke, but he stood straight and saluted Ian.

Ian looked to Renda. "Explain."

Renda crossed his arms over his chest and cocked his head to one side. "The Council gave Seria the ship."

"Seria?" Ian was sure he'd killed the man. He'd certainly intended to.

"We had no intention of serving under the bastard, but the Council fortified the island's defenses. Now the only people who can lift the enchantments are the Council's most trusted advisors." Ian almost laughed to see Renda's smirk. "We simply waited until we were well past the island's defenses, then rid ourselves of him and his mates."

"You mutinied? But surely you know what I've—"

"We couldn't care less," Barra said with obvious bluster.

"Fools. Where will you go? What about your families?" Ian looked to Aine. How old was the boy? Ten? Eleven?

"They know what they're doing, *Captain.*" Barra's jaw was tight, his brow furrowed. Ian couldn't help but admire him. He'd taken his punishment for letting Taren escape as a man would, and he was still loyal. More so, perhaps, than before.

Ian nodded solemnly. "Stand down and head off the *Witch.* Lower the sails. Rider won't fire if he knows me to be safe." Ian motioned Renda to stay, then told Barra, "Take the helm. They'll want to raft alongside."

"Sir?"

"They're allies, Barra. And if you've chosen to move against the Council, you'll need as many allies as you can muster." In spite of Ian's shock, his heart swelled at the knowledge that his men had chosen to follow him. But did they really understand what he'd done? He turned to Renda and said, "Come with me."

"Aye, sir."

Renda followed silently as Ian descended the steps to his cabin. "Tell me what happened. All of it," he snapped as he pulled some clothing from the armoire and began to dress.

Renda sat in one of the chairs in front of the captain's desk. "Not much to tell. We were told you helped the prisoner escape. The Council says you're a traitor—that you've spied for Vurin for years. We were ordered to bring you both back, dead or alive. Seria showed up before we could raise the anchor, waving his commission in our faces."

"You were the instigator?"

Renda shook his head. "Although I'd love to claim credit, it was Barra's idea. He and Aine came to me."

Ian was tempted to tell Renda how foolhardy he'd been to listen to Barra and Aine, but he asked only, "What did you do with the men?"

"Tied them up and left them on a small island not far from Lurat." When Ian raised his eyebrows, Renda continued, "Don't worry. We made sure they could escape in due time. Much as it was tempting to kill him and the other Council dogs, they're probably already back on Ea'nu, telling the Council of their woes."

Ian paced back and forth in front of the large windows, trying to assess the situation. But what could he do now? Perhaps Aine could go back to the island, but the others would surely be hung for their treachery.

"You worry too much," Renda said with a dismissive wave of his hand.

"Damn you! I've no doubt you'll land on your feet. But what of the others? What of the boy? Aine? If you had been captured—"

"We weren't captured."

"But where will you go? What port will welcome you? If you return to the islands, you'll be captured." Ian slammed a fist on the desk.

"Vurin will welcome them, as he'll welcome you."

Ian stopped pacing and stared at Renda. "What?"

Renda leaned back in the chair, his legs apart, arms resting comfortably on his thighs. "Just what I said. He will welcome us."

"And how would you know this?"

"Because you, dear friend, aren't the only spy amongst our people." Renda pursed his lips in obvious delight.

"What?"

"Just what I said. Do you think it a coincidence that I saved your pathetic hide from those fools?" The affection sparkling in Renda's eyes belied his strong words. No doubt he'd been waiting for this moment for nearly twenty years.

"Vurin?"

"Aye. I was ordered to stay behind and make sure you survived. He said he owed a debt to your parents and that you were… redeemable. Much as I disagreed—" Renda grinned and Ian saw true affection reflected in his demon eyes. "—I told him I'd watch over you."

IAN leaned over a table covered with charts, but he wasn't really seeing them. He was still getting used to the strange path his fortunes had taken since his men had fished Taren out of the water six weeks before. He had never expected to set foot aboard the *Phantom* again, and yet now here he stood, in his own cabin, captain once more. His ship. No longer the Council's tool.

Yet again, Renda had come to his aid. Even now, after Renda had explained that he'd been spying for Vurin for more than two decades, Ian still found it difficult to fathom. "Vurin asked me to watch over you. Keep you safe."

Ian had been tempted to point out that Renda had made lousy work of it, having left him in the Council's prison to rot for nearly two years. Ian knew Renda had been given little choice. If he'd fought to have Ian released, he'd have drawn attention to himself. Much like what he'd done with Taren, Renda had walked a fine line between duty and self-preservation. Neither of them would have been of much use to Vurin and the mainlanders dead.

The thought reminded him of Taren. What would he say to Taren? *You didn't lie about why you rescued him.* He also hadn't told Taren the truth. He'd received his orders from Vurin too late to prevent Taren from being imprisoned. Taren spent weeks rotting in that prison, hopeless and suffering, because Ian had not trusted Taren with the truth.

At least Renda had been honest with his wife all along. She had escaped the island and would meet them on the mainland to be reunited with her husband. Now Ian had little hope of the same with Taren. Not that he and Taren had confessed their love, but Ian had hoped in time, they might be more to each other. *Goddess, please don't take him from me now.*

Someone knocked at the cabin door. "Come," he said without looking up. He could sense Taren's presence even before he entered.

"Rider asked me to tell you that the *Sea Witch* will be getting underway shortly."

"He did, did he?" Ian wasn't sure if he was pleased that Rider had sent Taren to him or if he wanted to berate the man for interfering so blatantly in his personal affairs. By sending Taren, was Rider giving him another chance to convince Taren to come with him to meet Vurin?

"Aye."

Ian finally met Taren's gaze. "You'll be leaving with them, won't you?" He hadn't intended it to come out as a question; he hadn't wanted to betray his own deep disappointment.

"Why would I leave with them?" Taren asked sharply. Ian could sense the hurt in Taren's words. "Or have you changed your mind?"

"I... no. I thought perhaps, after what you'd learned, you would not wish to come with me."

"My wishes have nothing to do with this." Taren wore a hard expression, although Ian still sensed a vulnerable softness beneath. "I'm indentured to Rider. I go where he tells me to go until my contract is paid in full."

Taren's words stung, and Ian realized that he himself had provoked this response. He hadn't meant to challenge Taren; he'd meant only to harden himself against the inevitable. Why had he doubted Taren wanted to stay with him? He shook his head and ran a hand through his hair, which was still slightly damp from the water. "I am sorry."

"Did you think I expected you to sacrifice yourself and release me?" Ian winced to hear Taren's bitter laugh. "I am only glad you *did* release me."

"I waited too long." Ian shook his head and exhaled. "I waited to get you out of that place when I knew what they were doing to you. I waited for two decades, knowing what the Council had become. Watching them justify what they were doing to my people." Ian walked over to the large windows and looked out at the rolling waves. How many times had he escaped to those waves so he could avoid the truth? From his safe haven aboard the *Phantom*, he'd found it easy to ignore so many things.

"I hoped the Council would see reason and release you," Ian continued as he turned around and faced Taren once more. "But I knew they wouldn't. Anyone from the mainland is suspect. Anyone who isn't loyal to their cause is a sympathizer. I'm ashamed to admit it was easier to let them have you and hope for the best. But it's me they wanted all along, Taren. Or people like me."

"People like you?"

"Ea who hope to reunite our people—who want to free the islanders. The Council knows we're lurking in the shadows, waiting. For years they've been trying to find the traitors in their midst." Ian offered Taren a wistful smile. "I knew you were no traitor. I knew it because I am a spy. You were right. I'm the one they wanted, not you."

"But how… if you were on the island? How did you…?" Ian saw comprehension come swiftly. "Rider. The stories Bastian told me of how you were enemies. They were lies."

"Aye." Ian drew a long breath. "Rider helped me send word to Vurin. He would leave the messages where I might find them, outside the island's enchantments, and I in turn would give him my response."

Taren's face grew pale. "So this. Us. Are we a lie as well?"

"No." Ian took Taren's face in his hands, forcing Taren to look him in the eyes. "Never."

"But you and Rider… you were lovers."

"Yes. But not for years now. Decades."

Taren pushed Ian's hands away.

"You must believe me. You know him well enough."

"I believe you."

Thank the goddess. Ian pulled Taren against him.

Taren shuddered as if his body was fighting its response, but he did not return Ian's embrace. "Tell me," he said after a moment. "I need to hear the truth from your lips. All of it." He pulled away and sat in one of the chairs.

"Do you know of the war between the islanders and those who chose to return to the mainland?" Ian asked after a brief pause. Taren nodded. "You were born during that war. A child of those who sought to reclaim their land from the humans. I was about your age when we fought each other, Ea against Ea. Brother against brother. My parents were caught in the middle of a civil war, having made their home on the mainland."

"Why did the Council send them to watch the humans?"

"My parents were the last in a long line of sentinels. When the Ea fled the mainland—when the colony there was destroyed—my great-great-great-great-grandparents stayed behind. For hundreds of years, the Dunaidh family kept watch over the humans and reported back to the island Ea. We took human names, learned their ways, lived amongst them. But my parents, like their parents before, remained loyal to the Council. They were brave." Ian stopped and shook his head.

"The islanders were fearful of the humans, and for good reason. They learned our secret and destroyed the mainland temple centuries ago. We still have reason to fear the humans—don't get me wrong—but this time, the real threat was not a human one." He knew he sounded bitter, but he didn't care—he'd lived with the pain of his secret for too long now. He didn't know how else to feel.

"When I was a child, some of the Ea began to return to the mainland from the island. Only a few at first, but their numbers grew quickly. I, like you, knew nothing about my people. My parents feared that if I did, I might share our secret with the humans. But when I first transformed, they had little choice in the matter. They introduced me to the children of the mainland colonists, and I spent my life in two worlds. In school, I was human. I learned human ways, I learned their science, even their gods. But with my family, I was Ea. I played with the children of those few Ea who returned. I swam with them. I loved them as my brothers. I celebrated the Ea feasts and worshipped the goddess.

"The Council believed our race would perish as they had almost done hundreds of years before. They refused to let any more of the islanders leave. But those who wished to return were strong willed. Their leader, Vurin, went before the Council to ask them to let those who wished to leave go. When he was imprisoned, his followers attacked the Council. The war began.

"My parents were recalled to the island not long after. They sailed back to Ea'nu to plead with the Council to work with the colonists for peace. The Council wouldn't listen. They branded my parents traitors for suggesting that Vurin and the others had a right to choose their future. What did my parents know of the island and its safety? They were contaminated by the humans. They'd been gone too long." Ian closed his eyes and took a deep breath. The pain of grief still weighed heavily upon his heart. "The Council executed them."

"Gods, Ian. I can hardly imagine…."

"I stayed behind on the mainland. My parents wanted me to stay, and I didn't challenge them. I think they knew what might happen when they returned to the island, and they wished to keep me safe. I didn't mind. I was young, carefree. In love."

"Rider?"

Ian nodded. "We studied together at the royal college for nearly three years. I saw no difference between us, Ea or human. Rider guessed my secret, of course." Ian laughed to cover his pain. "I was careless, naïve. But when I learned of my parents' deaths, I knew I had to avenge them. I had to leave Rider.

"They imprisoned me. 'Mercy', they called it." Ian shook his head. "Some mercy. I spent two years rotting in that prison. I nearly died. I *wanted* to die. But Renda heard of my illness. He knew nothing about me, but he healed me and convinced the Council to let me serve aboard the *Phantom*. I agreed to fight alongside the islanders."

"Renda?"

For the first time, Ian smiled. "Aye. He too had sworn his allegiance to Vurin and the mainland Ea. Vurin asked him to watch over me, knowing what I might face when I returned. Renda healed me when I was sick and dying in Dubra Prison. He persuaded the Council to allow me to prove my loyalty by serving aboard the *Phantom*. I was little more than a slave, shackled and watched at every moment. But when the captain and quartermaster were killed in battle, Renda and I were the most experienced sailors. Renda was a healer. He refused to captain the *Phantom*, but he insisted I do so."

Taren stood and walked over to Ian. The last thing he expected was Taren's kindness. "You blame yourself for my captivity." When Ian did not respond, he continued, "What were you to do? If you'd rescued me, they'd have known you were a traitor, and you might have died yourself."

"Perhaps that would have been better."

"No." Taren spoke forcefully. "I don't believe that, and neither do you."

"You've forgiven me." Ian managed a tight smile.

"You've been honest with me. What more can I do but forgive you?" That Taren was so forthright, so accepting, surprised Ian.

"There is one more thing I need to say," Ian began after a moment, knowing he must speak the entire truth about his feelings for once. "But it's not easy for me."

"Say it, then, and be done with it."

How Ian loved the way Taren approached life with a slave's strength and the spirit of a free man, never looking back. He envied Taren that. Servitude had not diminished Taren's kind heart and loving spirit. "Our people are dual natured. As a man, my reason controls. As a beast, I desire things I sometimes am ashamed of."

"There is nothing shameful in desire. Rider taught me that."

"No. But when both combine, I… I can become quite possessive. I do not wish to share you."

Taren's eyes grew wide with recognition. "You're jealous."

"I…. Yes." Ian forced himself not to look away. He was strong. He did not shrink from the truth.

Taren reached out and brushed Ian's cheek with his long fingers. "If you did not wish me to sleep in Rider's quarters, why did you not tell me so?"

"I had no right. You are not mine." Then, realizing how Taren might misconstrue what he'd just said, Ian added, "Not in that way. You are not a slave, nor are you indentured to me."

"I am—"

"No!" Ian grabbed Taren by the shoulders, surprising himself with the force of his response. "I do not wish a slave. If you will not come with me willingly, you might as well leave with Rider."

Taren said nothing but stared at Ian in obvious confusion, his brow knitted and lips parted.

"Do you not understand? I want you like this—fearless and free to speak your mind. If you choose to be with me, I will gladly have you. But I will not have your submission. I want far more than that." Ian still regretted having tried to force Taren to submit to his will and eat from his fingers. He would not give in to his baser needs again. He would give Taren the respect he deserved. But first he would make Taren understand. "Our people will never be slaves to men. I don't understand how you came to be sold, but I won't abide it. If you choose to return to Rider now or when the year is up, then I will accept your choice. But make no mistake: it will be your choice, neither mine nor Rider's."

Renda entered a moment later. "The *Sea Witch* is departing," he told Ian.

"Thank you." Ian followed Renda to the door, then turned back to Taren and said, "Time to choose, Taren." Ian did not wait for Taren to decide but left him without another word. He would have his decision soon enough, he knew. Best to give Taren time to think.

Up on deck a moment later, Ian watched as the men aboard the *Sea Witch* prepared to release the lines that bound the two ships together. Rider stood by the gangplank spanning the short gap between the ships, waiting for him, Bastian at his side.

"Thank you," Ian said as he extended his hand in friendship. "For trusting in me."

Rider shook his head. "I always have. You just chose not to see it."

Taren walked over to them and stood by Ian. "Aye," Taren said. "We often choose to overlook the obvious." He inclined his head to Ian nearly imperceptibly, but Ian understood that he'd made his choice. Ian struggled to mask his emotions as Taren stepped forward and saluted Rider. "Fair winds, Captain. Until we meet again."

Rider turned to Taren, the edges of his mouth curving faintly upward, his eyebrows raised.

"I will keep my word," Taren said. "I will return to you in a year." Ian had expected nothing less, but Taren's words pained him.

"Be well, Taren." Rider turned and crossed to the *Sea Witch*, leaving Bastian behind.

"Captain." Bastian offered Ian a soft smile. "I know you will keep him safe."

Ian nodded. Taren raised a shaky hand in salute, but Bastian did not hesitate—he embraced Taren and held him for a moment, then followed Rider to the *Sea Witch*. A few minutes later, the ropes released, the two ships drifted apart. Ian, who had joined Renda amidships, watched as Taren stood and waited until the *Witch* was out of sight.

TWENTY-THREE

TAREN stared out the aft windows. They were close to Raice Harbor, judging by the rocky shore visible in the distance. In spite of Ian's reassurances, Taren felt nothing but turmoil as they approached land once again. He had made his choice to stay with Ian, but he feared a life of his own choosing. The thought that at the end of the year he would return to Rider comforted him. He'd lived his entire life without having to make his own decisions. It had been far simpler that way.

Soft lips brushed the back of his neck, causing Taren to shudder. He hadn't even noticed Ian had entered the cabin. "I was hard on you, wasn't I?"

"Yes. No." Taren shrugged. "I don't know."

Ian put his arm around Taren's shoulders, a gesture that settled Taren's pounding heart.

"I must tell you something," Taren said. "You were honest with me. I owe you the same."

Ian raised his eyebrows in question.

"I lied when I said my wishes had nothing to do with staying with you—that I stayed because Rider ordered me to." Taren rubbed his neck and took a slow breath.

"What other reason is there?" Something in Ian's expression made Taren wonder if he hadn't already guessed, but wanted to hear it from Taren's lips.

"I wished to stay with you. I—" Taren forced himself to meet Ian's gaze and hold it. "—I was happy at your side." *More than happy. I felt as though I were home.*

The faint hint of a smile upon Ian's lips spoke of warmth and understanding. "I am glad," he said. "I hoped you might say that. Much as I wish you to stay with me, you are not my slave."

Heat rose in Taren's cheeks. Ian, perhaps guessing at Taren's discomfort, changed the topic. "We have received word from Vurin's sentries. Renda will sail the ship to the enclave. We will join them there in a day or two."

"But how…?"

"The enclave is only a few hours away for a strong swimmer."

"Oh." Taren chuckled at his own foolishness. Of course the sentries would have swum to meet them! "Sometimes I forget… it all seems so dreamlike at times."

Ian kissed him, a reassuring gesture. "It will take time. But you will have that time. There is so much I want to show you." He released Taren from his arms, then began to undress.

"Are you coming with me?" Ian's eyes sparkled. Taren realized once again that he had misunderstood. They would swim to shore. "Although I'd be happy to indulge your human desires before we leave, if you wish."

"I… ah…." Taren knew he was much too excited about making landfall to think about anything but leaving the ship.

This time Ian laughed, a full-throated laugh that seemed to rumble throughout the cabin. By now he was gloriously naked, causing Taren's cock to assert its interest and making his britches uncomfortably tight. "Well? What'll it be? Shall we swim, or shall I ravish you first?"

Taren felt his own grin as the last of his trepidation evaporated in the face of Ian's offer. "Both?" he suggested as he pulled his shirt over his head. A moment later he dove into the water after Ian.

IAN'S family's home was built on a secluded cove outside the city. More of a cottage than a house, it was hewn from white stone and covered in vines dotted in red, yellow, and fuchsia flowers. Little grass grew in the front yard; instead, beds of flowering gardens nestled around a pathway of stone and shell. The powerful smell of salt spray and the perfume of the flowers added to the heady sense of freedom Taren had felt as they'd swam from the ship.

Taren sensed Ian's excitement to see his childhood home. Ian ran up from the shore, unabashedly naked, pausing only to bend down and reach around a large stone near the entry to the house to retrieve a metal key. Taren, panting, caught up with Ian just as he opened the front door.

"Vurin pays the caretaker," Ian said, clearly having anticipated Taren's question. "But no one has lived here in twenty years." Ian stepped over the threshold before motioning Taren inside, then began to open the windows to the breeze.

Simply appointed, the cottage's décor called to mind Ian's quarters aboard the *Phantom*. Utilitarian furniture, free of any decoration save for the tooled feet and arms, filled the brightly lit rooms. Faded but sturdy fabric covered the windows. The cottage smelled of the ocean, with a hint of freesia from the gardens.

Ian moved slowly about, his frame almost too large for the small interior. He paused at the fireplace, where a portrait of a young woman hung. Taren knew this must be Ian's mother—Ian had inherited her dark hair and green eyes, as well as her heart-shaped face. Her expression too recalled Ian. Strong but kind. Intelligent. Ian reached out to touch the painting, his mouth tight, the tiny lines on his forehead more pronounced. He looked haunted and pained.

Taren rested a hand on Ian's forearm. "She was very beautiful."

"Aye." Ian took a long breath, then smiled. "If I'm not mistaken, there are clothes upstairs. Wait for me."

Taren explored the room while he waited for Ian, stopping from time to time to admire the paintings. Ian's parents had loved the sea—Taren could tell this from the many depictions of the ocean and the shore. Ian's father had likely been a sailor in his youth, judging from the number of canvases that featured ships, many of a similar design to the *Phantom*.

A woman's portrait caught Taren's eye. It sat on a table in the corner of the room, next to several others. Not much bigger than his palm, the painting featured a golden-haired beauty dressed in a simple white gown with a crown of flowers in her hair. "My great-great-great-grandmother," Ian said as Taren picked it up. "One of the last of the Ea priestesses."

Taren compared the woman's face to Ian's. But for her flaxen hair, she could have been Ian's sister. Even more than Ian, the woman reminded Taren of Owyn, from his dreams. Taren held the painting up to the light to get a better look, noticing for the first time the necklace she wore—a black stone, like a piece of glass, hung from a silver chain. The stone hung at the edge of the valley between her breasts.

Without thinking, Taren ran a thumb over the stone. The sudden fear took him aback. His hands felt cold and he lost himself for a moment, his mind wandering.

"Taren!"

Taren looked up to see Ian leaning over him, his jaw tense with obvious concern. Taren realized he was now seated on the settee by the front window of the cottage, his head propped on several pillows. Had he fallen asleep?

"Yes?"

"I asked if you were all right, but you didn't answer." Ian's voice was slightly rough, as though he were waging an internal battle to control his emotions.

I've frightened him. "I'm fine," Taren said quickly, sitting up. He noticed the portrait had fallen to the ground, the glass having broken on the stone floor. "Gods, Ian, I'm so sorry. I must have dropped it."

Ian shook his head. "The glass is easily replaced. But you…. One moment you were standing there, the next you collapsed."

"I am quite thirsty," Taren put in, hoping to dispel Ian's fears. "Hungry as well." It was partially the truth, although he knew that neither thirst nor hunger had been to blame. Something about that painting had startled him. Something familiar. He rubbed his eyes and for an instant saw Owyn's face looking back at him. Owyn. Of course! The woman's hair was the same color as Owyn's. *But that was a dream.* He brushed the thought away.

"If you're well enough, we can walk into Raice Harbor. There'll be a tavern serving food. But if you can't walk, I can—"

"I'm fine. No need to worry. I always seem to be hungry after I transform."

Ian nodded, clearly pleased to have a reason for Taren's weakness. "Aye. My mother used to say I ate more than both she and my father on the days I spent with my friends in the water." He laughed. "I'm sorry. I should have been more considerate—this is all so new to you."

THE walk to the edge of the harbor was an easy one, mostly downhill. They ate well, washing down their dinner of fresh fish and potatoes with a hearty ale. It had been so long since Taren had eaten anything but hardtack and salt fish that although he guessed their meal to be quite average, Taren thought it was the best thing he had ever tasted. Afterward, they walked down to the harbor. Taren smiled to see the *Witch* safely at anchor.

"You miss them."

"Aye. My life aboard the *Witch* was a full one." Taren glanced over to the tavern where he used to live. "A far better life than the one I knew here."

"Rider told me how he found you," Ian said as he squeezed Taren's shoulder. "Would you like to see your old home?"

"No." Taren tensed with fear to imagine himself back at the inn once more. Could they take him back there? He'd rather die than return.

"You needn't worry. Rider also told me that he came to an agreement with the tavern's owner several months after he took you. He paid your indenture in full, and then some."

Taren looked up at Ian, uncomprehending. "He… what?"

"He paid your debt, Taren. They cannot claim you."

Rider had done that? But why? His throat tightened as he understood that Rider had fully intended to give him his freedom—his *full* freedom—at the end of his three years. His eyes burned and he was thankful that the darkness hid his reaction.

"There's something more, Taren," Ian said, his hand still on Taren's shoulder, reassuring as ever. "Something Rider told me you should know once we were safely back on the mainland. It isn't a pretty thing."

"Aye." Whatever it was, Taren told himself he would face it. He wouldn't go back to living in the shadows, no matter what his future.

"Borstan the Rigger. Seems he sold you to save his own neck."

Taren shook his head. "You've not told me anything I didn't already know."

"There's more, I'm afraid."

"He's dead?" Taren wondered aloud.

"No. But Rider spoke to him."

Taren could just imagine what might have transpired. The old man never had a bone in his back. He'd have cowered before the pirate captain, given him anything, *said* anything. "No doubt he babbled like a madman."

"Aye. But he told Rider about how you came to be with him. He admitted that your parents never sold you to him."

"He… he never owned me?" Taren's gut clenched when he heard this, bile rising and burning his throat as his anger grew. He clenched his teeth and pulled away from Ian, unsure how to handle his increasing rage.

"No. You are and always were a free man."

"Free?" The word felt foreign upon his lips. How many times had he been told he was a worthless piece of refuse, first by Borstan and later by Madame Marcus and the others at the inn? How his parents hadn't wanted him—worse, that they'd sold him into slavery for their own selfish reasons?

"Free." Ian wrapped strong arms around him in a warm embrace.

Taren hadn't realized until that moment he was shaking with rage. He struggled to free himself from Ian's grip. "I must see him."

"That you must," Ian agreed. "But not tonight. Tomorrow, in the light of day."

"No. I must see him now. I want to—"

"Kill him?" Ian offered Taren an understanding look.

Taren ceased his struggle and let his body go limp in Ian's arms. Gods, but Ian was right! If he saw Borstan now, he might do something rash. "Yes," he whispered before closing his eyes and allowing Ian to pull him tighter against his chest.

"We will go tomorrow."

"We?"

"Aye. I will come with you. Not to make certain you do not harm him—you are too kindhearted to do him harm, even if he has brought it upon himself—but to give you my support, should you need it." Ian kissed the top of his head.

Taren's tears fell unimpeded, and for once he didn't fear that Ian would push him away for his childish lack of self-control. Within Ian's arms, he felt warm, safe. Loved.

TWENTY-FOUR

"TAREN! Boy! You've come back to me!" Borstan stood in the doorway of the tumbledown shack, his expression one of happiness. Taren knew better—he could see fear burning brightly in the old man's small eyes.

Taren walked past Borstan into the one-room hut, Ian moving to block the old man's path as he tried to escape. "Sit," Ian said in a voice that rattled the single glass window and caused Borstan to shake nearly as much. Borstan had no choice but to obey. Shoulders slumped, gaze on the ground, he found a rickety chair and sat, resignation apparent in every bone in his ancient body.

"Look at him," Ian commanded after a moment. "Look at the man you once called your son. Look at him and beg him for his forgiveness."

"Forgiveness? But—"

"I know the truth, old man," Taren said. He felt surprisingly calm, the tempest that raged in his heart the night before having left smooth seas in its wake.

Taren hadn't been back here in nearly five years. Then, this place had been comforting: a home. It pained Taren to realize that he'd have been happy to spend his childhood in this one-room building. Regardless of his position in life, Taren had been reasonably happy here. He'd worked hard, but he'd enjoyed the work.

"You can't know how I feared for you, sending you to that terrible place. But they said they'd hurt me, that they'd break my bones. And you know my heart broke when you left. I was so lonely, I didn't have no reason to carry on, my heart was so heavy with grief 'n' all."

"Silence!" Taren snapped. He didn't want to hear Borstan babble—he was tired of the pathetic lies spoken only to save his own skin. He didn't need more lies; he needed answers.

"I didn't mean it! I swear! I wouldn't have sold you if I'd had a choice."

"But I was never yours to sell, was I, old man?" Taren thanked the gods for Ian's solid presence behind him. Without Ian, he'd have been tempted to strike Borstan. "All those years, you lied to me. Told me my parents sold me to you, that my life was yours."

Borstan looked ancient. He trembled as he spoke, fear rolling off of him like the surf retreats from the shore. "I didn't mean you no harm by it, son." No doubt he feared Taren would do him harm, because he cowered and made himself small.

"You don't deserve to call me that."

"Tell him the truth, Laxley. After all your lies, it's the least you can do." Ian's voice resonated with anger, but his hand remained on Taren's shoulder, comforting and warm.

Whatever fear Borstan felt in Taren's presence, Ian clearly frightened him more. He glanced about the room, perhaps hoping to find a way past Ian and Taren. He reminded Taren of a cornered animal, pathetic and small. The realization that he had once loved Borstan as a son might love a father made Taren feel sick. Had he been so desperate for kindness that he hadn't seen the truth?

Borstan clasped his withered hands in his lap, turning them over and wringing them. "She came to me. Your mother. She was sickly. Hurt. I dunno." He looked up at Taren imploringly—seeking forgiveness? Absolution? "I... I told her I didn't need no boy to help me, that she should take you somewhere better. You know, in town, where you might be of service when you grew.

"She told me it was too dangerous. That there were people who would hurt you. She begged me to hide you. Said your father was strong. Smart, too. She gave me money. Gold coins—lots of 'em. I paid one of the women to help me until you were old enough."

"She just left me with you?" It was true, then, he'd been unwanted. It didn't surprise Taren to learn this, but it still pained him to hear it. He'd hoped.... No, he'd *dreamed* of something different.

"She said you were special. That I needed to keep you safe. She was right. You were smart too, and a good worker." Borstan's eyes shimmered. "She promised she'd come back for you if she could, but I knew she wouldn't. They found her dead the next day, not far from the shore. She's buried in the cemetery by the inlet."

Taren swallowed hard. Had she known she was dying? But if she were Ea, why hadn't she transformed and healed her body?

"Did she say anything else?" Ian asked when Taren didn't speak for some time.

"Nothing. Except that she wanted me to give you something, Taren. I'd right forgotten about it." Borstan got to his feet and shuffled over to the bed, pulled a small box from underneath, and dusted it off as he walked back over to them. He opened the box and drew something out, then handed it to Taren: a necklace made of rocks and shells.

Taren fingered the necklace, noting the simple thread that held it together was beginning to fray. If it had been valuable, Borstan would have sold it as he'd sold Taren to the innkeeper years before.

Taren glanced at Ian, whose lips were tight. He had to wonder if Borstan really had forgotten about it or whether he'd withheld it because giving it to Taren would have raised questions.

They left shortly after, Taren too overcome with anger and grief to remain longer in Borstan's presence. "I want to see her grave," Taren said as they walked back toward the port.

Ian said nothing but instead put his arm around Taren's shoulder.

There was no headstone, of course. His mother would have been afforded only a pauper's burial, laid to rest in an unmarked grave. Still, Taren placed the flowers he'd picked by the shore atop the soil, then kneeled and pressed his hands to the ground, wanting to touch her.

He imagined her, green-eyed, with long black hair, her skin the color of the moon. He could almost hear her laughter and see her smile as she'd held him in her arms. He blinked back his tears and offered a silent prayer to the gods that her rest was peaceful. He resolved to learn more about her. He hoped she knew he was safe.

LATER, Taren lay against Ian's chest. They hadn't made love. Perhaps Ian had understood that Taren needed something else. Patience. Trust. Comfort, even? Taren had come to realize something as he listened to Borstan's pathetic excuses and outright lies: he loved Ian. Not as a brother, as he now loved Bastian, nor as he loved Rider. He loved Ian as a man. And if perhaps someday Ian might find it in his heart to return that love, Taren's happiness would be complete.

"The necklace. You recognize it, don't you?"

"Aye." Ian exhaled a soft breath, as if he too shared Taren's grief for his mother's fate. "The style is Ea, but the shells are unfamiliar to me."

Taren allowed his hand to stray to the necklace, which he now wore around his neck. Ian had insisted they have it restrung that afternoon, and Taren was glad now. However little it was, Taren would wear it as a reminder that once, he *had* been wanted. Loved.

"Are you ready to meet your future?" Ian asked after a pause.

"My future?"

"We will leave for the enclave in the morning. There is nothing more to be learned here."

Taren shifted slightly in Ian's embrace. "What does Vurin want from me?"

"I don't know." Ian kissed Taren's hair. "But he is a good man. You have nothing to fear from him. I promise."

Taren met Ian's gaze and offered him a tight smile. He wasn't sure why, but he *was* afraid. Something lurked beyond his understanding, and it frightened him. A greater truth. An inevitability.

"Don't leave me," Taren whispered. *I can't do this alone.*

"I will be there with you. By your side. I promise you'll not be alone in this."

Taren closed his eyes and pressed his cheek more firmly against the smooth skin of Ian's chest. "Thank you," he whispered.

TWENTY-FIVE

THE next morning dawned warm and sunny. They left on foot, taking nothing but food and water for the day-long trip. "We need nothing more," Ian told Taren with a smile. "The villagers will provide for us as long as we stay."

Taren wondered when they'd rejoin the crew of the *Phantom* and sail again. In spite of his curiosity about the Ea settlement, he knew Ian was as eager as he to be on the water once more. Ian had spoken little about his plans for the ship and her crew except to say that Vurin did not expect them to remain in the village for long.

"Where will we sail?" Taren asked as they walked the road that led along the shore. "Will you patrol these waters, as you did for the islanders?"

Ian shook his head. "Perhaps. I honestly can't say. I intend to speak of it with Vurin. If Renda believes the islanders are a threat, then we may well patrol again. Seria will do his utmost to convince the islanders that Vurin's people mean them harm."

"Do you think Vurin will try to return to the island by force?"

Ian shook his head. "Vurin has no wish to return to Ea'nu. He does not believe we belong there."

Taren was about to ask Ian where Vurin believed the Ea belonged when they crested a hill and Ian stopped walking. There, where the trees were the thickest, Ian turned to face Taren. "The village is hidden in much the same way as the island," he said. "It's an ancient technique known only to a few Ea. The wards are called Kur'it—enchantments that hide our people from the outside world."

"Have the Ea always hidden themselves?"

"No. Not until they were attacked by humans, centuries ago." Ian lifted his hand to a place between two of the largest trees, causing the air there to ripple like water. "Our ancestors hoped to live alongside the humans. There are stories of hybrid Ea and human children, more powerful even than our people. Longer lived. Perhaps they still live, although I've never met one."

"How long do Ea live?" Taren had wanted to ask this question for some time, but he'd been afraid. He wasn't sure why, but it troubled him.

"More than twice as long as humans. We grow like human children, but then our bodies age slowly. Perhaps in the same way our bodies heal injury, the transformation heals what cannot be seen inside of us."

"The humans," Taren said. "The reason they attacked the Ea... was it this?"

"Perhaps. There are few accounts from that time left to us. On the island, there have long been rumors that the humans kept Ea as slaves, but they are untrue. The Council found it convenient to perpetuate the stories—it helped keep the islanders docile. The people tolerated the Council's heavy hand because they feared what they might face beyond the island's waters." Ian shook his head. "As to the truth of what happened nearly a millennium ago, only the legends and ruins remain."

Ian took Taren's hand and raised it to the barrier. "Let me show you how to enter the wards," he said. The air beneath Taren's palm felt thick and slightly warm. His skin tingled with the touch, although it did not hurt. "A human would feel nothing, but he would not be able to pass. He might notice this, but then his mind would tell him to walk around this place. Later, he would remember nothing."

"Now imagine the sea," Ian prompted.

Taren complied—it was never difficult to imagine the open water. He thought of the sound of the surf as it pounded the rocks, the way the light filtered in rays until it touched the bottom, where it glittered as sand. The sensation against his skin intensified, then abated. Ian nodded, and they both walked through a strange blanket of white into a small clearing that overlooked a valley nestled between high hills. Neither spoke, but the backs of their hands brushed as they moved.

The forest thinned as they descended into the valley, the scent of pine needles mingling with the sweet scent of grass and the tang of smoke from burning wood. In the distance, Taren saw a small village outlined in green fields, animals grazing as a hawk soared above in slow circles. The stone houses were tightly spaced, the roofs thatched in dense pine that caught the sunlight and shimmered. Taren stopped and stared.

"Welcome to Callaecia, Taren."

Callaecia? But how was this possible?

"Taren, are you all right?" Taren heard the concern in Ian's voice. He turned and offered Ian a reassuring smile.

Callaecia. How could he explain to Ian that he knew this place? That he remembered it nearly as well as the harbor and the home he'd shared with Borstan? That he had traveled every foot of the roads crisscrossing the hills, that he knew every crag and dimple that dotted the land? That he had swam in the small cove that led out to the ocean? This was the village from his dreams. "It's beautiful" was all he said. It was the truth.

They reached the base of the hills sometime later, having taken their time to enjoy the warm summer sun and the cool breeze from the ocean. Sometimes Taren thought he could hear the laughter of children from the beach like an echo in his ears. He caught a hint of movement in the distance and turned, expecting to see something—he wasn't sure exactly what. A familiar face, perhaps?

The village consisted of a neat circle of stone cottages with thatched roofs, no more than three dozen by Taren's reckoning. Many of the houses looked ancient, many hundreds of years old. Older buildings stood beside newer ones, the difference evidenced by the lighter color of the limestone blocks that made up their outer walls. The architecture reminded Taren of Crias'u, on the island of Ea'nu. But where the island dwellings had been crumbling, these appeared well cared for. Neatly tended gardens of flowers and vegetables created a colorful contrast to the white stone, and the heady smell of bread baking and fish cooking made Taren's stomach growl.

A main street paved in stone and shells ran through the settlement, familiar and straight, the smaller streets little more than simple dirt paths. Taren saw few horses, all of which grazed, and he guessed that horses were not used for transportation but for working the fields that surrounded the enclave.

A tall figure—a man—walked toward them as they drew close to the first houses, causing Ian to quicken his pace. Dressed like a peasant in simple trousers, a linen tunic, and sandals, the newcomer nevertheless stood straight and proud, his presence commanding even at a distance. Ian offered the man his hand and said, "Vurin. It's been far too long."

"Ian." Vurin smiled and clasped Ian's forearm, then embraced him as a father might welcome home a long-lost son. The lines that formed around his green eyes bespoke deep friendship and admiration.

Something inside Taren relaxed, his body reassuring him of Vurin's kind heart. Vurin appeared at least as old as Rider, but from what Ian had said, Taren knew he was nearly a hundred years old. He was taller than Ian but just as broad, with high cheekbones, a long jaw, and hair the color of night. Not handsome by any human measure, but he radiated a cool confidence that made Taren take note. Taren wondered vaguely if there wasn't some hierarchy of Ea, like some of the animals he'd learned about in books. The more powerful the animal, the more dominant. Perhaps this explained his own awkward beginnings with Ian.

"This is—" Ian began, but Vurin stepped forward and pressed his fingers to Taren's face.

"Taren," Vurin finished.

Unsure what to make of Vurin's strange greeting, Taren said nothing. After a moment, Vurin smiled and shook his head. "My apologies, Taren. I'm being quite rude." Taren took Vurin's offered hand and Vurin clasped it warmly. "Welcome. We will speak later, but for now you must rest. No doubt you are tired from your journey."

Several small children gathered around them as they entered the village, curiosity plain on their chubby faces. From the number of people who came out to greet them, Taren guessed that the settlement had fewer than two hundred inhabitants. No humans—Taren sensed this even before they had reached the first of the houses. The feeling was much the same as when Taren had first come aboard the *Phantom*.

"Ea can sense each other's presence," Ian explained when Taren asked him how he could feel this with such clarity.

The villagers were obviously curious, but although he'd expected they'd be wary of him, Taren felt nothing but welcomed. Vurin, perhaps sensing Taren's surprise at the warm greeting, explained, "Their lives—*our* lives here are insulated. We meet few newcomers, and as you can see"—he gestured around them—"there aren't many of us."

What began as a simple dinner behind Vurin's cottage became the center of village activity. Taren watched the thrill of recognition dance over Ian's face as one by one the villagers introduced themselves. Taren had never seen Ian so happy to discover how many of the men and women he'd known survived the war. Many asked questions about the island, most of which Ian declined to answer except to say that there were many good people who lived on Ea'nu, and that he hoped someday they too could meet their brethren in peace.

The crew of the *Phantom* had arrived two days before and were already settled into some of the empty cottages. It surprised Taren how quickly the townspeople had embraced them as their own. Taren watched as Aine spent most of the meal surrounded by several young girls, his face blushing furiously as they giggled and asked him about the ship.

"Aye," Aine said, standing a bit straighter as he spoke. "We took the ship from Seria and his men. Gave it back to her rightful captain."

"Weren't you afraid?" one of the girls asked with wide-eyed wonder.

"A sailor must face his fear," Aine blustered, blushing once more as he caught Taren's eye across the table. Taren smiled back at him and nodded his approval.

Ian put his hand on Taren's waist. "I fear for him," he said. "And for what losing the *Phantom* will mean for those left behind. His parents are good people. I'm only sorry you weren't able to meet people like that on Ea. There are many."

"Will Vurin move against the Council to free people like them? Attack the island?"

"I doubt it." Ian shook his head. "Too many of our people died for him to want to risk the lives of those who survived. He believes we have the means to liberate the island from the Council without resorting to violence."

Taren glanced over at Vurin, who was studying him with interest. In that moment Taren was sure that whatever Vurin had planned for his people was somehow linked to his own future. What had the old woman said? *"The fates will find you, Taren. They always will."* Taren reached for his belt and fingered the dagger he wore there. Ian had returned it to him before they'd left the *Phantom* two days before.

"I have no doubt this belongs with you," Ian had said. Taren had not protested—he knew Ian was right, even if he didn't understand it.

THE celebration went on for hours, well beyond sunset. Tired and overwhelmed by the activity, Taren slipped away from the table and wandered over to the edge of the village, to the hill that overlooked the cove. The moon cast a shimmering veil of light over the water below. Taren longed to transform, but he'd promised Ian he would wait until the morning. Instead, he lay on the ground, inhaling the sweet scent of the grass and the ocean as he gazed up at the stars and listened to the waves. He closed his eyes and dreamed.

"YOU are home, Treande," Owyn said as he embraced him tightly. The familiar scent of incense permeated Owyn's clothing. Taren loved that smell—it always reminded him of Owyn and of the peace he found in Owyn's company.

"It's been too long since I've held you."

Owyn just laughed. "I leave you to your own devices for a few hours and you sound as though it's been an eternity."

Taren reached up and brought Owyn's lips to his own. He closed his eyes and lost himself in the kiss, wishing it would never end. Something was coming, and he feared the future more than he could express. Taren had spent the night before praying to the goddess for enlightenment. He'd prayed that their lives here would be blessed and that their people would prosper. His prayers had done little to allay his fears.

Owyn stroked his hair and kissed his cheek. Before he knew it, Taren's eyes welled up with tears.

"Owyn. Goddess, if you ever left me, I don't know what I'd do!"

"OWYN, my love," Taren murmured. "Don't leave me."

Ian, who had been stroking Taren's hair as he slept curled up on the grass, pulled his hand abruptly away. He leaned back on his hands and looked up at the stars. Faint bands of clouds had begun to cover the night sky.

Owyn. He'd heard Taren speak the name before, although never so clearly. Was Owyn the love of which Vurin had spoken? Hours earlier Vurin had taken Ian aside, when Taren had been busy listening to Aine tell him about the village girls.

"Thank you for bringing him home," Vurin had said. "I prayed he was safe."

"Then you knew of Taren?" Ian asked.

"Aye. The old priestess foretold his birth and of his return to embrace his destiny. 'He will discover the love that has waited for him here,' she said. She also told me he would be greatly tested."

"Then his parents…?"

"I handfasted them. I consecrated Taren to the goddess when he was born." Vurin's pain was obvious.

"He doesn't know."

"I'll tell him, when the time is right. There are many truths he must learn, not the least of which how his parents sacrificed themselves to protect him."

"And this love?"

Vurin just offered Ian a sad smile and squeezed Ian's shoulder. "He must learn that for himself. No man can dictate the ways of another man's heart. But if the priestess foretold it, we can be sure whoever owns Taren's heart will stake his claim."

Ian forced both his conversation with Vurin and his jealousy from his thoughts. Too many times he'd ignored the goddess's plan for him, and he'd finally learned it was useless to fight. He'd pushed Taren away when he'd first found him, and yet each time he'd run from Taren, the fates had seen fit to reunite them. He'd tried to run from his own gift, and yet he'd used it to save Taren's life as well as his own. He'd tried to deny the strong feelings he had for Taren, and yet the thought of returning him to Rider at the end of the year already pained him more than he cared to admit.

No. His fate and Taren's were inextricably intertwined. No matter how far he ran, he could not run away. He knew his place was at Taren's side. He would protect Taren—the goddess willed it. If all he could give Taren was his safety, so be it.

Gently, he gathered the sleeping Taren in his arms and cradled him as he walked back toward the village. Taren murmured in his sleep and buried his head in the space between Ian's shoulder and neck. *Laugh all you wish,* he told the fates. *I already love him.*

TWENTY-SIX

TAREN watched the slow rise and fall of Ian's chest as he slept beside him. He remembered falling asleep on the bluff and dreaming of Owyn. He'd hoped to speak to Vurin, but whenever he tried, it seemed Vurin was in the midst of another discussion, his eyes never meeting Taren's. Taren needed understanding, if not all the answers he sought. He would not wait any longer.

The soft breeze caressed his bare skin as he rose from the bed and dressed silently. He leaned over Ian and kissed him sweetly on his forehead, pausing to embrace the warm emotions that seemed to accompany thoughts of their time together. Then, taking care not to wake Ian, Taren slipped out of the cottage in his bare feet, his shoes in his hands.

Vurin's house was dark but for a light in the back window that opened onto Vurin's study. The room was tiny and filled to brimming with books and papers. Vurin sat in an old armchair covered in threadbare fabric, wearing eyeglasses and holding a book. He wasn't reading the book. He was looking up at Taren through the window. *Waiting for me.*

Vurin smiled and gestured Taren inside, setting the book upon a small table. "Taren. I'm glad you came." Vurin pointed to a chair that faced his own, then rose to tend the fire. The logs, once disturbed, glowed and snapped. A small flame rose to illuminate Vurin's face, which appeared pale and drawn. The smell of the wood reminded Taren of his time spent with Borstan as a young boy. How he'd loved to lie on the carpet in front of the fireplace there, reading a book as Borstan snored, having fallen asleep.

"You seek answers," Vurin said once he'd sat down again.

"No more than you, I'd venture."

Vurin laughed. "I deserve that, don't I?"

Taren said nothing. Vurin wanted something from him. The knowledge that for once in his life he had something valuable to offer gave Taren pause. He wasn't sure how he felt about it. Part of him wished Ian were here beside him, and yet he hadn't asked Ian to come.

"May I get you something to drink? Wine, perhaps?"

"No. Thank you."

A long sigh escaped Vurin's lips as he leaned back in his chair and ran a hand through his hair. "Ian doesn't know, does he?"

Taren schooled his expression, unsure of how to respond to Vurin's question. "I don't know what you mean."

"He doesn't know about the dreams."

Taren swallowed hard and his heart began to race. How would Vurin know of his dreams? Had he somehow read his mind?

"I am sorry, Taren. I've frightened you. Sometimes I forget that you did not grow up with us. Forgive me for my audacity." He leaned over the table and poured himself a small glass of wine that appeared almost black in the dim light of the fire. He studied it for a moment, swirling the liquid about, then took a sip. Taren had the distinct impression that Vurin too was uncomfortable and was taking the time to form his thoughts. "I am a mage," Vurin finally said.

"A mage?" Taren had heard the word before, of course, but he'd never really understood its meaning. "You mean you're a magic user?"

"It is similar to magic. There are those of our people who have certain gifts. The healing gift. The power to defend. The ability to communicate with animals. The gift of sight." With these last words, Vurin looked directly into Taren's eyes. "Many of these gifts have been lost or forgotten over the centuries." He motioned about the room, then continued, "We live as the humans do. We have adopted their culture, their ways. But our gifts remain."

"How did you know about my dreams?"

Vurin took another sip of his drink. "My gift," he said after a moment, "is empathy."

"Empathy?"

"Aye." Vurin laughed and shook his head. "Not a prized gift, by any means, although it serves me well. It is the ability to sense the emotions of others. Some are able to impart emotion. Even pain."

"Pain." Taren immediately thought of Seria. If such gifts existed, no wonder the humans might fear the Ea.

"You have experienced this?"

Taren took a deep breath as he willed his dread away. "In the prison. Seria... touched me."

Vurin frowned but said nothing.

"Can you do this too?" Taren asked.

"Yes." Vurin waited a moment, then added, "There are darker sides to our gifts. The mages were once our teachers, our priests. But when the Ea fled the mainland hundreds of years ago, many of the mages perished. The Council forbade us from teaching our children. The mages taught us well, but without them to guide us...."

Taren shivered in spite of the warmth from the fire. "What did you sense when you touched me?" he asked, eager to leave his memories of Seria behind. The nightmares were more than enough of a reminder.

"I sensed someone. Another soul, and yet the same."

"I don't understand."

"Of course you wouldn't. You grew up amongst the humans. You learned of their beliefs, their superstitions, and you were taught about their gods. Even our own people have forgotten the old ways. When they left the mainland for the island, so much was lost." He sighed audibly, then finished his wine. "May I show you something?"

"I... yes."

THE moon cast shadows over the ground as they walked past the houses to the outskirts of the settlement. Taren couldn't shake the sensation that he knew this place—the feeling was stronger now than it had been when they'd first arrived. The memory seemed to grow stronger the longer he spent here. The houses were slightly different than he remembered. He wondered if he were dreaming even now. When had it become so difficult to separate reality from dreams? He'd been a bit of a dreamer before he'd met Ian, but now his dreams dogged him every waking hour, the slightest reminder in this living world awakening another memory from his dreams.

They continued on until they reached a small hill, far enough from the town that only the barest hint of the roofs was still visible. Vurin said nothing, perhaps knowing that Taren needed silence as he took in the familiar countryside. Taren was thankful for this—he felt both overwhelmed and confused, knowing he was on the brink of a revelation so powerful, he needed to steel himself for its truth.

And then he saw it. Not much more than a pile of stones at the apex of the hill. But when he looked at it for a second time, he saw far more than just rubble: he saw a building hewn of white stone that shone in the moonlight. He saw the temple flicker into being, solid and seemingly immutable. The same temple he'd seen in his dreams.

"Gods." Taren hadn't intended to speak the word aloud.

"You know this place."

"Aye." Taren struggled to find the words to explain what he'd felt since he set foot in the village. "But not just this place. The hills… the cottages… the way the road through the village veers toward the woods. The smell of the ocean. The way the grass felt beneath my feet as I walked the cliffs…. It all feels so familiar. Sometimes I feel as though I've dreamed this all before."

"Perhaps you have." Vurin offered Taren a kind smile. "But I sense this troubles you as much as it pleases you. Why?"

"I'm afraid."

"What do you fear?"

Taren considered this for a moment, then said, "I'm afraid I won't be able to return. That I'll lose myself in my dreams." Even now, he felt the dreams begin to pull him back.

Vurin squeezed Taren's shoulder. "I'll be here should you need me. Take your time."

Taren nodded, then continued to wander around the ruins, sometimes seeing the high walls, sometimes the broken and blackened stones at his feet, as if he inhabited two worlds. He stopped a few yards from the entrance—or what had been the entrance—held there by some invisible force. The world around him dissolved and what was night now became day.

HE HEARD screams and ran toward the temple, his heart pounding, his fear great. Why had the humans come with their swords and fire? He had to get to the temple and find Owyn before it was too late. Owyn would know what to do, what to tell their people.

He stumbled over a rock and nearly fell face-first onto the road, but broke his fall with his hands. In the distance, he saw the thatched roofs of the village ablaze. Soldiers rode through the empty streets on horseback, weapons drawn. Men and women fought back, giving both the very young and very old more time to flee to the harbor. The smell of death was everywhere, mingling with the smoke.

Flames rose skyward from the temple, the white stones of its outer walls scorched. The soldiers had come here first. He'd only left the temple a few hours before. It was Owyn's birthday and he'd gone to the market to find him a gift. Owyn had kissed him and left to gather an offering for the evening's ceremony.

"Oh Goddess! Owyn!" He saw Owyn lying on the temple steps, his body so still that Taren had to remind himself that he sensed Owyn's presence. He was still alive. "Owyn! Goddess, Owyn!" He took Owyn's bloodied face in his hands and kissed him. "Where are you hurt?"

He needn't have asked. He saw it then, the gaping wound on Owyn's chest. He pressed his hand down and tried to stem the flow of blood. He was a strong healer but even he knew he was powerless to save Owyn. He'd get Owyn to the water. If he transformed, he'd live. Gently, he began to lift Owyn into his arms.

"No. Leave me. Save yourself and the others."

"You'll die if you stay here." He wouldn't leave without Owyn.

"You'll die if you take me. And there are still those who can make it to the water. They need your help. They will need you to lead them to safety." Owyn's voice was weak. Blood bubbled at his lips like the froth of a wave on the sand, remaining behind after each breath.

"Then I'll die." He wouldn't live without Owyn. He couldn't.

Owyn took his hand and shoved something hard and cold into it. "Take the stone from me."

"What? No. It will kill you."

"Take it. My life is nothing if the stone is lost."

Taren took the knife from Owyn and stared at it—it was the same knife he'd found on the beach! But how was that possible?

"No!" Taren shouted as he tossed the weapon aside. He began to lift Owyn again, but this time Owyn touched his hand to Taren's chest and released his power. The pain took Taren by surprise and he nearly fell

backward. Taren had only seen Owyn use his power once, and although Taren knew it was a warning, not meant to injure, it was still a shock.

"What did you do that for?" Taren demanded.

"Treande. Beloved. You mustn't let the humans find the stone. That stone is the salvation of our people." Owyn offered him a wistful smile. "Please. You know what you must do. You cannot let me die without retrieving it. You know what will happen."

Taren felt hot tears on his cheeks. Of course he knew what he must do! But to lose Owyn was like losing his heart. And the stone….

"Damn the stone!" he shouted, his anger not for Owyn but for the goddess herself. How could she have permitted this to happen? Let the stone die with Owyn, if that was the goddess's wish; he'd not take Owyn's life!

"We are not meant to stay here. The goddess has shown us the way."

"The goddess has abandoned us," Taren hissed. "We've done nothing to deserve this. And you… you have served her with all your soul. If she cared for her people, would she let us die here?"

"Our people will survive. You will help them. But you must not leave without the stone. You must take it from me." Owyn's eyes shone with love, although Taren saw it only through his tears and the thick smoke. "You must keep it safe. You know the prophecy."

"I can't…."

"You must. Please. Take the stone and go to the others. They need you now."

Taren gritted his teeth and fought more tears as he retrieved the dagger. He ran a single finger over the hilt and said a prayer to the goddess that he would see Owyn again. Then he bent down and kissed Owyn. In the distance, he heard shouts and screams. Why hadn't he heard them before?

"Beloved. I will be with you. Always." Owyn smiled up at him. "But for now, you must let me go."

Taren nodded dumbly, then bent over and kissed Owyn once more. Owyn's cold hand met Taren's cheek. "Forever, beloved," he whispered.

Taren lifted the dagger. His hand began to tremble and, with it, the blade. Goddess! Help me do this. I haven't the strength of my own.

Taren drew a deep breath and, using his right hand to steady the blade, plunged the knife deep into Owyn's heart. Owyn's gasp of pain and Taren's cry became the same sound, wending upward to the sky. Owyn's chest began to glow. Brighter it grew, until Taren had to look away. The sound from Owyn's lips faded with the light.

When Taren looked back, he knew Owyn was gone. Over his heart was a small stone that glowed faintly blue, strung on a silver chain. Through the blur of his tears, Taren took the stone and hung it from his neck. He touched Owyn's cheek. Already his skin felt like ice.

On the horizon, a tiny band of light had formed. The sun had begun its slow ascent. The stench of fire and blood burned Taren's nostrils as he bent over Owyn's body and sobbed.

It began to rain.

"TAREN?"

Taren slowly became aware that he was lying on the grass, his body wracked with pain. Overcome with grief, he sobbed, gasping as tears streamed down his cheeks.

It had rained in his dream. It was raining now as well. Hadn't the sky been clear when they'd climbed the hill to the temple? Taren struggled to comprehend where he was.

"Taren?" Vurin knelt beside Taren and touched him gently on his back. Taren looked up at him, embarrassed and confused. "What did you see?"

"See?" Taren repeated dully. He looked back down, expecting to see Owyn's body. He lifted his hands to his face. There was no blood. He reached for the chain around his neck but felt nothing there. What had just happened?

"You possess the gift of sight, Taren."

"Sight? Then what I've seen—that was the future?"

Vurin shook his head. "The past. The goddess guides you to the future. Only she knows what will come to pass."

Taren sat back on his heels and shivered. "It wasn't a dream?"

"Not a dream. That much I can sense."

"But the temple. The blood. The stone. Is that my past?" Taren struggled to make sense of the vision—if it was a vision at all. He still wasn't sure he believed it.

"You saw the stone?" Vurin's face looked ghostly pale. "Tell me. What did it look like?"

Taren struggled to remember—it was difficult to put the image of Owyn's bloodied body out of his mind. "Small. Rough. Like glass, but black. Not much bigger than my thumb." It came to him in a blaze of recognition: he had seen that same stone in the portrait of Ian's great-great-great-grandmother.

"Ian," Taren whispered.

"You know the truth, Taren. You've known it for some time, haven't you?"

Taren took a deep breath and looked past Vurin toward the water, feeling suddenly weak. Clearly sensing this, Vurin put his hand on Taren's shoulder to steady him. "Come. You must rest now, Taren. We will speak more of this later."

"You know about this stone?"

"Aye. A fair bit. But that is too long a story for tonight. Later, I will tell you what I know." Vurin stood and offered Taren his hand.

Taren took it without protest. He wasn't sure if he'd have had the strength to rise of his own accord.

"There will be time enough to speak of it later, I promise."

TAREN slipped back into bed as the sun began to warm the fields. Ian was still asleep, but he stirred as Taren wrapped his arms around his chest and pressed his face to Ian's back. Tears threatened, as they had done since he'd awoken from the dream. The pain that had begun in his chest now spread to his entire body. Not a physical pain. This pain ran far deeper. And yet—

"Find what you were looking for?" Ian asked in a voice thick with sleep.

"What?"

Ian tensed and pulled away from Taren. "You smell of grass and of fresh air."

"I took a walk."

"I see." Ian clearly did not believe this.

Taren yawned and reached for Ian, wanting the solidness of his body—he needed the reassurance of Ian's touch.

"You still haven't answered my question. Did you find what you were looking for?"

"Yes." Taren kissed Ian's lips, then brushed his fingers over Ian's skin. *Something I've looked for longer than you can imagine.*

Ian tensed and turned away. Taren held his breath for a moment, trying to understand Ian's apparent change of heart. He reached out to touch Ian's cheek and felt his jaw tense. "Ian?"

Ian did not reply.

"Ian?" Taren sat up in the bed as the feeling of dread intensified. Had Vurin told Ian about Treande? Taren wondered if his gift frightened Ian as well as it frightened him.

"I won't keep you from him."

The pain Taren sensed in Ian's heart cut him to the quick. "Him? But I—"

"You saw him tonight, didn't you?"

"Vurin?"

"Owyn."

Taren gasped.

"I heard you speak his name. It's not so surprising that you would go to meet him," Ian continued before Taren could respond. "Vurin told me you were fated to return here. It's why he asked me to rescue you, though to be truthful, I'd have done it anyway. I didn't want to lose you. And when he told me the old woman predicted you'd find him here, I knew I'd have to let you go."

"Old woman?"

"The mage. The last of the oracles from the time when our people fled this place for the island. She died when I was young. She told Vurin you would find your soul's mate when you returned to the village."

An oracle? Taren thought of the old woman he'd seen, the one who had given him the dagger. What had she said? *"He seeks to avoid that which is destined, and you are determined to run."* She had been talking about them, he was sure of it.

"No," he said. "You don't understand." He didn't know what to say, but he knew he must say something. "Owyn isn't who you—"

Ian's laugh sounded both pathetic and bitter. "I can't compete with the goddess's plan for you. If she wants you to be with him, I can do nothing to stop it."

Taren reached for Ian, but he pulled away and climbed out of the bed.

"Ian." Taren ran a hand over his mouth, his eyes filling with tears. "Please. Listen to me."

Ian stopped at the window, the moonlight tracing the outline of his naked body. Taren slid out from the blankets and embraced Ian from behind, lacing his hands through Ian's and kissing his bare skin. Ian shivered and breathed deeply, leaning back to press his body against Taren's, then pulling away just as swiftly. "What is there to say?"

"More than you know." Taren steadied himself and mustered his strength. He'd already kept the secret too long; he just wasn't sure how to tell it. "I went to see Vurin tonight," he said, hoping Ian wouldn't notice how his body trembled with trepidation. "I... since the prison, I've... I've had dreams. Or I thought they were dreams. Vurin showed me that they weren't. They're memories." Taren closed his eyes and said a silent prayer to the goddess. Never before had he called upon her for strength—until today, he hadn't understood his need to do so.

Please. Don't let me lose him now, when I've finally found him again!

"Vurin told me about our peoples' gifts." Taren sighed audibly. "He told me that I have a gift. The gift of sight. I thought he was mad." Taren looked away as he struggled to form the words. "I'm nothing. No one. A slave. Neither human nor Ea."

Ian turned and stared at Taren. Whatever he'd expected Taren to say, it was clearly not this. "I won't have you say that. You know you're not a slave. You're one of us."

Taren smiled sadly. "I wouldn't have believed it myself until tonight. And much as I know the truth of my birthright, I still am a slave in my heart."

Ian shook his head and brushed Taren's lips.

"Vurin took me to the ruins of the temple. I.... Everything is so familiar here. The hills, the village, the water. I've been here before, Ian. I know this place as well as I know Borstan's shack. I lived here. And not as a child. As a man."

Ian's eyes widened when he heard this. His lips parted, but he did not speak.

"I didn't meet Owyn," Taren continued, hoping with all his heart to ease Ian's fears. "But when I saw the temple.... It was there. Solid. No longer in ruin. I could touch it." Taren looked down at his hand, once more expecting to see blood on his fingers.

"Owyn was there, in my vision. He was dying." Taren's eyes filled with tears. He tried to fight them, but he was too tired, too overcome with grief to do anything but let the pain possess him.

Ian reached out and brushed Taren's tears away, then gathered Taren into his embrace. "You don't need to do this. I promise I won't stand in your wa—"

"Ian. Goddess! Don't you see?" Taren clasped Ian's face between his shaking hands. "You feel it too, don't you? I've known you before. Known your touch, your kindness, your heart. I've known your *soul*, Ian.

"The old woman on the island called me Treande." Ian's eyes grew wider. "I *am* Treande. Or I was. His soul lives in mine. I don't understand it, but I know it's true." Taren pressed a hand to Ian's chest, over his heart. "And you... your soul is *his* soul. Owyn's soul lives in you. He promised he would find me again. And you have!"

"I...," Ian began as he put his hands over Taren's. "No. It's not possible." But his expression told Taren that he knew the truth the instant Taren spoke the words.

"Let me show you," Taren begged. "Please. I can do this. Vurin told me how."

Taren led Ian outside. The first rays of morning had begun to paint the hills pink and orange. The sound of a rooster echoed from one of the nearby buildings, and the fresh scent of the grass rose to meet Taren's nostrils with each step of his bare feet. "Come," Taren said as he walked between the houses to face the rise that overlooked the water. He clasped Ian's hand tightly, feeling the warmth travel from his hand to Ian's. "Do you see it?"

Ian gasped. Taren knew he saw it too—the stone cottage at the edge of the cliff. A whiff of smoke rose from the chimney. Tiny flowers of blue and pink dotted the green hillside. When Ian spoke, it was soft, barely a whisper. "I once dreamed of building a house on that hill."

Taren squeezed Ian's hand.

"Taren. I'm such a fool. I thought—"

Taren's lips silenced Ian's words with a kiss full of promise. Taren's fingers brushed the rough skin of Ian's cheeks. "There can be no other for me," Taren said as the kiss broke. "You understand that now, don't you?" Taren saw love in Ian's gaze.

"Yes." Ian spoke the word in an undertone.

"Perhaps someday the goddess will bless us with that house."

"Someday?" Ian's voice had a wistful quality. Taren guessed he understood his hesitation.

"There is more for us in this life than building a home together, Ian. The goddess demands more." Taren's thoughts strayed to the necklace and the black stone. He shivered as he pushed away the memory of Owyn as he died.

Ian wrapped Taren into his arms. For the first time, Taren noticed Ian's cheeks were wet. "I will keep you safe," Ian murmured against Taren's neck. "I swear it."

No, Owyn, Taren thought as he drew a long and shuddered breath. *This time, I will keep you safe.*

SHIRA ANTHONY, in her last incarnation, was a professional opera singer, performing roles in such operas as *Tosca*, *Pagliacci*, and *La Traviata*, among others. She's given up TV for evenings spent with her laptop, and she never goes anywhere without a pile of unread M/M romance on her Kindle.

Shira is married with two children and two insane dogs, and when she's not writing, she is usually in a courtroom trying to make the world safer for children. When she's not working, she can be found aboard a 35' catamaran at the Carolina coast with her favorite sexy captain at the wheel.

Shira's Blue Notes Series of classical-music-themed gay romances was named one of Scattered Thoughts and Rogue Words' "Best Series of 2012," and *The Melody Thief* was named one of the "Best Novels in a Series of 2012." *The Melody Thief* also received an honorable mention, "One Perfect Score," at the 2012 Rainbow Awards.

Shira can be found on:

Facebook: https://www.facebook.com/shira.anthony

Goodreads: http://www.goodreads.com/author/show/4641776.Shira_Anthony

Twitter: @WriterShira

Website: http://www.shiraanthony.com

E-mail: shiraanthony@hotmail.com

The Blue Notes Series by SHIRA ANTHONY

http://www.dreamspinnerpress.com

The Blue Notes Series by SHIRA ANTHONY

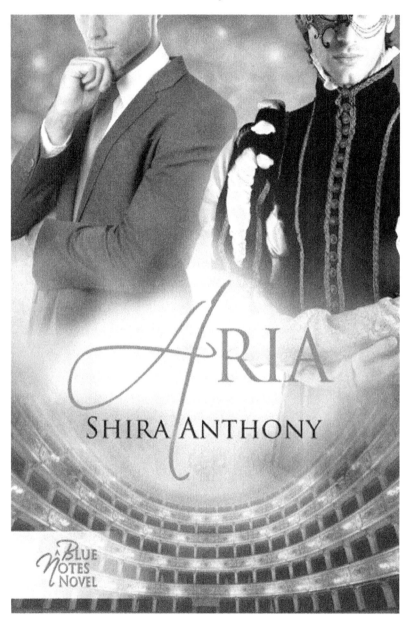

ARIA

SHIRA ANTHONY

A BLUE NOTES NOVEL

http://www.dreamspinnerpress.com

The Blue Notes Series by SHIRA ANTHONY

THE
MELODY
THIEF

SHIRA ANTHONY

A BLUE NOTES NOVEL

http://www.dreamspinnerpress.com

The Blue Notes Series by SHIRA ANTHONY

PRELUDE

SHIRA ANTHONY
VENONA KEYES

A BLUE NOTES NOVEL

http://www.dreamspinnerpress.com

Romantic Fantasy from SHIRA ANTHONY

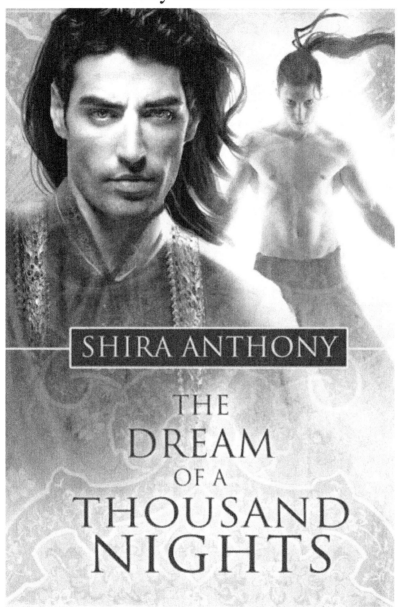

SHIRA ANTHONY

THE
DREAM
OF A
THOUSAND
NIGHTS

http://www.dreamspinnerpress.com

By SHIRA ANTHONY and EM LYNLEY

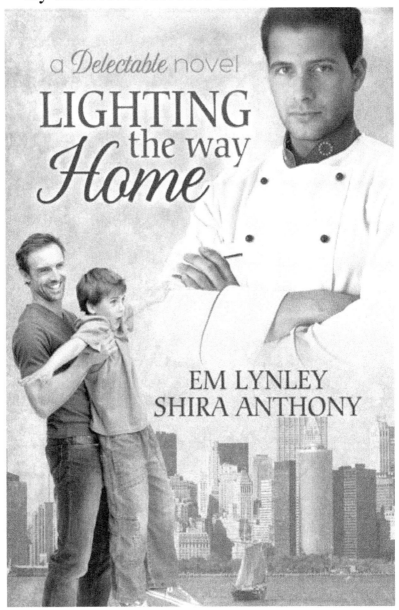

a *Delectable* novel

LIGHTING
the way
Home

EM LYNLEY
SHIRA ANTHONY

http://www.dreamspinnerpress.com

CPSIA information can be obtained at www.ICGtesting.com
Printed in the USA
BVOW06s0128121115

426835BV00007B/50/P